Ronald Hardy is a Londoner who began his professional life as an accountant specialising in taxation, then turned to writing. He lives in a cottage in Surrey with his wife and two children, but he travels far and wide to provide the background for his books. In writing *The Men from the Bush* he spent two months following the River Niger to its watershed, walking 'into the dark side of the sun' and gathering the facts about the cult of Ju-Ju. For his story of *The Iron Snake*, the building of the Uganda Railway at the turn of the century, he trekked most of the six hundred miles from Mombasa to Lake Victoria, retracing the old caravan and trail routes through desert, bush, swamp, forest and mountain range. For *The Face of Jalanath* he made five high-altitude ski-tours in the European Alps.

Two of his novels have won major literary prizes – *Act of Destruction* received The James Tait Black Memorial Book Prize and *The Savages* won the Putnam $15,000 Award in America in 1967.

The Face of Jalanath

RONALD HARDY

SPHERE BOOKS LIMITED
30/32 Gray's Inn Road, London WC1X 8JL

First published in Great Britain by
Cassell & Co Ltd 1973
Copyright © Ronald Hardy 1973

Published by Sphere Books 1974

TRADE
MARK

Set in Intertype Times

Printed in Great Britain by
Hazell Watson & Viney Ltd
Aylesbury, Bucks

ISBN 0 7221 4308 7

This is for Joyce, Christopher and Christine

The Karakoram Range of the Himalaya forms the northern mountain mass of Kashmir. It is a rampart of rock and ice and giant peaks that extends from the Hunza to the Shyok. But the rampart is also a frontier, and beyond it in the north-east the moraines fall to the Chinese province of Sinkiang. There are passes through the Karakoram, old trade routes that once carried merchandise at great altitudes into China and Tibet. Now the routes are closed and only the Red Guards watch from the edge of their secret land.

East of the Karakoram Pass, in the Indian zone of Kashmir, is a place named Dhalabat. It is built one thousand feet below the line of perpetual snow. No one can recall its origins. Once, perhaps, it was a mountain village, serving the needs of pilgrims and merchant traders. Now it is the School of Snow and Mountain Warfare.

CHAPTER ONE

This was early May and already the streams were greyed with melted snow. The streams were above him and below him and when the truck turned through the loops in the ascending road he could look down and see the fall of the streams and the three lakes on the valley floor and the fleece of mist that lay across the farthest of them. Then, when the nose of the truck swung again, the snow ridges appeared for a moment above the terraced slopes. Wild indigo was spilled on the slopes like violet shadow. He shut his eyes, inhaling with a kind of hunger the sweetness of the Himalayan air. Somewhere there were pine forests. He could not see them but their essence was on the wind. The recognition stirred his senses. I would always know it, he told himself. If I were blind I would know it. That word of universal fear brought its own swift reaction. He opened his eyes. The ridges tilted with the angle of the truck. He tapped the driver's shoulder. 'Stop here,' he said.

He left the truck, crossed the road to the lip. The driver cut the engine. He stood in silence, that silence of great spaces which, now, was broken only by the freshets of snow water that were threaded down the grain of the slopes. The lakes in the valley were as small as coins. Down there the heat, imprisoned in the rock wall of the valley, would be building. There were fishing boats and walnut men casting their seines in meshes of sudden light against the sun. There were the painted boats that dredged for lotus roots and water chestnuts. And later in the year the floating rafts of earth that were already planted out and tied in flotillas across the breadth of the lakes would begin to yield, and a man, watching from the shores, might believe that the water had put forth a garden of flowers and fruit. He felt his eyes flood, the exile's sense of return. 'Seven years,' he said aloud, bitter at their loss. 'It is seven years.'

The driver's boots scuffed behind him. He bent, picked

a flower from the drift of primulas that grew down from the lip. He said without turning, 'Once, on one of the expeditions, I kept a note of all the trees and flowers.' He smiled. 'Even the Latin names.'

The driver was silent. Then: 'Captain Farran.'

'Yes?'

'I saw the name-tag on your pack.'

He did not answer. There were rhododendrons in the fold of the slope, the yellow stems of bamboo. Wind stirred his hair. The coldness of the glaciers was in it. The question came.

'Are you Richard Farran, the climber?'

It had begun with those words. The voice was Petrie's.

'Richard Farran?'

'Yes.'

'The climber?'

But the words were not questions. They had the flat quality of statements. The rainstorm was gathering, the Exmoor sky so livid in the west that the heather was turning brown in the sullen light. Petrie's face was out-lined dark against the sky, against the dead colour of the heather. He stared at it, at the globules of sweat in the short white moustache. He began to walk. The man's raincoat rustled behind him.

'My name is Petrie.'

He lengthened his stride. Ahead the moor rolled like a brown sea into mist. Petrie's feet were thudding in the sodden grass.

Rain began. Farran moved into the cover of an oak. Petrie came out of mist, bowed under the lash of rain.

'It is a large moor,' Farran said coldly. 'And there are other trees.'

Petrie smiled. He removed his tweed hat, shook out a spray of rain. He had pomaded silver hair, cheeks that had gone malarial in the yellow light. He plucked the coloured feather from the hat-band, squeezed out a bead of water between the tips of sensitive fingers, then reshaped it. There was something foppish in the action.

Farran said with distaste: 'Mr Petrie—'

'Brigadier.'

Farran watched the moor. It shuddered in rain. The oak-tree roared.

'Don't you believe me?'

10

He turned, stared into Petrie's face. Authority had made its visible imprint. 'I believe you,' he said.

Petrie replanted the feather. He said reflectively, 'At the age of thirty-five – your age, Farran – I was already a full colonel. You, on the other hand—'

Farran went out into rain. The air of the drowning moor was thick with vegetal scents. Petrie's voice spoke from the shadow of the oak. 'Three pips isn't much to show, is it?'

Farran buttoned the storm-collar of his coat. Petrie emerged from cover.

Farran said with sarcasm, 'You'll spoil your feather.'

They stared. Animosity stood like a barrier between them.

'I'll walk with you to Exton,' Petrie said.

Walking, the rain now violent, Petrie asked, 'How long is it since you climbed in the Himalaya?'

'Seven years.'

Petrie nodded. 'Seven years.' The voice went sour. 'That was the Nanda Devi affair.'

They stopped. Petrie's tweed hat was saturated. Rain runnelled down his lemon cheeks.

'Not an affair,' Farran said with anger. 'A climb.'

'Three men died. Two on the French rope, and a Sherpa. I will give you their names. Mithois, Griot, Nima Badri.'

The three faces swam for a moment behind the blurring rain. 'You have a good memory,' Farran said. He watched Petrie's eyes. They were clever, bright like a bird's.

Petrie smiled. 'I have a good file.'

A file. The man was growing in stature, becoming more formidable with every word. This walker in the rain had the smell of power.

'In the year before that,' Petrie said, 'you led the climb up the Muztagh Tower.' He held up two fingers. 'Two were lost, Erländer and Weiss.'

The faces joined with the others, like a procession of the dead. He turned away, strode through rain. Petrie called after him, 'And Kamet. Remember Kamet?' He did not stop. 'Three men gone,' Petrie called. 'Three.' The numeral was flung about in the squalling rain. 'Shall I give you their names?'

Farran stopped. 'No, don't,' he said. 'Don't.' It was like a plea.

Petrie joined him. Their trousers flapped in wind. Farran said, 'I was never blamed. I am not a—' He was silent.

'No,' Petrie said. 'None of those words. But you are a jinx.' His voice softened. 'That's true, isn't it?'

'So they say.'

The rain eased and the sky took a paler light.

'We'll talk about it later,' Petrie said kindly. 'In your room.'

Later Petrie came to him. This was late evening and darkness flowed like smoke across the moors. There was a scent of mildew in the hotel room. He lighted the gas-fire and, kneeling, heard Petrie enter. Petrie carried glasses and a bottle of Cognac.

'Will you drink?' Petrie asked.

'A small one.'

Petrie, too, knelt by the fire, began to turn the glasses in its radiation. Farran adjusted the gas flow. There was a moment in which the wall mirror reflected the absurdity of their two kneeling figures. He stood, went to the window.

'A small one,' Petrie repeated. The glasses turned within his fingers so that lozenges of red light leapt on the walls. 'Don't you drink much?'

'Why ask? You have the file.'

Petrie poured Cognac. 'No dossier is ever complete.' He stood, proffered a glass.

Farran drank. Headlamps cut paths of light from the darkness of the moor, retreated. So the file had become a dossier? The word had an ominous ring, a word used by policemen. 'Who are you?' he asked with unease. 'What do you want from me?'

Petrie was silent. The room had darkened and Farran moved from the window to the light-switch.

'Leave it,' Petrie said sharply. He turned. 'Let's keep the fire-light, shall we?'

Farran watched him. It was a conspirator's face, with eyes and mouth that were fashioned for intrigue. He understood Petrie in that moment. Bargains must be struck in shadows, in muted voices. He went to the bed, sat.

Petrie said softly, 'The expeditions are over. You know that, don't you?'

'Yes.'

'You are thirty-five. A few more years' – he raised his

hand above his head to denote great heights – 'and it will all be inaccessible.' The hand fell abruptly. 'Beyond reach.'

'You made your point.' Anger resurged. 'Now get out.'

Petrie went to the fireplace, leaned across it so that his face and glass were pricked with red. He said, 'You'd have done well in the war, Farran. A command. A private army. A bit of danger.' He sipped Cognac. 'But peacetime soldiering?' He shook his head. 'You are a misfit. You are always at half-cock.' His voice took an infinite sadness. 'And that's a frightful waste, isn't it?'

Farran did not answer. The gas-fire hissed. Petrie swayed in and out of redness, his tongue flickering down into the Cognac with the delicacy of a serpent. He went to the window. Rain hit the pane like flung gravel. He said, 'But one war ends – and another begins. There is always an enemy, always a battlefield. In the light or in the dark. In a host of places.' He smeared condensation from the glass. 'Even on mountains.'

'Mountains are for the pure in heart, Brigadier. And on a mountain a man battles with himself. There is nothing else.'

Petrie came back from the window. He said softly, 'I could send you back to them.'

'To the Himalaya?'

'Yes. I have that power.'

Now the séracs shone like needles. This world of rock, snow and ice that tilted above the windshield was the evidence of Petrie's power. But, it seemed, power and guile were inseparable. 'I could send you back to them.' These murmured words were the lure. But in the morning the Brigadier was gone. There was no message. Only the bottle of Cognac, left like a gratuity on the mantelshelf, remained. He walked the moor for three days until his leave expired. But there were no feet to follow in pursuit, no tweed hat to bob through rain. Petrie was gone, and with him the remnant of a dream.

He rejoined his regiment. This was the annual training scheme. The rain had moved north and mud lay in the valleys of the Brecons. Everything went wrong. The schedules would not work and there were ludicrous pockets of confusion. In the early hours of the final day the 'A' Squadron barrack-hut exploded into flame. Later Kerr, the battalion commander, sent for him.

'You are the Adjutant,' Kerr said with fury. 'You are responsible.'

He shook his head.

'Yes. Responsible. You know the rule.' Anger had enspittled his mouth. 'No live ammo or pyrotechnics will be kept or taken into living accommodation.' He brandished a sheaf of stapled foolscap. 'It should be here, here in admin instructions, here for every bloody fool to read.' He swallowed spittle. 'But it isn't.'

'It is there.'

'It is not.'

'I tell you it is there—'

Their voices rose, ringing in the hut. They stared around them, as if aware of this echoing witness to their own violence. Kerr dabbed his lips with a handkerchief. He offered the sheaf and Farran took it. 'Then show me,' Kerr said.

He riffled pages. Someone moved behind the partition that divided the orderly-room. He heard the rasp of a cigarette-lighter.

'Well?' Kerr asked.

The clause was missing. 'I don't understand,' Farran said.

He searched the desk. Kerr's boot tapped the boards. 'It was in the original,' Farran said. He produced his hand-written draft. One of the sheets fell. Kerr retrieved it. The upper margin was ornamented with a range of mountains. Kerr, stared, held out the sheet as if it were infected. He said with disapproval, 'If you kept you mind on the paper-work—'

Rebellion rose. 'To hell with the paper.'

'You will not run an army without it.'

'That's right. I've heard you say it.' Then, in a parody of Kerr's pedantic voice: 'Paper is the oil of smooth administration.'

Kerr flushed with anger. Farran turned away. A shaft of sunlight touched the filing-cabinet and the tweed hat that sat upon it. He picked it up.

'You have a visitor,' Kerr said. He left and Petrie came, as if at a signal, from behind the partition. A cardboard cylinder was tucked between arm and body. He stood there wincing, ill at ease in the brilliant light.

'Let's go to the mess,' he said.

Farran gave him the tweed hat. 'You've lost your feather, Brigadier.'

In the mess Petrie said, 'We need a quiet place.'

Farran led him to the billiard-room. There was a three-quarter-size table, a smell of tobacco, a single window. Petrie locked the door, drew the curtains so that only a sliver of light cut the gloom. Then he switched on the table-light, laid the cardboard cylinder on the baize. Rolled paper protruded from the ends.

Farran said gravely, 'Is that my dossier?'

Petrie withdrew the roll of paper. 'You have a laconic tongue,' he said. 'It may explain your slow promotion.' He spread the paper into a square, placed a red snooker-ball on each corner. 'It is a map.'

Farran bent across it. Kashmir and the Karakoram lay beneath him. He bent lower. Familiar names and the little triangles that denoted the great peaks came into focus. He allowed his finger-tip to glide in sensitive explorations across the surface of the map, as if its contours might be felt. Emotion blurred his eyes, the blue-white whorls of the ranges ran like wet pigments. 'For a time,' he said, 'you made me believe it.'

Footsteps stopped outside the door. The handle turned. Petrie's head moved down into the orbit of the big metal canopy, his fingers across his lips and his cheek so low that it took a green tinge from the cloth.

Farran whispered, 'We could hide under the table.'

Petrie straightened. Displeasure touched his face. The footsteps retreated. He stabbed ill-temperedly at the map with one of his sharp, polished finger-nails. 'This is—?'

Farran bent across it. 'The Vale of Kashmir.'

Petrie plucked a ball from a pocket, spun it up the table. 'Kashmir,' he said softly, enjoying the syllables. 'Kashmir.' He caught the ball on its rebound. 'A beautiful name. It rings on the teeth like a gold coin.'

'You are a poet, Brigadier.'

Petrie spun the ball again, imparting side with an expert flick of the fingers. He gestured at the map. 'Take a north-east diagonal.'

'From the Vale?'

'Yes.'

Farran waited.

Petrie murmured, 'Talk to me about it. Just talk.'

Farran hesitated. Petrie, he knew, was exposing a wound. He stared around him, at the shadows and the locked door and the faint gleam of inter-squadron challenge cups. Beyond this room was Kerr's world of paper and army forms, the interminable schemes and courses that were a substitute for action, a sterile world where the colours gathered dust. He felt the walls move inward. Only the map had life. It lay there in the soft green light, rich as a landscape painting. He drew his finger across it, sensuously as if its texture was of silk. He let it rest above a small blue pool. 'Here,' he said, 'on the Lake of Dal—' The words released him. He began to speak.

There were houseboats on the lake. They were better than the hotels, and for a few rupees you could lie on a walnut cot and watch the distant snowfields through windows of engraved Chinese glass. Even here, on the breast of the lake, there was always the sandalwood smell of India and, if you were still in the valley when the monsoon rains came in June, the timbers of all the houseboats groaned like things in pain and the willows that fringed the lake stood in mist as if disrooted. Then, leaving the lake and climbing with the autobus road toward the Ladakh, you could pause above gorges that were filled with moving cloud and there, below the cloud, was the valley and the pagoda roofs of Srinagar and the wall of the Pir Panjal. Here, where the land was dissected and provided the cloud would open, you would see the shoulder of Nanga Parbat. This was the first of the climbers' mountains to reveal itself. These were the mountains that occupied a special area of the mind. Men had died in attempting them and other men were drawn to them as if they were shrines. They had none of the taint of tragedy. Men had gone to them like spirits disappearing into the unchanging whiteness, not for destruction but to be enfolded. So the mountains were sanctified.

'What rubbish!' Petrie said.

But it was true. Any climber who was not embarrassed by the true revelation of feeling would tell you that. Other mountains were malevolent. You felt it there like a tangible presence and, with these, men were drawn by a simple, magnet fear. There was never tranquillity, not even in that silent moment on the summit.

'A mountain,' Petrie said, 'is a mass of rock – no more and no less.' His voice took an edge of impatience. 'North-east, Farran. You have a long way to go.'

The diagonal would take you through the Burzil Pass, through the wing of the Great Himalaya and down into the Plains of Deosai. Here you were north of the cease-fire line and the Pakistani Army controlled the routes to the Karakoram. There were lines of tents under the Lombardy poplars and during the summer heat the transport crossed and recrossed the plains under plumes of orange sand. Skardu was the last and largest of the towns. Here you would organize for the trek and pray that your equipment was at the airstrip. Here they would sell you hashish in the shadow of the Fort or, if your tastes were unsophisticated, orchard apricots in green paper bags. The apricots were said to confer longevity, and the men of Hunza, in the north, were the proof of this. But, they would assure you with gravity, no quantity of apricots, not even a lifetime of the eating of them, would prolong your days in the Karakoram if the weather turned or the guardians were affronted. Here, too, you became aware of the dominance of the mountains and, with the crossing of the brown and rapid waters of the Indus and the rise of the land into coldness, they grew as if thrusting from the earth and sometimes the peaks shone like jags of glass that have been set as warnings in the top of an immense blue wall.

'Yes,' Petrie said. 'A wall. That is how I see it. A great fortification.'

Seven days' march would bring you to the greatest of all the glaciers. The Baltoro flowed from the heart of the Karakoram and was the union of many other glaciers. Here you would build the first of the important camps. There were alpine flowers and the pugmarks of snow creatures on the Baltoro and because of this evidence of life the glacier seemed always to present a face of peace. But above you was grouped an array of the world's highest peaks. At night you felt their menace, weight poised in darkness. At sunrise the glacier was reddened and, climbing above it, you would see the three Gasherbrum summits, the Teram Kangri and the Golden Throne, the Masherbrums and the cone of K2. Only the British could reduce a mountain of such feral power to a letter and a numeral. But some men called it Chogori, or corrupted this absurdity of a letter and a numeral to Kechu. Whatever name you gave it you would stand, alone above the river of ice, and reflect that this awesome place was the true roof of the world, that here—

The ranges again lost definition. He said, 'You know how to twist the knife, don't you?' Anger repossessed him. He swept his arm across the map so that the four red balls were spun to the farther cushion and, rebounding, burrowed into the map. It hopped like a live thing down the table. 'Send me back' – he heard the tremor in his voice – 'or leave me be.'

They were silent. Petrie recovered the map, smoothed it, replaced the balls. 'Are you a violent man, Farran?'

'No.'

'Are you capable of' – the voice became casual – 'an act of violence?'

'Against you, Brigadier – yes.'

Petrie smiled. Somewhere in the mess a metal object fell. He listened, as alert as a sparrow. Then: 'Where were we?'

'On the Baltoro.'

'Move east.'

'As the crow flies?'

'Yes.'

No crow would ever negotiate the Karakoram. But sometimes the choughs were seen, as black and predatory as ravens, as high as twenty-five thousand feet. Their shadows came like darts of black paper across the whiteness and, turning with the swiftness of their flight, you were disturbed by a strange sense of destination. The birds, flying east down the line of the chain, would pass through the cols that lay beneath the Karakoram Pass, crossing the cease-fire boundary into the Indian zone. There—

'There,' Petrie said, 'you may pause.'

Farran waited.

'Now move north.'

He drew his finger slowly across the Plains of Lingzi Thang, up again into the white areas of the map that signified the great altitudes. Petrie had moved away to the end of the table. He took a cue from the rack, arranged a red and a white in the jaw of a pocket, began to play a series of gentle cannons. Farran paused. Beneath his finger-tip was the segmented red line of the international boundary.

Petrie said softly, 'Where are you now?'

The balls clicked.

'It is all Karakoram,' Farran said. 'A wilderness.'

'Keep moving.'

The red line, drawn across the peaks and glaciers, had no geographical precision. It was the range, in all its varying depth, that was the true frontier. He slid his finger through the whiteness, down into the pale blue hatching and toward the puce areas of the lower lands. He paused again. The billiard-balls stopped.

'And now?' Petrie whispered. His head leaned into light so that Farran saw the pink scalp under the strands of silver hair.

'In China.'

Petrie's lips moved silently on the syllables, like a man mouthing a forbidden word. The cue was suspended above the table. Farran felt the tension that had, for a moment, charged the slender body. Then Petrie relaxed. The cue dipped so that its tip rested on the map, south of the red line. Farran bent. The tip moved back and forth, leaving a smear of blue cue-chalk.

'This neck of land,' Petrie told him, 'is bordered on the east by Tibet, and on the north by Sinkiang.' The cue scratched, a new blue river appeared on the map. 'Below the range there are lakes, rivers and plains. There is also' – he searched for a phrase – 'a military establishment. It is administered by the Indian Army and it provides special facilities for any friendly nation that is prepared to pay.' He put down the cue, began to roll the map. 'Farran, we are going to send you on a snow warfare course.'

'A course? Is that all you offer me?'

'Much more than that.'

Farran waited.

'I offer you – adventure.'

The truck had climbed and, now, they were above the tree line. This was the country of the shepherds, and the first of the flocks had been brought from the lower lands for the high grazing. Here the grass was still brown from the suffocation of the winter snows. There were drifts of

19

white. Stone cairns, built by pilgrims at the roadside, crumbled like memorials to dead gods.

The road lifted to the level of the snow ridge. He sat upright in his seat. Far below him were the crowns of Himalayan oaks, forests of pine, cultivated squares of buckwheat and Tibetan barley. Above and behind the ridge rose the wall of the high Karakoram. The sun was on the peaks so that they gleamed like spires of glass. He felt the beginning of excitement, the first burn of coldness in the lungs. Nothing had changed. This changelessness was the true spirit of the Himalaya. He watched with reverence. This was a private reunion and the seven wasted years slipped away from him in that instant like a discarded garment.

The truck stopped. It was very cold and Farran pulled the parka from his kit-roll, put it on. This was the moment when his fingers found the drawstrings and, in the tying of them, would always brush across the mended tear. The tear ran upward through the fabric from the strings to the armpit and it had been slashed when Erländer's crampons struck like a claw at the beginning of the fall. The line of twine stitches was ugly and ineffaceable, the cicatrice of an old wound. He waited for Erländer to make his brief appearance. The face smiled, then faded. The driver pointed across the windshield to the shallow valley that ran like a trench between the snowfields.

'Dhalabat,' the driver said.

Farran went to the edge of the road. Here the snow was thick and would remain until the thaws of August. The spoor of tractors was on the road, and the road ran in descending spirals to the valley. Dhalabat lay below him. He could see the village and the movement of men and asses in its single street. Snow defined the eaves of fret-worked houses, a Hindu temple, the shapes of cattle barns. This was an ancient place. He heard the notes of the temple bell, rising from the valley like the sound of antiquity. But around and beyond the village were the military installations. There were barrack-huts that were placed in geometric patterns, a covered park for snow-tractors, a firing-range, a fenced perimeter, a training piste that climbed through the piedmonts under a web of flood-light lamps and was lost in the mountains. An Indian flag rippled in the pale sun. West of the village, where the glacier threw a flower of green-blue light on the sky, a Weasel tractor came through the snowfields. Behind it and drawn on its traces were an equipment sled and a section of men on skis. He watched their approach, the moment when the Weasel was poised where the plateau ended above the slopes and the men moving out from the traces and into the final run that would take them down to the village, the small black shapes formed into a perfect vee and each man spurting a plume of upflung snow and hunchbacked under the heavy pack and the rifle needle-thin and slanted across it and, now, the section running for the village as fluid as a falling arrow. He felt their joy and he watched them until the slopes were empty and only the Weasel brought movement to the whiteness.

He returned to the truck. Wind was coming off the snow and he pulled the hood of the parka about his head. Ice sheened the road and the driver took the truck down very slowly in the lower gear. Now he could see a wider aspect of the village and, above it on the crag where the range unfolded, a monastery and the grouped white cubes that were the monks' cottages.

At the bend in the road there was a painted board, pinned on the rock-wall like an advertisement hoarding. It bore a regimental emblem and the words:

SCHOOL OF SNOW & MOUNTAIN WARFARE
Commandant: E. E. Hadji, Col.

CHAPTER TWO

Hadji stood, dabbed with a napkin at his lips. The mess fell silent. He said, 'Tonight, in this mess, we have thirty new arrivals. We welcome them.' His teeth gleamed for a moment within the fibres of his beard. 'There is of course a speech.' He twisted the napkin into a cone, the sallow fingers as dexterous as a waiter's. Then he placed it on the table, straightened his tunic, went to the fireplace. The mess watched him. Hadji, now, was outlined against the aureole of light that was radiated by the burning pine logs, his legs apart and the black beard thrust aggressively at them like a tusk. They felt his power. This was a formidable man. The eyes, as black and soft as grapes, roved the tables. Hadji smiled again. It was the head of a rajah, Farran thought. The dark green turban, perfectly folded, reshaped the forehead into a triangle of walnut skin. It lacked only the ruby that might be set against its folds.

Hadji said, 'Most of you are serving officers in the forces of the NATO powers. But here in Dhalabat you have no rank. Command starts here' – he tapped his chest – 'and runs' – his hand made a flowing movement across the turbans and sleek black heads at the central table – 'through a permanent cadre of the Indian Army. Remember that.' The grapes lost their softness. They glinted like coal. 'You are here to learn. A few' – his eyes rested on Farran – 'will give to us their own special skills. But each of you, no matter how distinguished, will learn a new art of war – war in an upper world where snow, ice, altitude and cold are the first of your enemies.' A hint of derision touched his voice. 'I pity you, for the lessons will be painful.' He pointed to the windows, to where the blackness of night enclosed them like a shutter. 'Out there, in these great white wildernesses, man is a weakling. So, firstly, you will learn survival—'

The memorized phrases washed across them. This was a performance. They listened, enjoying the resonance, the modulations of that deep and hypnotic voice as if it were a melody. Farran turned away his head. Around him were the dress regimentals of a dozen armies, blended by the tawny light of walnut-oil lamps into arrangements of tan, grey, blue, olive-green, maroon. Faces nodded behind wraiths of tobacco smoke. At one time, he judged, the place had been a grain and livestock barn. Iron rings hung on the timber walls. Above him the roof rose into a vault of cross-gartered pine, as lofty as a church. The floor, partly covered with rush matting, was of crude stone flags. The flags were stained dark from centuries of urine; and, indeed, the barn, warmed by the fire and the bodies of the assembled men, was pervaded by a faint ammoniac scent. There was a large adjacent room, reached through a central opening in two bamboo screens. Once, perhaps, it had been a store for winter feeds of dried iris and willow leaves. Now there were pictures on the walls, framed documents, a line of leather benches. He could see the edge of a draped billiard-table and one of its ornate, mahogany legs, the glint of bottles on a corner bar.

Hadji was saying: '—and then you will learn techniques. You will learn to navigate and preserve at all times your line of communications, to trek and ski and climb, to bivouac on a mountain face, to build a house of snow and erect a tent in the teeth of a blizzard, to maintain weapons and transport in sub-zero temperatures, to read the signs of danger in the skies and in the snows and in the icefalls, to use explosives and enlist the aid of a million moving tons.' His voice fell to an impressive whisper. 'You will learn through hunger, the heats of the high glaciers and the awful cold of the Himalayan night to sustain a minute but unquenchable spark of life. And finally you will learn that even when the spirit is as frozen as the limbs it is possible for a man to rise and move and *strike*.' The word echoed in the roof. They heard the logs shift in the fireplace, the sough of wind in eaves. 'All this you will learn.' He held out his arms in an orator's gesture. The hands groped at them through firelight like tan gloves. 'Thus armed you will return to your units, to your native lands. You will take with you, and teach, these indelible lessons.' His voice gained vibrance. 'Wherever the battlefields of the future reach across snowbound mountain frontiers you will meet your enemy, engage him – and prevail.'

Someone laughed.

Hadji's arms remained outstretched for a moment. He said softly, 'A man laughed.' The beard jerked, it was like a sign of anger. 'Let him stand up.'

No one moved.

'I am waiting.'

A chair shifted. A lieutenant rose.

'British?'

'Yes, sir.'

Hadji waited.

'Ardrey,' the lieutenant said. '95 Commando—'

Farran watched him. *Ardrey.* Somewhere there was a response to that name. He was young, young enough, it seemed, to laugh aloud at extravagance. He had a candid face, thick straw hair that might gleam in sun like a brass plate, a strong but slender body. When he moved it would be with grace. He stood there, facing Hadji, as straight-backed as a cadet.

Hadji said coldly, 'Was the speech amusing?'

'No, sir.'

Hadji touched his turban. 'Or was it the funny hat?'

The Indian officers smiled. There were seven of them. They were hosts, and because of this sat proudly and with dignity in their seats.

'How old are you?'

'Twenty-one.'

Twenty-one. As straight as a cadet. The word brought associations. The Academy, fierce young men joined in a military élite. Memory stirred. A NATO war-game in Norway, an avalanche accident to a British unit, the court martial of a young lieutenant. 'He won the Sword of Honour,' the Defending Officer had pleaded. 'And when disaster came he was only twenty-one—'

Hadji repeated it. 'Twenty-one.' Then, with derision: 'Do you laugh at us from some pinnacle of achievement?' He went to the table, poured water. Even the act of drinking was theatrical, the head tilted back, the legs apart, the tumbler seeming to lie balanced on his out-thrust beard. 'I will tell you the sum of your achievement,' he said. His eyes narrowed, as if he were recalling data from a document. 'A few Alpine climbs, a place in the British Army ski-team' – his voice took emphasis – 'and a certain winter exercise in Norway.'

Farran saw Ardrey flinch. The word had struck like a

24

blow. Now the mess was silent. Men toyed with cigarettes or glasses, watching, aware of an undertow.

Hadji said, 'Your last climb – where was it?'

'The Weisshorn.'

'The Weisshorn?'

'Yes, sir.'

Hadji stared. He had full red lips. In repose they lay in the blackness of his beard like cherries. 'Tell me,' he said with mockery, 'What did you do when you had scaled this terrible peak?'

'Do?'

'Yes.'

Ardrey smiled. 'I came down again.'

The mess laughed.

'And then?'

Ardrey shook his head. The questions were snares.

'I will tell you.' Hadji bent, kicked at the logs. Sparks showered his boot. 'A hotel' – the boot stabbed again – 'hot water, a meal, a Cognac. Am I right?'

'Yes, sir.'

'Sit.'

Ardrey sat.

Hadji said to him, 'You will not find hotel comforts in the high snows.' Then to the mass of faces: 'You are not in the Alps. Remember that. You are in the Karakoram. Study them. Respect them. Be humble. This is a place where the reckless die.' He began to pace through fire-light, the black poniard of a beard pricking the smoky air like a weapon. Stopping, he said, 'Two men among the new arrivals have experience of the Himalaya. Let them stand.'

Farran stood. Faces turned. A chair scraped behind him. Hadji nodded and Farran said, 'Farran. Royal Tank Regiment.'

'And?'

'Kemmerich. Second Rhine Army Corps.'

Kemmerich? Here? The familiar voice with its soft Bavarian accent had reached out, touching the surface of the mind like a brand. Erländer and Weiss began again their long and soundless fall down the ice wall of the Muztagh. 'I loved them. I loved them—' That was Kemmerich, crying piteously across the intervening years, Kemmerich of the pallid face that always burned brick-red in wind and glacier suns, Kemmerich kneeling in snow, disfigured with grief, tears that became lanes of ice. He saw amusement in Hadji's subtle eyes. He turned, stared into Kemmerich's face. Already the first burns lay like open knifecuts across the cheekbones. There was nothing in the eyes, not even accusation.

When he left the mess Farran walked through the lines to the edge of the camp. There was a half-moon and he could see the walls of the valley and the blurs on its faces where wind took and held the snow on the sky in trailing scarves. This wind, he knew, was the fringe of the southeast monsoon, bringing the warmth and dampness of the Bay of Bengal and laying snow in enormous mantles across the upper heights. Above him were the lights of the monastery. He watched them extinguish. Then he went to the barrack-room.

Hut Nine was the distribution centre for new trainees. There were thirty prepared cots, each with a palliasse, a thin grey pillow and a clothes locker. Oil-lamps hung from the rafters. There were two wood-burning stoves with metal flues, pyramids of split pine logs. He stood for a moment on the threshold. A sour-sweet smell, that compound of soap, tobacco, socks and gun-oil that characterized every barrack-hut he had ever known, touched his nostrils. Men talked, smoked, turned their faces into the sullen light. Some were in bed. Kemmerich was bent across the first of the stoves, feeding wood. Farran watched him. He wore long woollen underpants that were yellow with age. The wool threads were stretched tight across his powerful legs. An old warning murmured in the mind. 'Never let your legs get cold,' the German had told him. 'If the legs go you are finished.' But Kemmerich's legs would never go. They were abnormally thick in the calves and ankles, legs that had been built for rock and ice. These were the legs he had followed as a boy of eighteen on his first serious climb. He shook his head, as if in wonder at the passage of the years. Seventeen years since that time of testing on the red-brown spurs of the Pointe d'Amont, fifteen since the west wall of the Pic d'Olan, twelve since Kangchenjunga; and eight since the Muztagh. These and others he had shared with Anton Kemmerich. Then the fall had thrust them apart.

Kemmerich bent again across the stove. His crucifix swung from the neck in a swift ellipse of light. Farran walked between the cots, stopped. 'Hello, Kem,' he said.

Kemmerich turned. The face glistened with antiseptic cream. Farran saw that he had aged. The hair, once blond, was as pale as ash. The eyes were set deeper in the sockets, the cheeks leaner, the jowls more pronounced. His vest was open at the neck and the crucifix lay half buried in a frizz of grey-white hair. But the belly was flat and pads of muscle swelled on the chest and shoulders. He was as hard as teak. Farran searched the eyes for warmth. There was a moment when it seemed the German might respond, put out his arms in greeting. Then the eyes went cold as stones. Ghosts stood between them. Farran turned away, walked to his bed.

A sheaf of green, lithographed paper lay on the pillow. It was headed: ARMY SCHOOL DHALABAT. CAMP ADMIN. INSTRUCTION NUMBER ONE. There were twenty-seven numbered paragraphs and it was signed SYED ARIF, *Adjutant*. He sat on the bed, removed his boots, began to read. At all times, it announced, the language will be English. Trainees would be posted to one of the four companies Alpha, Beta, Gamma, Delta. For purposes of training each company would be sub-divided into sections and half-sections—

Farran riffled through the pages. Much of it was standard administration. There were locations for the Regimental Orderly Room, the Guard Room, the Fire Station; security rules for the vehicle pools, camp policing, the Armoury, the issue of weapons, compasses, binoculars and watches. Arms would not be left unattended, mess bills would be paid to the Mess Treasurer on the Friday of every week, no statement on any subject relating to the unit would be made to the Press without first obtaining clearance from the Adjutant—

Around him men were talking. Farran listened. Some were of senior rank. Yet here they were recruits, strangers in a strange environment. And like all recruits they explored each other, watched and assessed, reacted in their different ways. Later they would whisper confidences to

27

their neighbours, deliver small, secret parts of themselves in the intimacy of darkness.

He reached the final page. Three paragraphs were of special interest.

25. Pistes and open touring-routes are under the control and periodic inspection of accredited members of the IMF. One piste is floodlit and, subject to the discretion of the Adjutant, may be used for night training. Permission will be refused where (a) weather conditions are bad and/or (b) generator current is not available.

26. Only teams of three or more persons may travel beyond the northern perimeter of the camp. There are four refuge huts – Pingal, Dashti, Kulan and Jilga – each of which is stored with fuel, food and a radio transmitter. No team entering a refuge will leave without (a) signalling to base and (b) checking store reserves. In no circumstances will a team depart from a refuge if it is unlikely to reach base before nightfall.

27. Medical facilities are available at the monastery of Thyangjun under the directorship of Dr Joseph Shaw. All personnel will respect the silence of the monastery and the devotions of its inmates.

Farran put down the sheaf. The door opened. Wind retched upward from the throat of the valley. A man entered, beat snow from his shoulders. He walked to the stove. He wore fur gloves, a scarlet snow-suit. He removed the gloves and the hood, held out his hands to the heat of the stove. 'Arif,' he told them. 'Captain Arif.' He was young, very proud. He had a shy, handsome face, a complexion that glowed in the lamplight like a polished nut. He smiled at them. 'Is everyone happy?'

'Delirious.'

'Except for that bloody door—'

'—and the frozen taps.'

Arif showed his brilliant teeth again. 'It is for one night only. Tomorrow you shall have new quarters.' He wiped wetness from his cheeks. 'Have you all read the admin. sheet?'

'At least three times.'

'It is very distinguished.'

'Any questions?'

'Section twenty-five.'

Pages rippled.

'Tell me,' Arif invited.

'The IMF. What is that?'

'The initials signify . . .' Arif frowned. 'You must surely know?'

Heads shook gravely.

'It is the Indian Mountaineering Federation.'

'The what?'

Arif repeated it.

'You mean Indians climb mountains?'

Arif flushed. The hood had disturbed his hair. Black strands stuck out like antlers. 'This year an Indian team will climb Everest.'

'But we've already done that.'

Arif walked the length of the hut toward the second stove. He looked around him. 'If there is anything you need?'

'Women,' a man said. 'There will be a great need for women.'

Arif laughed. 'We have yaks, asses, goats, sheep. But no women.'

'I have never tried a yak,' someone said.

'It is a beautiful experience.'

'But one needs an orange-box to stand on.'

'And Captain Arif to hold its head.'

Arif laughed again. He was enjoying the baiting.

When he had gone Ardrey said, smiling, 'We ought not to do that. He's a very nice man.'

Farran studied him. He felt a sudden sympathy. We have things in common, he wanted to say; dead men in the files, preserved for ever like names on tombs. He said on impulse, 'Did you ever meet a man in a tweed hat?'

Ardrey looked up and Farran saw an immediate light of understanding. Then the eyes veiled. These were regions of the mind too raw to be touched.

When Farran left him Ardrey lay back on his cot, stared at the ceiling. Hadji's voice spoke again: '—*and a certain winter exercise in Norway.*' So Hadji knew. The bearded

29

head nodded, as if in answer to the question. Norway. The name, now, was a trigger. It scattered images in the mind, the ridge of Svaanastinde indistinct and the night opening around them like a pit and the patrol moving on the traverse and down the snow slope that was already ribbed and mottled by the gale, the crust breaking under the racquettes and above them the cliff of snow poised then moving, moving and the soft engulfing roar as the avalanche brushed them, men digging, voices that were flat with fear in the night. Someone whispered, 'Two missing. We can't get them out.' There was terror in the words. Ardrey turned on the cot. The whisper would never be silent, now, another, more clamant voice was speaking—

'What was the object of the patrol?' This was the Prosecutor.

'Contour navigation.'

'Were the men experienced?'

'No, sir.'

'Where was the patrol at the time of the accident?'

'On the eastern slopes.'

'Was this the selected route?'

'No.'

'Why had you deviated?'

'The weather came down.'

'Suddenly?'

'Yes.'

'Why choose east of the mountain?'

'It was the short way back.'

'Had you been warned of avalanche danger on the eastern flanks?'

'Yes.'

'And yet you chose that route?'

'I told you. It was the shortest.'

'But dangerous?'

'Yes.'

'You led the trainees into danger?'

A silence.

'Had you the equipment for a tented camp?'

'Yes.'

'Let us be clear. Could the patrol have camped until daybreak?'

'Yes.'

'Without danger?'
'Yes.'
'Then why go on?'
Another silence.
'Answer me.'
'I made an error.'
'Of judgement?'
'Yes.'
'Was there in fact a snowslip?'
'Yes.'
'Of which you had been warned?'
'Yes.'
'At what cost, Lieutenant?'
'Two men.'
The voice stopped. That was Norway. It was there, in those sunless snows, that the Sword of Honour lay buried with the two dead soldiers.

Farran awakened in the early hours. There were shafts of moonlight, dark areas where the fireplates of the stoves shed grilles of red light. He could hear men breathing, wind, the sound of snow decanting from the eaves. He got up, went to each of the stoves, fed them with logs. The boards were pleasantly warm against his naked feet. He stood for a moment by the stove that was adjacent to his cot, stared across it at the hut and the sleeping men. He had spoken only to Ardrey and Kemmerich. The rest were nameless. But he had watched and listened. The thirty men, he estimated, might divide into five West Germans, four French or Belgian, six Scandinavians, four Italians from the Alpine Regiment, three Canadian or American, eight British. The Western powers, it seemed, were aware of the white frontiers and the enemies that lay beyond. All these men were on a six-week course. But Petrie had promised him much more than a course. The voice, that voice of enticement, spoke again. 'I offer you – adventure.' Adventure? That was a heroic word, a word to run through a man's blood like an intoxicant – and a word of many meanings. Here it might mean exploration, deep reconnaissance into the great uncharted regions that spread north of Sinkiang and east to Tibet, the use of new weapons and new high-altitude techniques, even prestige climbs. But Petrie had spoken also of battles

31

fought in the dark, of an act of violence. And Colonel Hadji? 'A few,' Hadji had said with significance, 'will give to us their own special skills.' Their eyes had met, were held for a second in an awareness of a secret shared.

Soon, perhaps, Hadji would reveal himself.

CHAPTER THREE

At first light Arif came again to Hut Nine. He held three foolscap sheets. He pinned them to the wall, saying, 'These are lists. Read. Then take your kit to your allocated hut.'

Farran went to the lists. Men pressed around him. Huts Eleven and Fifteen each received twelve men. Six only were allocated to Hut Seven, and it was there that he found his name.

BETA COMPANY HUT SEVEN. PERSONNEL
ARDREY, A. D. (UK) 2nd Lt., 95 Commando, 189 Infantry Brigade
CRAY, E. C. (USA) Capt., Provost Corps
FARRAN, R. M. V. (UK) Capt., Royal Tank Regt
KEMMERICH, A. L. (West Germany) Major, Rhine Army Corps
LUC, J.-P. (Belgium) Capt., 66th Army Para Brigade
RICCI, A. V. (Italy) Lt., Alpine Regt

He turned away, stared momentarily into Kemmerich's unshaven face. Then he went to his bed, began to fold and stow his kit.

He was the first to reach Hut Seven. The barrack-hut lay on the east perimeter at the start-point of the training piste. It was very cold and his breath rode in plumes on the air. The sun was low in the valley and he stood at the door to the hut and watched the tide of red light flood the glacier. Inside the hut there were six beds, three large clothes-lockers, two hanging lamps, a central stove and a stack of cut wood, a Primus cooker and a drum of kerosene, an assortment of pans, cutlery and crockery, a wash-basin and three ewers, a shower with a torn plastic curtain. There was also a cupboard. A duplicate of the hut register was stuck with adhesive tape to its centre panel. Opening it he found provisions: some tins of jam, meat and sardines, sacks of rice and barley flour with Srinagar stencils, quantities of clarified butter, biscuits, lentils, cooking-oil. He closed the cupboard door, chose

33

the bed that was farthest from the entrance, dropped his kit and pack upon it. Men were entering.

He turned from them, began to unpack. Ardrey's face swung across his vision and a kitbag thudded on the adjacent bed. Someone opened the stove, pushed in wood. Smoke billowed. They would move around, Farran knew, make noise, test the water-taps, the draughts, the stuffing in the palliasses, the weight of blankets, the capacity of lockers. But they would also make judgements. Friendships would begin, frictions develop. Wherever soldiers were gathered in close proximity this was the pattern. He put clothes into the nearest locker. 'Share?' he said to Ardrey.

Ardrey nodded.

A locker, a book, a confidence – something shared was always a preliminary. He heard Ricci say to Ardrey, 'Did you bring books?'

'A few.'

'If one could—?'

'Any time.'

Ricci smiled with pleasure. He was as youthful as Ardrey, with fine brown hair that arrowed down into a widow's peak, a fair, north Italian skin, audacious eyes, restless hands that flickered rapidly through the medley of clothes and articles that was strewn upon his bed.

But others were quick to establish private territory. Farran could hear behind him the voice of Ethan Cray. It came huskily above the general murmur, the scrape of boots. '. . . and there is one hell of a down-draught. So' – knuckles rapped the window pane – 'at night we can cover it. That is all I am saying.'

'And I am saying that I cannot sleep in a darkened room.'

This was Robert Luc, the Belgian para.

'I have the bed under the window—'

'Yes. But that does not make the window your personal property—'

'No?'

'No.'

The knuckles rapped again. '*My* bed. *My* window—'

'We shall see.'

The voices seemed to collide. The American's was throaty, the voice of a man with a polyp on the chords –

34

or a taste for whisky. Luc's was sibilant, the words so clearly enunciated, so sharp there was an impression the tongue cut them out as if with a blade. Cray said, 'Yeah. We'll see.' Farran turned. Cray loomed black against the square of white light. He was very big, a man of perhaps thirty years. He lit a cheroot. He had the face and body of a boxer; the neck ridged with muscle, thickened features, little whorls of scar-tissue around his eyes, a head so brutally cropped that it bristled like a brush. His face turned toward Luc, toward the light. Farran saw the conflict in it, the belligerence that still flared in the eyes. Then Cray relaxed. He offered a cheroot.

Luc shook his head.

Cray said gently, 'We'll change beds, huh?'

Luc turned away. This one, Farran decided, would give nothing, accept nothing, forgive nothing. There was something tensile in the man, some force that lay coiled like an imprisoned spring. He had thin dark lips, gaunt jaws, a profile that was as sharp as a hatchet. He removed his leather jacket, placed it on the bed. Then he began to empty his canvas bag and the Sabena holdall, placing each item on the blanket with meticulous care, as if precision, even the symmetry of arranged objects, was important to him. Every movement was very slow. This is how you will climb, Farran thought; the hands and feet as deliberate and unvarying in their rhythm as those of a man moving through water.

Now Luc was arranging his toilet articles. These too were carefully placed; a shaving-brush, coarse yellow soap, a shallow leather case about eight inches square. He opened it, re-aligned the contents. Then he put it, still opened, on the bedside locker. Farran saw that it contained a number of cut-throat razors. He crossed the room to the locker, stared down at the case. It was old. It had a worn blue velvet lining and, on the velvet, an indecipherable gold crest. There were eight razors, each with a yellowing bone handle. Seven of them lay in compartments. The eighth was clipped into the lid.

'They're very good,' he said with interest.

Luc nodded.

'And old.'

'My father's – and his father's before him.'

Farran took one out. Displeasure touched Luc's eyes.

He opened the blade. There was a Sheffield trade-mark. 'English,' he said.

Luc nodded again. 'One for each day of the week.'

Farran replaced the razor. 'And the eighth?'

Luc smiled. It was like a grimace of pain. Farran unclipped the eighth razor. It was longer than the others, heavier in the hand. He opened it, turned it in the window light. Sun touched the steel with red. There were seven minute nicks in the bone of its handle. He ran his fingernail down them. Luc reached out, took the razor from his hand, returned it to the case. The dark lips closed. Arif came in.

'Listen,' Arif said. He held a roll of paper. 'You have two weeks. Two weeks in which to acclimatize, to learn the terrain. Subject to standing rules you may do as you wish. Walk, ski, climb.' He tossed the roll on to Kemmerich's bed. 'This is a map. It is clearly marked with routes, altitudes, the position of the refuge huts. All danger areas are coloured red. All climbs are coded according to severity.' His face became serious. 'You will study this map, commit its references to memory. This is your first and most urgent task.' He pointed at Farran. 'You, Farran, are appointed section leader. You will attend Admin. at 0800 hours each morning. There you will receive weather forecasts from both Radio India and Radio Pakistan. You will then file a written plan to your section's daily route. This is a basic safety requirement. Clear?'

'Yes.'

'Which of you have experience of the *langlauf* ski?'

All except Cray raised their hands.

'Here we use nothing else,' Arif said to him. 'You must practise very hard.'

He opened the food cupboard, took a fistful of flour, held it poised above the sack. 'We give you your dinner. But that is all. Other meals' – he allowed the flour to sift through his fingers – 'you must yourselves prepare.'

He opened the hut door. Sun struck his sleeve, turning the nylon vivid red. Behind him the snows rose in broad white fields. He stood there, his face faintly quizzical. They waited. Tension grew. Arif raised his face to the warmth of the sun. Cray said in the silence, 'Is this all you can tell us?'

Squads were grouping on the lower slopes. Voices came. Arif said seriously, 'From here on, whatever you do you do together. Share your skills. Give freely to each other. If a link is weak then make it strong. Live, move, work, think as a team.' He pointed at them. 'Not six men – but one. Do you understand?' He pulled his hood about his ears, held up a finger. 'Two weeks. The sun and snow are perfect. Be patient. And be happy.'

They were happy. In that fortnight of freedom, the weather holding good and the snow firm, Farran led the section daily from Dhalabat. These were joyous days in which the muscles hardened and the cold burned in the lungs like a flame, days in which the six men ski-toured within the immense rectangle that was formed by the refuge huts. 'The only way to ski,' Farran told Ardrey. The boy's face was pink with health. 'No lifts, no machines. Just your own two legs. Six hours' trek. And then—' He pointed down the glacier, across the troughs and plateaux that shelved above the village. This was always the ulti- mate in joy, this down-hill run to home, the light failing and the nightfall reaching like a scarf at the heels and the column weaving before it as if in flight, the skis hissing and the breath clouding and the tiers of snow, rock and ice shifting like painted scenery and, then, the slow curve above Dhalabat and the swift and undeviating schuss in which the column broke and each man raced, poles tucked and body bent, towards the gilt-and-tile roofs. 'Christ, this is marvellous,' Cray would say, panting. 'Goddam marvellous.'

But at sunrise of the fifteenth day filaments of cirrus cloud leapt in red explosions on the eastern sky. Already wind was clawing furrows in the powder snow. Arif, pointing, said to Farran, 'It is a bad sign. It will become very violent.'

The weather had changed; and with it the regimen of training. At noon a man came from the orderly room, stood for a moment on the wooden steps, then descended and walked toward them.

Arif said with sympathy, 'Your time of suffering has begun.'

The man was squat, very wide and powerful. He wore a fur jacket and a Peruvian bonnet. Unbuttoned ear-

flaps lifted in wind to beat his yellow cheeks. He came
out of sun, a square of fur against the brilliance. He had
a mongol face, a flat nose with cavernous nostrils. Mandarin whiskers hung like black wires down the corners of
his mouth. The fumes from a hundred cooking-pots had
glued the fur of the jacket into greasy spikes. Wind
brought its evil smell. When he neared them they saw that
the pocks and craters of an extinct smallpox marked his
cheeks.

He did not speak and Arif said softly, 'This is Dorje.
He has no rank, no papers, no origins except these mountains. Even his name is the name we gave him. He is only
Dorje. But he is unique. He is indestructible. Listen to
him. Learn from him. He will teach you how to stay
alive.'

Dorje watched them from behind his clouding breath.
He stood in silence. They heard the putter of the engine
to the hoist. The empty hooks swung up the slope and became small with height. Arif bowed to Dorje with a kind
of respect, walked away. Dorje continued to stare. The
eyes were currants set in puffs of yellow flesh. Mist was
filling the valley and through it the snowfields gleamed
like cliffs of chalk.

Jilga was the farthest of the refuge huts, and it was to
Jilga that Dorje took them. The hut was built, where
snow would not bury it, under the lee of the rock buttress
that leant above the Thieng glacier. The glacier ran like
a river of milk into wastes of snow and ice. There were
hot springs on the south shore of the glacier, and above
the springs the steam rose on thermal currents and was
turned into rains of ice. The hut was scoured by wind.

'Wind is the worst of your enemies,' Dorje told them in
his lisping English. 'Worse even than the mist.' He had led
them then to where the wind was funnelled from the
glacier. For three days they trekked into this howling
throat of wind. Here the wind was an animate thing. It
assaulted. It numbed the brain. It pounded the lungs. It
drowned them in noise. 'Your enemy,' Dorje shouted.
Wind took his words, fragmented them. 'You want to
escape, heh? To sleep, heh? To lie down and—' Wind
flung the word like a whiplash around them. 'Die . . .
die . . . die—' The head shook so that the Chinese

whiskers swung their particles of ice. 'Oh, no, you not going to die. You going to live.' He had begun to laugh, showing his carious teeth. 'And you not going back to that lovely hut. Oh, no.' The mittens gestured at the white canyons that enclosed them. 'You going to build your little house right here.' In that savagery of wind, the light draining from the glacier and the gale rising, he taught them to cut the snow bricks that would form an igloo; and there in the snow house, limbs entwined, the bricks sweating and their own body-heat sustaining them, they lived through the Himalayan nights.

There were days, too, when Dorje led them into mist. This was a silent world. 'Stop now,' Dorje said. They had stopped, the scarlet parkas vaguely seen against the moving grey walls. 'Listen,' Dorje said. There was no sound except the rasp of breath. They had stood there waiting. But Dorje did not move or speak and the mist filled their noses with its smell of graves and they felt the pressures of the wilderness, its utter deadness and their own fragile founts of life. Panic rose. Dorje whispered, 'No tracks. No landmarks. No sounds.' He was silent again. Then, mocking: 'Perhaps you are already dead.' The fur shape retreated into mist. They heard his boots crunch, stop somewhere beyond their vision. The walls moved inward. 'For Christ's sake!' Cray shouted. Dorje's ragged shape came out of mist, groping like a bear. 'You see?' Dorje said. 'You are afraid.' He tapped his wrist-compass. 'Have faith in the navigation. Nothing else can save you now.'

Dorje retaught them as if each man was a novice. From misery grew knowledge. They spent two weeks based on the Jilga hut. Then, when the gales died and the land revealed itself in brilliance, Dorje led them into new and unmapped regions. These were trials of speed. 'Out there,' Dorje told them, 'the most quick route is not always the straightest line, heh?' Now the land was falling and there were long and rhythmic runs down the breast of the glacier, Cray competent now on the slender, heel-free blades of the *langlaufen* and the team so prac-tised that, running, it seemed to swing like a linked chain on the glacier of ice. Here, on the bank of the Thieng, above the moraine trough, they pitched their tents. And

39

here, where the peaks were low and the altitude supportable, they made their climbs.

At the end of June Dorje brought them back to Dhalabat. In those weeks the summer had crept upwards from the valley. There was green around the village and the streams smoked in sun.

In the Orderly Room Hadji gestured at the window and the angry sky. 'Red sky in the morning. Farran—' He stroked his beard: it gleamed with brilliantine. 'You know the proverb?'

'We are not sailors, Colonel.'

Hadji frowned. He pointed at one of the chairs that faced his desk. Farran sat. There were six manila files on the desk, each with a superscribed name. There was also a tweed hat. Petrie came in his furtive way from an inner room. He stood there wincing in the brilliant light. Farran flicked the tiny pheasant-plume that was stuck in the hatband. 'You found your feather, Brigadier.'

Petrie sat, turned his lemon face from the light. He wore a hairy suit, a regimental tie, brogues. The material of the suit glinted with flecks of gorse-and-heather colour. He looked very English. He said, 'I kept my word.'

'Yes.'

'Are you enjoying it?'

Farran nodded.

'There is a price to pay.'

Farran smiled. 'Adventure? That is not a payment.'

Petrie stared. Hadji came from the window, sat. The green turban bent across the desk. He aligned the files, naming them aloud. 'Farran. Cray. Kemmerich. Luc. Ardrey. Ricci.' The tan fingers riffled pages. The room was silent. Petrie rose, went to the window, adjusted the plastic venetian blind so that the sun was diffused, sat again. His face relaxed in mellow light. Farran waited. Across the turban and through the gap below the blind he could see a slope and a section of men in red combat suits motionless on the brow. He watched the NCO glide down the slope, the swift snow-spurting christiania where the slope levelled and the flowing movement in which the man crossed the poles into a triangle and, swivelling the barrel of the NATO automatic rifle, brought it to rest

40

between the grips. The voice came faintly: 'This is the snap firing position. Now you do it.'

'Cray,' Hadji said. 'Begin with Cray.'

Petrie unbuttoned the jacket of his absurd suit. A pipe was stuck into the waist of the trousers. He withdrew it, stared into the empty bowl, began to suck. Hadji listened with distaste. Then to Farran: 'I am asking you for an assessment. A personal assessment of each of these five men.'

Farran said slowly, 'To make a judgment—'

'Yes?'

'—one would need to know the nature of the mission.'

Petrie made a liquid noise in his pipe, smiled.

'Cray,' Hadji said.

'Very strong,' Farran said. 'Very good on rock.'

'And on snow?'

'Fair.'

'No more than that?'

'No.'

'How important is this?' Petrie asked.

'It depends on the climb,' Farran said. 'Everest is a snow mountain, for example. So you'd need to be good on snow.'

'And you wouldn't take Cray?'

'No.'

Hadji turned more pages. 'Kate's Needle and Devil's Thumb – both in British Columbia. King Peak in the Yukon. And Mount St Elias in Alaska.' He looked up. 'These are Cray's listed climbs.' The voice took an edge of contempt. 'Not quite the Himalaya, are they?'

Farran said stubbornly, 'If it's a rock climb I'd take him.'

Hadji was silent for a moment. Then, quietly: 'It is a rock climb.'

Petrie said, 'But much more than that. Much more than a climb.'

Farran waited. Petrie withdrew the stem of the pipe, gave his secret smile. A thread of spittle swung from the mouthpiece. Farran felt his temper rise. He said with insolence, 'It tastes better with tobacco in it.' He saw anger glitter in Petrie's sparrow eyes.

Petrie said coldly to Hadji, 'I told you, didn't I? I told you he has a tongue.' The spittle dropped to his knee.

41

Hadji said, 'Let's get back to Cray. Let's consider temperament.'

When they reached the Kulan hut Ardrey lighted the stove and Luc checked the food stores. Ricci patched the window where the glass was broken. Cray dumped his pack, then went outside. Farran followed. This was evening and red light came down the col like pigment squeezed from a tube. Cray stood in snow, watching the scenery and the way in which the pinnacles of Weche glowed. He held a silver flask and the silver was red in the light. Farran saw him unscrew it, the quick jerk of the head when he drank.

Cray offered the flask.

'No.'

Cray took another drink.

'You have quite a thirst,' Farran said.

Cray shook his head. 'Not really. Just a few little drops on the tongue. That's all.'

'But often.'

Cray turned. The eyes flared. 'Yeah, that's right. Often. Little and often. That's how I like it. It keeps me feeling good.' A pulse throbbed in his neck. 'You some sort of temperance society?'

Farran did not answer. Cray drank some more Scotch. His face was red; red in sunlight, red with anger.

Hadji repeated Cray's words: 'It keeps me feeling good.' He closed the file. Then: 'Have you ever seen him drunk?'

'No.'

Petrie filled his pipe. 'A lot of men like whisky.'

'Yes,' Hadji agreed. 'But does he *need* it?'

Petrie looked up, stared at Farran across the pipe.

'He needs it,' Farran said.

Hadji made a note. Then he tapped the second file. 'Robert Luc.' He opened it. 'Robert Jean-Pierre Luc.'

Farran saw again the trim body of the Belgian, moving slow as a sloth across the rock-face. 'As a climber – first-class.'

'And as a man?' Petrie asked.

'A savage.'

This was the Pingal refuge and, after nightfall, the hut warm and the lamp yellow, Dorje sleeping and they

42

seated around the pinewood table, Robert Luc took the shovel and left the hut.

Ethan Cray laughed. 'Man could get his ass froze on a night like this.' He laughed again and the whisky-scent rode for a moment on the smell of burning oil.

Farran watched them. The low, hanging lamp shed its light on their faces. There was a second in which past and present fused, in which other faces came gaunt from cold and effort into lampglow. The years were filled with faces such as these: the same stubbled lips, the same burned and buffeted skins, the same pale circles around the orbits where the goggles had been. How many climbs? How many failures? How many summits? How many cabins where men had grouped in intimacy at a wooden table in the yelling night? He felt his years in that moment. Then Cray lighted a cheroot and the scratch of the match restored him. Ardrey turned a page of his paperback. Ricci's fingers combed his hair in the restless gesture that was characteristic of him. Kemmerich explored the whorls of cream that were daubed across his sore red cheeks. In the shadows on the floor Dorje's ogrous face snarled in sleep.

'Let's play poker,' Cray suggested. He searched for cards. Then he rose, went to Luc's rucksack, found the pack, returned. Ardrey smiled, touched his book, shook his head. Cray began to deal. The door opened, closed on a shriek of wind. They heard the scuff of Luc's boots. Cray dealt more cards, his thick fingers stabbing through the wash of yellow light. Then Luc's shadow touched the edge of the table and the shovel came from height, descended very slowly until it rested in the centre. A crust of snow fell to the wood. Cray stopped dealing. Luc did not speak. The blade of the shovel moved precisely around the table, drawing the four hands of cards into the centre. Then it lifted, poised now above the undealt cards that remained in Cray's left hand.

'Drop them,' Luc said softly.

Cray did not move.

'Bad luck to take another man's pack,' Luc said. 'You ought to know that, Cray.'

Cray expelled a plume of smoke.

'You poisoned the cards.'

Cray smiled.

'Drop them,' Luc said again.

Cray did not move. Farran saw the tremor in his cheek.

'Cray?' Luc whispered. He waited. More snow fell from the shovel. They heard it patter faintly in the silence. Cray blew out smoke. Luc brought down the blade of the shovel across Cray's knuckles. Cray screamed in pain. The cards scattered. Violence leapt like a flame through the hut, Cray swinging and Luc thrusting with the shovel, the lamp rocking and the yellow light palpitating with its movement and Dorje's grotesque shape coming from the floor like an awakened bear.

Petrie smiled. 'Men often quarrel.'

'Especially at high altitudes,' Hadji said.

'Wait,' Farran said. 'There is more.'

Hadji shook his head impatiently, pushed away Luc's file, replaced it with another. His finger underlined the inscription, but it was Petrie who spoke. 'Kemmerich,' he said.

Farran was silent.

'Well?' Hadji asked.

Farran shrugged. 'His record speaks.'

'Yes. And with eloquence. But a record illuminates only the past. Don't you agree?'

'Yes. But he is still good.'

'He is forty-five,' Petrie said.

'I tell you he is still good.'

'But past his best?'

'He is unchanging. He is like iron. He is as good as I have ever known him.'

Hadji opened the file, repeating the words slowly. 'As good as I have ever known him.' He wrote them down. Then: 'Let's consider the relationship. You and Kemmerich.'

Farran waited.

'You were once close friends,' Petrie said.

'Yes.'

'You shared many things.'

'Yes.'

Hadji leaned forward. 'But this again is of the past. Dorje reports that you do not even speak. True or false?'

44

'True.'

'But why? Is there dislike?'

'No.'

'Distrust?'

'No.'

'What then?'

Petrie flicked flame across the bowl of his pipe, peered through the first wraith of smoke. 'A memory,' he said. 'It stands between them.'

Hadji turned pages. 'The Muztagh Tower,' he said. 'A fall. Two deaths. Some repercussions.' He looked up. 'But a long time ago.'

Farran said nothing. Outside the hut the red combat suits flowed through glare. Laughter came distantly.

Hadji said quietly, 'Were you at fault?'

'Yes.'

'You accept the blame?'

'I accept it.'

Hadji's face softened. 'I like that, Farran. To acknowledge guilt, to live with it. Perhaps that is the only real penance.'

Petrie grimaced. 'But there were others,' he said. 'You have many burdens, Farran.'

'No. Only the Muztagh.'

Petrie smiled sourly.

Hadji said, 'Let's stay with Kemmerich.' Then to Farran: 'Won't he forgive you?'

'No.'

'Have you asked him?'

'Not in words.'

Between the Jilga and the Dashti huts the land ran down in wide fields of snow. There were no overhangs, no shadow, no bad places, nothing to oppress; only the immense but gentle valley where, running freely and without wariness through the troughs of reflected sun, the spirit lifted in response. He had stopped to adjust a binding and, kneeling and turning the knife-blade in the head of the screw, he saw below him the run of the team and Dorje's pigtail whip once like a thong across the vision. Then the team was gone and he stood, removed his hood, allowed the wind to play for a moment in his hair. He did not

45

attempt to follow. He stood there, unmoving, enjoying the silence and the empty land.

Then he heard the song.

It came from above and behind him, so distant that it came and went in phrases. He turned his head, listening. The song strengthened. Kemmerich's baritone voice rose and fell, filling the valley, dying in the snows, flighting again. His eyes blurred with tears in that moment of recognition. The simple melody of the lied clutched him like a pain. Kemmerich had always sung; sung himself down through the snows, sung whenever the joy was incontainable.

Kemmerich turned the shoulder of the mountain, a small black figure ski-ing very slowly on the whiteness, poles tucked loosely under the arms, face lifted to the sun. The figure passed below him. He watched it, listening to the swish of blades and the lilting voice. Then he turned, traversing down into the channels left by the skis, following the voice. He knew this song. It had lain in the memory; and, now, the words came easily and he began to sing, his own voice joined with that of Kemmerich. In those moments of harmony it seemed that the years of estrangement had been shed, that he and Kem would sing again through the days of perfect snow.

But it did not last. He heard his own voice, now flat and solitary in the stillness; and he knew that Kem was silent. Kemmerich stopped, turned deliberately, so that he faced away from the trail. He, too, had stopped, staring at the German's back, at the white hair that was frizzed on the brick-red neck, waiting in the breath-pluming air for Kemmerich to turn, to smile, to hold out a hand. But Kemmerich did not turn; and he, Farran, had gone hunched and miserable down toward Dashti.

But you could not tell this to Petrie and Hadji. He waited and Hadji said seriously, 'You must try. You are members of a team. You have a mission. You will need each other.'

The olive fingers reached for two of the three remaining files, exhibited them, one in each hand, like a man offering objects for sale, and said, 'Ardrey and Ricci. The leaven of youth.' He dropped the files. 'How do you assess them?'

'Surely you have all this from Dorje?'

'We want it from you.'

Farran considered. 'They are both very young—'

'And—?'

'In the Himalaya I would not normally take a man below the age of twenty-five.'

'Why not?'

'This again depends on the climb. The bigger mountains demand exceptional powers.'

'And what are these powers?'

'Endurance.'

'Yes?'

'And patience.'

Hadji was amused. 'And don't the young possess these powers?'

'Not often.'

'Let's not generalize,' Petrie said. He sucked at the pipe, turning its glistening mouthpiece into a lance of sun. 'Take Ardrey.'

Hadji watched a bead of spittle form. 'Yes,' he said with distaste. 'Take Ardrey.' He held up a hand, pulling down a finger with each enumeration. 'Cold. Wind. Exposure. Extreme physical effort. The hazards of rock and ice.' He raised an eyebrow.

'He will endure,' Farran said.

'But there are other dangers,' Petrie said mildly.

Farran saw their eyes meet. Petrie puffed smoke, retreated again into his secret world.

Farran said coldly, 'If there are dangers of another nature I should know them.'

Petrie smiled and Hadji said laconically, 'You too must practise patience.' He opened Ardrey's file, scrutinized it. Then, without looking up: 'Do you know this boy's record?'

'Yes.'

'I refer to the incident in Norway.' He looked up.

'I know of it,' Farran said.

'Does it remain with him?'

They had left the Thieng glacier and, moving out from the icefall, made a slow traverse across the grain of the slope. The land glared; but below them where the descent was negotiable was the magenta shadow that was thrown by the shelf. On the shelf and poised like a mantle about

*to slip was the snow. Even at distance they could see the
weight of the mantle, its instability.*

*Dorje stopped them before they reached the shelf,
pointed. A fissure ran like a knife-cut horizontally across
the mantle.*

'Christ!' Cray said.

'Yes,' Dorje said. 'And it is new.'

They stared in silence.

*'Enough snow there,' Luc said, 'to bury a regiment of
men.'*

*Farran saw Ardrey flinch. The words, he sensed, were
tearing like barbs at the surface of his mind. Dorje, too,
was watching. He removed his goggles, and Farran saw
knowledge in the mongol eyes.*

*'Well?' Dorje said to Ardrey. 'What do we do, heh?
You tell us.'*

*They waited. Luc knocked ice from his bindings with
the spike of one of his poles. The sound beat echoes on
the walls of the shelf.*

*'Getting hotter,' Ardrey said. Anxiety strained his voice.
He held out an ungloved hand into the sun. 'Maybe hot
enough to start it.'*

'So?'

'So we wait. Until it is colder.'

'We make a camp and wait?'

*'Yes.' Ardrey stared up at the snow and its deep blue
fissure. 'It would be – prudent.'*

Dorje frowned.

*'Prudent,' Farran repeated. The word sounded ludi-
crous. 'It means careful.'*

*Dorje nodded. Ice swung on the points of the mandarin
whiskers. 'Yes,' he said, 'it would be prudent.' The voice
took scorn. 'Women are prudent. But we are not women.
We are soldiers.' He pulled down his goggles. 'So we
go. Now.'*

*Dorje kick-turned, led them swiftly into the shadow of
the shelf. In the shadow Ardrey fell. Farran stopped. The
binding was sprung and Ardrey knelt, began to fumble.
The fingers were too rapid. He looked up once and Farran
saw the patina of sweat on his cheeks. Ardrey pushed up
his goggles, stared over Farran's shoulder up the rock wall
to where the edge of the snow mantle glowed with a
luminous blue light. There was a moment in which there*

48

*was no intelligence in the eyes, only a blankness behind
which the brain drowned in cataracts of snow.*

'But he was right,' Hadji said. 'In the Karakoram you
do not take a chance. How many times have I said that?'

'It wasn't caution,' Farran said. 'It was fear.'

'It will pass,' Petrie said. 'Whatever he had he will
regain.'

Hadji tapped Ricci's file, smiled. 'You will never accuse
this one of caution.'

*Below them the snow slope narrowed down toward a
ledge. Molars of black rock defined where the ledge ran. A
thin ribbon of snow girdled the rock. Below the ledge was
cloud; and when the cloud broke and was dissipated by
wind they could see the chasm and the purple texture of its
depth. After the ledge the snow broadened again, ran and
grew into a plateau.*

*'Too risky,' Farran said. 'You'd have to turn on a six-
pence. We'll go back.'*

*He turned, led them sidestepping back toward the ridge.
But Ricci had not followed. Cray spoke and, locked on
their edges against the fall of the slope, they looked down,
saw Ricci's crouching figure on its downhill run. 'Oh, my
God,' Ardrey whispered. The figure swooped for the ledge.
They heard the rasp of metal when the upper ski scraped
the rock, Ricci's exulting cry. Snow spurted out, was
swallowed in cloud. Then he was through. They watched
him run easily on to the plateau. He stopped, turned,
waved. Even at distance they could see the laughter in his
face.*

*'Did you see that?' Cray asked. He began to tremble
from reaction. He dropped a glove, retrieved it. Then,
shouting: 'You fucking idiot!' The shout echoed in the
chasm, rebounding in the great chamber of rock and ice:
. . . ing . . . ing . . . ing . . . ot . . . ot . . . ot . . .*

*Later they rejoined Ricci on the plateau. Farran went
to him. He felt sick with anger, with relief. 'You disobey
again,' he said, 'and, God help me, I'll send you home.'
(Do I have that power? he asked himself.) But Ricci put
back his head and laughed. It was all enormously funny.
The teeth flashed and laughter-wrinkles formed in webs
around his eyes. He was irrepressible. Farran could not
sustain his anger. He felt his lips smile in response.*

'I'll race you home,' Ricci said.

Hadji gathered the files. 'Five men,' he said. He began again to enumerate, pulling down fingers, choosing words. 'Ethan Cray. Slow, powerful, aggressive, craving whisky, detesting Robert Luc. But a bull of a man whose physical strength you may come to need.' He removed Cray's file, exposing another. 'Then Luc himself. You named him savage.' He opened the file, riffled its pages, shut it with a kind of contempt. 'And savage he is.' The red lips curled. 'Read this history – and you will not turn your back on Robert Luc.' He discarded the file, depressed another finger. 'Anton Kemmerich.' He shrugged. 'Ageing, of course. But of such immense experience. You will come to value his judgement and his counsel. Let us hope the years are not already traitors in his muscles.' The file slid. 'The boy Ardrey. Such ability. Such promise.' Sorrow touched his voice. The turbaned head shook with regret. 'And then this tarnish on the Sword of Honour. But the qualities that earned it are still there, aren't they? Be sure you use them.' He was silent for a time. Then, smiling, he tapped the fifth file. 'Alessandro Ricci. Impetuous and reckless. But a handsome, warm, accomplished boy. So he will always disarm you.' The smile vanished. 'But he thirsts for danger. That is the story of his life. He needs risk like Cray needs whisky.' Hadji leaned forward. 'But remember – to dare is often to win.'

Hadji placed the five files on the extreme of the desk. Then he took the sixth, drew it toward him. The rosebud mouth smiled. The turban made a little obeisance to the file. When the name came it was in round and vibrant syllables. 'Richard Makepeace Victor Farran.'

Petrie smiled and, watching them, Farran saw that they would enjoy his dissection.

Hadji opened the file, read for a time, grimaced. 'At home,' he said, 'your battalion commander is highly critical.'

'Ah—' Petrie said with satisfaction.

Hadji began to read aloud. ' "Not a good regimental officer. Listless except on physical pursuits. At times insolent—" '

Petrie nodded in agreement.

' "Disrespectful of authority. An abrasive element in the chain of command—" '

Petrie nodded again.

' "—does not conceal his pathological dislike of Army forms." ' Hadji smiled faintly. 'I know that feeling, Farran.' He turned pages. 'Here is something better.'

Petrie frowned.

' "Ample evidence of courage, tenacity, initiative, survival ability, navigational skill." ' He turned more pages. 'Most of the major climbs—'

'And not a few disasters.' This from Petrie.

'But Dorje praises you,' Hadji said. 'As a climber, as a leader.'

He stood, went to the window, jerked up the sun blind. Sun flooded in. Petrie flinched in glare as if from a blow, moved his chair. Hadji watched the slopes. A squad lay prone on reindeer skins, rifles levelled, awaiting an order. Hadji said without turning, 'What are your politics, Farran?'

'Isn't it in the dossier?' Insolence had edged his voice. He felt Hadji's disapproval. He said, 'I have none.'

'No politics?'

'No.'

'No party affiliation?'

'I told you. No.'

'Surely you have allegiances?'

Farran nodded.

'What are they?'

An NCO shouted. They heard the volley. It was like an execution.

'What are they?' Hadji repeated.

'The Queen—'

'Yes?'

'—and the regiment.'

'Are you being funny?' Petrie asked. He knocked out the dead tobacco from his pipe. There was petulance in the quick thrusts of his fist.

Farran smiled and Hadji said, 'No man can be neutral.' He turned from the window. 'Well?'

Farran shrugged. 'If you put it like that—'

'I do.'

'Then I hate the bloody Reds. Is that what you want me to say?'

51

'If it's true, yes.'

Petrie looked up from his pipe.

Farran said, 'I suppose it's true.'

Hadji went to the desk, touched the five files. 'Will these men follow you?'

'Yes.'

'To the limit?'

'Why should they? Men go to the limit for what they believe in, to defend the people and things they love.'

Petrie sniffed. 'What piffle! Men suffer, make sacrifices, die for any number of reasons.' Cynicism glinted in his eyes. 'Money, vanity, a decoration.' He looked sideways at Farran. 'Or when failure or circumstances have made them' – he searched for a word, the fingers of his right hand kneading as if on a ball of putty – 'malleable.'

Farran felt his anger surge. He said to Hadji. 'Why don't you get Indians to do the job?' He tapped his chest. 'There is nothing here we should defend.'

Hadji sat. He said gently, 'You love the Himalaya, don't you?'

'You know I do.'

'So you'd defend them. That's what you said. A man defends that which he loves.'

Farran smiled. 'They are big enough to defend themselves, Colonel.'

Hadji smiled too. Then seriously: 'Forget your island coast.' He thrust his beard at the window, to where the high snows climbed into cloud. 'That is the true frontier – wherever your enemy waits.'

They were silent. Hadji collected the files, stood, went to a steel cabinet, dropped them into its upper drawer. He locked it, turned. Petrie flicked his lighter, stared across its flame. Farran knew he was dismissed. He said, 'You must tell us soon, tell us of our mission.' He waited, but Hadji and Petrie said nothing. 'These men,' he said. 'They will lose heart. You have to tell them.'

Hadji stroked his beard. He crossed from the cabinet to the desk. The turban moved through a sun shaft and, for a moment, it gleamed like an emerald. Hadji sat, swivelled his chair, made a circle on the calendar that hung on the wall behind him. 'Four days,' he said. 'Then watch my Orders of the Day.'

CHAPTER FOUR

On the first of the four days Arif brought the Weasel tractor to the door of Hut Seven. Behind the Weasel was an aluminium sled; and on the sled, shrouded in tarpaulins, was a mound of equipment.

'The final exercise,' Arif told them.

The Weasel drove east, towing the squad on a slow descent to where, five miles beyond the camp, there were cliffs of basalt rock. Holding to the traces and his face turned to the warmth of the early sun, the skis hissing softly through the corrugated spoor that was left by the tractor, Farran watched the cliffs grow larger. They were scoured by wind and there was no snow on the faces, only the long upward reach of green-brown strata.

Arif stopped the Weasel on the scree slopes that ran from the cliffs. He climbed down.

'Not another cliff assault,' Luc said wearily.

'Yes,' Arif said. 'But with a difference.' He pointed. 'Remove your skis. Then strip the sled.'

They built their skis and poles into two pyramids, then stripped off the tarpaulins. There were six new packframes on the sled, an assortment of ropes, North Wall hammers, pitons and pulleys, some tents and bivouac tents, an Army mountain stove, a drum of kerosene, food stores. Farran examined one of the packframes. It was larger than standard, a very strong skeleton of moulded plywood. Under the frames were six rectangular iron shapes. He touched one, stared, looked up at Arif.

'A simple pig-iron weight,' Arif said. He smiled. 'Take one off.'

Farran hooked his fingers under the object, lifted. The dead weight of it wrenched at his muscles. He held it poised for a moment, then dropped it in the snow.

'Come now,' Arif mocked. 'It is only sixty pounds.'

Cray went to the sled, picked up another of the iron cubes, tossed it easily into the snow.

'And the rest,' Arif said.

Cray tossed them out.

'One for each of you,' Arif said. He pointed to the face of the nearest cliff. 'You see the ledge?'

Farran followed the direction of his finger. The ledge at distance was no more than a dark scar in the coloured strata. It traversed the cliff from a point low on the right to its outlet on the left, achieving a rise of perhaps one thousand feet.

Arif kicked one of the pig-iron shapes. 'The purpose of the exercise,' he told them, 'is to convey these weights safely across the face.' The smile left his eyes. 'You will assume that the objects represented by these lumps of iron are of immense value. It will be a disaster of the first magnitude if one of the objects or the man carrying it is lost.' He watched them seriously. Wind leapt through the tarpaulins, cracked them with the sound of pistol shots.

'In that case,' Farran said, 'it would be wise to fix a rope.'

He went to the sled, took out a coil of nylon rope, sufficient pitons and karabiners, stuck his hammer into his belt. Then he set a packframe on the edge of the sled, lifted one of the iron cubes, settled it in the frame. 'Help me,' he said; and Cray came forward, hefted the frame onto his shoulders. He staggered. His knees bent under the weight. He buckled the chest-strap, walked a few paces. The lifeless weight of the pig-iron bore down, tilting him back on his heels so that his boots broke through the snow crust. He looked up at the cliff, feeling then the first disquiet.

He watched the team struggle into their own loaded frames, walk, pivot, turn, adjust themselves to the weight. Then he led them up and across the scree to where the cliff rose.

He removed the frame, dumped it in the snow. Then he began the climb, moving lightly and rhythmically over the face. The cliff faced south and already the ice of the night melted in sun, running in rivulets down the basalt. But the rock was hard and firm. He enjoyed the climb, the scents of rock and ice, the burn of sun on the nape of the neck.

He reached the start-point of the ledge. He looked down. The Weasel, painted in its black and white camouflage, crouched like a small striped insect in the snow. He hammered in the first of the pitons, secured the rope. Then he moved slowly up the ledge, fixing pitons, snapping on the steel rings of the karabiners, threading through the rings the uncoiling rope.

The ledge ran up to a wide arête. He reached it in thirty minutes. Below him ribbons of mist were breaking in sun-heat. From here he could see the village and the camp, the frozen staircase that was the glacier. He remained there for a minute, savouring the silence. Then he made a rapid descent, checking the tension of the rope, the security of the spikes.

At the foot of the cliff the squad was waiting. He manoeuvred the packframe onto his shoulders. Arif nodded. They began the ascent.

The first toehold, the first downward thrust of the leg warned him of the effort they must make. For a time it seemed that the weight of the pig-iron would drag his fingers from the rock. He tightened his grip, gained a foot, then another, inching his way up the bare brown slabs. This was pain. The plywood frame bit through the layers of parka and jersey into his collar-bones, into the flesh of his shoulders, into his spine. The frontal strap constricted. He could not expand his chest against its grip. His lungs were starving in the thin air.

'Rest now!' Arif shouted.

The shout was distant, heard against the sound of his own gasping respiration. He clung there, teeth bared. Sweat runnelled his back into the division of his buttocks. Through the waves of exhaustion he felt the drag of the monstrous iron crab that was pinioned to his back. He locked his knees. Somewhere below him the team sobbed and retched on the wall.

They spent two days and nights on and around the cliffs. They learned to hate the pig-iron cubes – and finally to control them. They marched on racquettes through the snow fields, climbed, glissaded with the weights down the slopes, even manipulated them on pulleys across the basalt faces. They padded sections of the plywood frames so that they would not bite. 'But it don't get no lighter,' Cray complained. 'And sixty pound of iron is nothing like sixty pound of pack.'

Arif came again at noon of the third day. They were brewing tea. Arif walked across the snow, accepted a can, smiled at them quizzically. Farran nodded in answer to the query in his eyes, and Arif pointed at the cliff and said, 'Show me.'

They began the climb, Kemmerich leading, moving now with confidence under the pig-burdens, each man taking pride in the slow but certain progress. There was no wind coming off the glacier and the sun burned in an unclouded sky. Even the candles of ice that glimmered deep in the fissures had begun to drip. Farran heard Arif's voice call faintly from below, 'It is good. It is good.' He reached the ledge, pulled himself on to it, began the careful shuffle that would take him up the narrow lip to the arête.

Now the sweat was running. But it was not the sweat of fear. The packframe weights could be managed – this was proven. Bone and muscle, skill and training had responded. But here, high on the green-brown wall, the mind was liberated. The questions came. What were the objects to which Arif had referred? What could be so heavy and so valuable? Could they be weapons? And if so, what weapon weighed exactly sixty pounds? What was their destination? He turned his head, looked down the ledge to where the coloured bonnets of the team clung like alpine flowers. He felt a sudden emotion, almost of pity. These men were now his responsibility. What were they involved in? Petrie's voice warned again within him: *There is a price to pay.*

It was then that he saw the chough.

The bird came out of the sun, its shadow soaring on the cliff. He heard its wingbeats, and the first wave of vertigo ran through his body. He strengthened his grip on the rope. 'Keep still,' he told himself. 'It will leave.' Sweat formed inside the rims of his goggles. He pushed them up so that they lay propped on the wool of his bonnet.

He listened. The sound of the wingbeats was gone. No shadow rushed on the cliff-face. He looked up to where Kemmerich waited thirty feet above him. Through the film of sweat he could see the German's thick woollen calves, the foreshortened body. He began to climb, Kemmerich taking in the rope and belaying it around a jutting rib of rock.

The bird came again.

He turned in panic and the pig-iron shifted suddenly in its frame. He felt himself totter, the pull of the terrible iron weight that would pluck him from the wall. The rope ripped the bonnet from his head. Bonnet and goggles dropped into the void. 'Help me!' he screamed. The bird sank through the shifting angles of rock and sky. The pig-iron slewed again, jerked him from his hold. He fell until the rope went taut. There was a moment in which he swung in space. Then he felt the knee-grazing pain as his body scraped across the rock. Blood ran down his shin. He found a hold, a purchase for his boots. He clung there, staring at the details of the rock, his face cold in the sun-heat. He heard Cray's voice say distantly, 'You okay up there?' Then Kemmerich's face leaned out of the sky, so close he could smell the perfume of the sun-cream. He felt the German's arm encircle him, holding him, restoring him.

He made himself look down. They were waiting on the wall. He could see the alarm in their faces. He searched for the chough. He said to Kemmerich, 'Has it gone?'

'Yes.'

The arm was still about his shoulders. He felt it tighten; as if, for a second, it had become an embrace. But he could not be sure. The arm withdrew. He nodded at Kemmerich. They made their way slowly up the ledge.

Now the glare struck at his unprotected eyes. The sun came off the snow meadows, enveloping him in a brilliant and unrelenting light. He narrowed his eyes, striving to exclude the glare. He felt the first needles of strain.

That evening they struck camp. This was always one of the good times; Arif pointing the Weasel into the setting sun, the nightfall near the light so red that the parkas glowed like poppies in the snow, the team relaxed in the traces, and ahead in Dhalabat the prospect of hot water, coffee, log fires in the mess.

But for Farran the return was spoiled. There was no serenity. The nausea still rocked in his stomach like some liquid residue of fear. Kemmerich was at his elbow, leaning back on the second trace. They did not speak. But near to Dhalabat the road was rutted. Their skis converged on a single channel of frozen yellow snow, and for a time their legs were joined and they rode together the undulations of the land.

Farran said softly, 'It was like that on the Muztagh. It has always been like that. The one thing that can throw me. Did you know that, Kem? A bird. A ridiculous, in-

57

quisitive sod of a bird hazing me on a climb. The only thing.'

He heard in his voice the plea for understanding. But Kemmerich was silent: his eyes went to the parka and the mended tear, this visible reminder of Erländer's death. The ruts diverged and the skis parted. He was alone again. He said tiredly, 'I'll have to tell Hadji. It's only fair. I'll quit.'

At the camp he removed his skis, stacked them in the rack at the flank of Admin. Hut. Arif and Hadji were standing by the steps. He went to them.

Hadji said accusingly, 'Your eyes are sore.'

'I lost my glasses.'

Hadji stared at his temple and the crust of congealed blood. 'What happened?'

'Something you don't know about,' Farran said. He wiped his watering eyes. 'Something you don't have in that bloody file.'

Hadji waited.

Farran hesitated.

'Well?' Hadji asked.

Beyond the angle of the hut he could see the ridges of the high Karakoram. Soon they would darken into silhouette. But now the sundown red suffused their snows. The old yearning rose. He could not relinquish them. He could not.

'Well?' Hadji said again.

'Nothing,' Farran said.

He walked away.

In the morning at first light, the reveille whistles blowing and he drinking tea by the hut window, he saw the concern in Ardrey's eyes.

'Your face,' Ardrey said.

Farran went to the wall mirror. A monstrous image stared back at him. The glare of those hours on the cliff had left a snow ophthalmia. His eyes were filmed and sunken. The flesh around them was puffed into dark swellings. Burns ringed the orbits. He turned away in disgust and Ricci, coming from his bed, smiled and murmured, 'Horrible.' Then, seriously: 'You must see the medic.'

Later that morning he climbed the road that wound

upward from the camp to the monastery of Thyangjun. Nearing he saw that the monastery was divided by a high stone wall. To the left of the wall were the monks' cottages, a group of pines, a temple with fretworked eaves and painted timbers; to the right of it more cottages, some huts, a central building with new stonework and big windows.

It was very quiet. Farran paused at the top where the road branched, looked down the crag to the valley. Snow had fallen in the night and the patches of winter-bleached grass were gone again. But the streams moved and shed their ice, smoked in the heat of the early sun. He could see the camp and the village, the western snow slopes, the moving hoist and its swinging anchors, Sno-cats and Weasels towing men out into the white lands.

He walked to the gateway. A captain of Royal Marines with a slung arm and a contused cheek came out, nodded, began the walk down. A board was nailed to the pillar. It read:

DHALABAT MILITARY HOSPITAL
Director: Dr Joseph Shaw

'Look to the left,' Shaw said.

Shaw's face was formless in the dark areas behind the ophthalmoscope. Farran could smell the tobacco on his beard. The deep voice murmured, 'Now to the right. Now into the light itself.' There was a pause. Shaw put down the ophthalmoscope. 'Are you very sensitive to light?'

'Yes.'

'Has this happened before?'

'Once.'

Shaw left him, drew the curtains and then the blinds. Sun revealed the surgery, the big X-ray machines that occupied half the floor space. He remained by the window, combing with his fingers his mane of fading hair. His profile was dark against the brilliant pane. It was a good profile, very strong. Like a stone statue, Farran thought, whose features have been eroded by time. He was a big man. Heavy shoulders strained inside a tight white surgical coat. Chemical stains had drawn on the coat a chain of amber islands: it was like an antique map.

'I can find nothing wrong,' Shaw said. 'No scarring.' He came from the window, went to a cabinet, explored an assortment of bottles. He selected one. 'In a day or so it will pass.'

Shaw bent across him, squeezed drops into the corners of his eyes, massaged the lids so that the fluid would spread. Farran's vision blurred. The powerful hands seemed to swing like heavy brown tools. Then the vision cleared and he saw near to him the right hand and its mottling of grave-spots, the atomizer that was poised in the fingers. 'For the burns,' Shaw murmured. He closed his eyes. The spray hissed across his face. When he opened them he saw that Shaw had gone to the window.

'Come over here,' Shaw said.

Farran joined him. Outside snow and sky were fused in glare. He put on his sunglasses. The giant Kashmiri peaks marched across the window. They stood in silence.

'They call it the roof of the world,' Shaw said softly. He put together the tips of his fingers so that his hands formed a gable. 'But I don't see it like that.' He disengaged the fingers. 'I see it not as a roof but as a' – he searched for an image – 'as a great fortification.'

Farran turned. The words were familiar. His mind fled backward. *A wall*, Petrie had whispered. *That is how I see it. A great fortification.* Shaw's eyes were narrowed against the sunlight: he could not see their expression.

Shaw pointed at the north-east Karakoram. 'Across that,' he said, 'is Sinkiang. The old maps print it as Chinese Turkestan. We worked there for many years.'

'We?'

'Mrs Shaw and I. We were missionaries.' He turned abruptly from the window. 'I'll show you the hospital.'

They left the surgery, began to walk. Shaw took his arm, guided him through corridors, a laboratory, past cottages that were connected by canopied walks. Icicles dripped. Nut-brown faces peered from the windows.

'We take a few rich merchants from Srinagar,' Shaw explained. 'They pay through the nose, of course.' He smiled. 'But it helps our funds.'

He opened the glass door that led into the central ward. A dozen men, Indian and European, occupied the beds. Some were in traction. An Indian doctor and a nurse with a red caste-mark on her olive forehead stood at the foot of one of the beds.

'Dr Azfar,' Shaw said. 'My assistant.'

Azfar nodded. He was small and thin with flat black hair that glistened like a varnished boot. He held an X-ray photograph in one hand, a white surgical coat in the other. He said sulkily to Shaw, 'You took my coat again.'

Shaw smiled. 'Did I? Then we'll swop.'

They exchanged. Shaw slung the coat over his shoulder. He was wearing a dark-blue jersey with a roll collar. The coarse yarn was stretched very tight across his barrel chest. He looked like a fisherman. Azfar gave the photograph to Shaw, put on his coat. Shaw held the photograph up to the light. Azfar waited, his thin hands driving nervously down the white coat, their sharp tips navigating the amber islands.

Shaw returned the picture. He said gently, 'You'll have to reset it.'

Azfar flushed. They left the ward. Farran looked back as the door closed. Azfar was staring at the picture, like a painter appalled at the evidence of his own lack of talent.

Shaw said, 'He's a good physician. But no good at bones. He's too fragile.' He held up his muscular hands. 'You need strength and confidence to deal properly with fractures.' He held open another door. 'Every week,' he said, 'we get three or four broken limbs. They also send us cases from Gulmarg – that's another of the Indian Army mountain warfare schools.' He closed the door. Now they were on the edge of gardens. Sunlight touched his beard, exposing the white strands that were entwined in it. He said seriously, 'This is a frontier, Farran. Never forget that. Everywhere men are learning to defend it.' He reached up to the eaves, swept off with his forearm its decoration of icicles. 'Last week,' he said, 'an icicle dropped clean into a man's eye.'

Shaw led him through the gardens. There were paths of worn stone, shrubs coming into bud, descending shelves of granite down which rills of water ran to fill a lily-pool. A miniature wooden bridge spanned the pool. It was like a scene from a Chinese willow-plate.

'Mrs Shaw tends the gardens,' Shaw said. 'We get three months of flowers. Then the cold comes down again.'

They passed from sun into the shadow of pines, out again into an area of flagged walks and raised stone troughs. Alpines bloomed in the troughs. Shaw stopped to admire them, touched the petals of a gentian. Then he pointed at the path that skirted the lily-pool. They followed it to where two ancient walls formed a right-angle. An iron gate was set in the rear wall; and beyond the lateral wall that divided the hospital from the monastery rose the triple roofs of the temple. There were four graves in the angle, each with a headstone and a stone surround. The soil within the surrounds was freshly dug. Primulas grew. Three of the headstones were green with age. The fourth was smaller, more recent. The inscriptions on all of them were very clear, as if someone had, with devotion, kept them sharp and free from fungus.

Shaw stood in silence. Farran sensed his sudden withdrawal. He read the first of the epitaphs. *The Reverend John Reagh. Died of the Cholera, 17 September 1892.*

Shaw murmured, 'As you can see, we were not the first missionaries to come to Dhalabat.'

Farran nodded. He had felt a momentary affinity with the bones that lay in the grave. The day and month of Reagh's death coincided with those of his own birth-date.

'That was the time of the great cholera epidemic,' Shaw said. 'We still have Reagh's own record. He had gone down in Srinagar. The town was stricken. There was nothing for sale in the shops except bolts of white cloth for winding-sheets. He got infected and was dead within a few days.' He pointed to the adjacent stone. 'His wife Millicent followed him a week later.'

They moved to the third headstone. 'A mystery, this one,' Shaw said. He read the inscription aloud. *'Martin Ian Clements. Captain, 9th Lancers. Answered the Last Bugle, 21 May 1857.'* He turned. 'We have no record of this man. We know only that his regiment was stationed at Umballa, that the Indian Mutiny was flaring through the land like a bush-fire, had in fact reached Delhi ten days before his death.' Shaw spread his hands. 'What was he doing here, three hundred miles from his regiment?' Shaw smiled. 'None of this matters, of course. It was a long time ago. But one hates a mystery.'

At the fourth grave Shaw's face went cold. Farran bent

to the small headstone. *Alan Francis Shaw. Born and died Christmas Day, 1954.*

'Yours?' he asked.

Shaw nodded. Farran saw the pain in his eyes. A monastery bell rang a single silver note. Shaw stared at the temple, at the grave, at the temple again. He stood there blinking in the sun. Farran felt the man's unbearable aloneness, knew then that Shaw had brought him to the tiny graveyard to share for a moment a private grief.

Shaw opened the iron gate. A path led from the gate around the rear of the hospital. Above them the mountainside was ragged with pines. They walked in silence. Then Shaw said, 'We stayed on for a few years after the Reds took over. But it couldn't last. There was no one now to listen to the Christian message. The China Inland Mission had had its day and the priests were leaving. Then the violence began. Kate and I were among the last to go. She was six months pregnant. We had' – he hesitated as if words had become fearful – 'we had – experiences. I could not tell you how they repaid us for all our years of service. Toward the end of 1954 we crossed the Pass of Zoji La into Kashmir. There were heavy snows and blizzards. She had a bad time. And when the boy came he was premature, too small and weak to survive.' Shaw stopped, pulled at his beard. 'For me that was the final irony. On Christmas Day we might surely have expected a gift, don't you think? Was that too much to ask?'

Farran did not answer. He looked across Shaw's shoulder at the hospital and its outbuildings. There had been no sign of a chapel. Shaw, it seemed, saw the question in his eyes. He said harshly, 'Don't expect cassocks and dog-collars and Onward Christian Soldiers. This is no longer a mission. It is an army hospital – no more than that.'

Farran left him at the entrance gate. He began the walk down to the camp. Below him on the slope where the snow was still good the squad had made a slalom. He stopped, watched them for a time. Cray was falling heavily on the tight turns. His thick laughter rose.

A bell rang faintly in the monastery. Farran zipped his parka. Then, on impulse, he turned, stared back up the path to the hospital.

Shaw's jersey made a dark-blue patch on one of the windows. A woman stood at his side. They were very close and her head was inclined against his shoulder. They were watching him.

That night in Hut Seven Farran was awakened by the sound of motor traffic. He got up, went to the window. Yellow headlamps cut paths of light from the darkness. The noise swelled. An armoured car, two covered trucks and another armoured car came from Admin. area, swept past the hut. He looked at his watch. 'Three in the morning,' Ardrey said behind him. They went to the flank window of the hut, wiped condensation from the glass. From here they could see the curve of the road, its sheen of black ice, the whorls of red light that were spilled from the tail-lamps of the convoy.

The convoy stopped two hundred yards down the road by Number Two Armoury. The door of the Armoury opened, forming a rectangle of light. A man came from the interior, stood for a moment in the entrance. He was in silhouette and they could not see his face. But the head was turbaned. The figure turned and the light drew a sliver of green down the folds of the turban. It was Hadji.

Now men were unloading the trucks, crossing and re-crossing the headlamps with a succession of shrouded shapes. Two Indian soldiers stationed themselves on either side of the door. The convoy commander gave a document to Hadji. They saw him read it, nod, sign it, return it. Then he locked the door, stared at the sentries, said something to one of them, went to the first of the armoured cars, climbed in. The convoy commander followed. The convoy left. The sound of the engines died. Snowflakes leapt on wind, broke against the window. The sentries stood unmoving in the darkness.

CHAPTER FIVE

In the morning Farran and the team went to Admin. Hut. Hadji's Orders of the Day were always posted at seven o'clock. Most of the squad and company commanders were there. Four foolscap sheets were pinned to the board. The Orders began with the usual preambles; the weather reports and forecasts, the day's arrivals and dispositions, route warnings and prohibited areas, a few acid comments on breaches of discipline and training procedures, a request for the prompt payment of outstanding mess bills. Then, under the head of *Drills, Lectures and Expeditions*, were twenty-four listed items.

Farran read them. Item Nineteen said simply:

> Capt. R. M. V. Farran's squad
> (Beta Company) will attend at
> Number Two Armoury at 1400
> hours. Subject: Demolition.

At five minutes before two o'clock Farran led the squad to Number Two Armoury. Sun bathed the camp. The afternoon sessions were beginning and the roads were filled with men. Trucks and tractors drove out and upward from the camp toward the receding snowline.

Two sentries guarded the entrance to the Armoury. Arif stood between them, as grave and important as an usher at a banquet. 'Remove your parkas,' he told them. 'Then sit.'

They entered the hut. The windows were shuttered. Light was shed from four electric bulbs that hung on flexes from the metal struts that braced the roof. Eight chairs were arranged at one end of the hut. They removed their parkas, sat, stared around them.

There were the usual Armoury stocks; wall-racks of 7.62 automatic rifles and Sterling sub-machine guns, stacks of stencilled ammo- and magazine-boxes. There was a wooden issue-counter behind which a quartermaster and his sergeant would normally stand. But behind the chairs was a projector: it pointed above their heads to the screen that was set on the wall at the opposite end of the hut. Around the screen and on two adjoining walls were pinned rows of very large black-and-white photographs. They formed a continuous frieze of snow, ice, glacier and mountain panoramas. A diagrammatic map was stuck with adhesive tape to the face of the quartermaster's counter. There were no names or references on the map, only coloured segments of white, blue and brown. A table and two chairs had been placed near to the screen. A white pointer lay on the table. In the centre of the hut were two long benches. Crude wooden legs protruded from the skirts of draped tarpaulins. The tarpaulins were moulded into strange humps and depressions by the objects they concealed. To the right of the benches two aluminium sleds were aligned on the floor; and piled in the sleds were the six plywood pack-frames they had used in training.

They heard the sentries salute. The door opened. Cold air gusted. Colonel Hadji and Petrie entered, marched down the hut to the table. The squad stood. Hadji turned, smiled, made a downward motion with his hand. They sat. Petrie placed his tweed hat on the table, pinched its crown into shape. Hadji removed his white combat parka, threw it on the ammo boxes, picked up the pointer, murmured something to Petrie, put it down again. Behind them Dorje's voice was grunting in the entrance. Arif closed and bolted the door. Then he and Dorje entered, sat apart from them in the two remaining chairs.

Farran looked sideways into the mongol face. Dorje took off his Peruvian bonnet, stuck it into the breast of his fur jacket. His pigtail lay curled on his shoulder like a thin black snake. Farran caught the fetid smell of the fur, moved an inch. Dorje bared his decaying teeth. At the table Petrie, seated primly, stroked his tweed thighs. Hadji's turban was an emerald under the overhanging bulb. The hut was very quiet. They could hear the whine of the generator. Then Hadji nodded to Petrie, sat. Petrie stood, took his pipe from his pocket, pointed it like a gun at the squad.

'Each of you,' he said, 'is a serving officer in the army of a NATO power. You were in fact selected from the armies of five separate nations. That selection was deli-

66

berate. And in the context of your mission this sharing of political responsibility is of immense importance. Before you leave this hut you will understand why.' He sucked at the mouthpiece of the pipe, pointed it again. 'I have to remind you as serving soldiers you are bound to secrecy. Nothing you learn today will be divulged or communicated to another party, now or in the future. You will not discuss your mission except among yourselves or with the other parties present in this hut. You will not mention any objective or location or code-name or map reference in the hearing of another party. For the remainder of your time in this camp you will not convey by word or deed or attitude that you are engaged in anything other than a normal training expedition.'

Petrie was silent for a time. He scratched with the mouthpiece of the pipe in the silver sidewings of his hair. Then he said, 'I have to make this clear. Nothing in your contract of service or in your individual oaths of loyalty requires you to commit a hostile act against a nation with which your country is not at war. Although you came here with an obvious foreknowledge of an . . . ah . . . clandestine act you still retain' – he emphasized it – 'you still retain at this moment of time a freedom of decision. You must exercise that freedom now. I can only say that your mission involves the territory and interests of a Communist power, that you will, while in that territory, be in very considerable danger. If any man feels that for moral or personal or political reasons he cannot continue then he must say so now. Once a man has learned the nature of the operation he is committed.' Petrie raked again with the pipe. 'I am going to fill a pipe, give you time to think.'

Petrie packed tobacco in the bowl, flicked his lighter. He stood there, coaxing the pipe, watching them over the flame. No man moved or spoke. Smoke curled. Petrie nodded, pocketed the lighter, bowed formally to Hadji, sat.

Hadji rose, picked up the pointer, went to the diagram map. He drew the tip of the pointer slowly north through whorls of blue and white until it rested on the zig-zags of a broad red frontier line. He said, 'Here in the Indian zone of Kashmir we are bounded to the north-east by the Chinese province of Sinkiang, and to the east by Chinese Tibet.' He smiled. 'This is geography.' The smile died. 'But we can express it in another way. We can say that here in

Kashmir we are bounded on two flanks by an ancient and implacable enemy.'

He left the map, walked a pace toward them. He said earnestly, 'On the changing Indian scene only this, this inbred fear of China, remains unchanging. Fear. I am not ashamed to use that word. It is born in us. We live with it. For fifteen years we have fought them on the white frontiers. We have killed – and been killed. The fighting flares. It dies. It flares again.' He shrugged. 'To the world these are border skirmishes. To us they are battles in a developing war.' He began to swish with the pointer against his thigh, as if some old emotion had recharged him. 'The dragon is no longer asleep. It is stirring. It is reaching out.' His voice fell. 'And the fire in its jaws is that of the thermo-nuclear weapon.'

Hadji thrust his black beard at them, beat his thigh again with his pointer. Then he relaxed. He returned to the table, put down his pointer. He said, smiling, 'And now for some natural history. Come back with me through time to the year of 1893.'

Hadji clasped his hands behind him, half closed his eyes, 'Imagine if you can the end of that distant summer. We are in the High Himalaya on the slopes of the valley of Nandakna. We are not insensible to beauty and we observe the wild roses and the honeysuckle, the shepherds and their flocks of horned sheep, the torrent of green water that surges through the gorge beneath us.'

Petrie grimaced, tapped impatiently. Cray whispered, 'Jesus, he's off again.'

'Above us,' Hadji continued, 'is the peak of Trisul. Indeed it is the snow-water from Trisul's glaciers that fills the gorge. We reach the ridge.' He pointed at Farran. 'What do we see, Farran?'

'We see Kamet,' Farran said.

'And?'

Farran searched his memory. 'Nilkanta. The Mana Peak. Dunagiri.'

Hadji nodded. 'We also see Maithana. Remember that name. It is significant.' He paused. 'So there we stand, high on the ridge, looking across the Gohna Valley and the gleam of the river Birahi Ganga toward the huge dolomite face of the mountain. All is silent. The scents of the valley rise. It is a place of peace.'

Petrie shook his head sadly, took the feather from his hatband, began to clean his fingernails with its quill point.

'But the peace is illusion,' Hadji said. 'For we are about to witness one of the world's great natural catastrophes.' He raised a hand to his ear. 'We hear a faint rumbling. It is like the sound of an avalanche or the first tremor of an earthquake. It seems to come from Maithana. And as we stare we see the face of the mountain change, slip and break into new contours. We watch it fall to the valley floor.'

Hadji dabbed his lips with a khaki handkerchief. 'Can you picture that scene? The sky dark with dust. Rocks as big as houses shot like cannon-balls at the valley walls. A million birds flung across the sky. The river spewing outward in two giant waves.' He shook his head. 'It defies the imagination. But this was not the end. For three days the falls continued. At the end of that time no less than twelve million cubic feet of rock had fallen, the Gohna Valley was blocked and the river lay dammed behind a rampart of rock and debris one thousand feet in height.'

Hadji folded the handkerchief into a square. 'For many months the monsoon rains, the mountains and their glaciers fed the river. It spread behind the dam into a lake three miles long. And through the winter, the spring and the summer the lake continued to rise until it began to lap at the very top of that rocky dam.' His voice hushed. 'At just before midnight on the twenty-fifth of August 1894 it overflowed. At first it was a stream. Then the enormous weight of the lake, penned back for so long a time, pressed against the dam. It broke. The lake was released. It emptied like a smashed basin suddenly shooting out its contents. And a flood of water, three hundred feet deep at the point where it broke the dam, roared down into the Alaknanda Valley. Imagine that seething mass moving through the night at a speed of thirty miles an hour. It must have come out of darkness like a giant tidal wave. Bridges, roads, temples, crops and villages were swept away. And finally the wall of water reached Srinagar.' He paused for effect. 'That city was utterly destroyed.'

Hadji stared at them for a time. Then he turned abruptly, sat. He dabbed again at his lips. He said to Petrie, 'I could do with a drink.'

'I'm not surprised,' Petrie said dryly. He rose from the

table, winced under the glare of the naked bulb that hung above his head, then moved away from it. He said, 'So much for Maithana. The geologists, of course, wrote learned explanations. The angle of the mountain slope, they said, exceeded the dip of its dolomite strata, and this produced the slip. Or some such jargon. But we at home use a simple term for natural disasters.' He pointed with his pipe. 'What is that term, Ardrey?'

'An Act of God, sir.'

Petrie nodded. 'An Act of God.' He gave his secret smile. 'But we can learn from the Almighty.' He glanced at the benches and their shrouded shapes. 'We can even flatter him by imitation.'

Petrie returned to the table. Hadji stood, gestured to Arif. Arif said something to Dorje. Both rose, went to one end of the longer of the two benches.

Petrie said, 'Will someone help?'

Farran and Cray left their chairs, went to the opposite end of the bench. Each took hold of an edge of the tarpaulin. Arif nodded. They lifted. There was a moment in which they held the tarpaulin high above the bench. Miniature mountains, snows and plains lay exposed beneath them. Water gleamed. Then Dorje tugged and they carried the tarpaulin to the side of the bench, placed it on the floor.

'Good,' Hadji said. 'Gather round, please.' He picked up the white pointer, sloped it on his shoulder as if it were a rifle, went to the model. Luc, Kemmerich, Ardrey and Ricci came from their chairs.

They stared down. Hadji watched them, an amused smile playing on his cherry lips. The model was perfectly made, richly coloured. At the southern end ice-caps rose as sharp as teeth. Between the caps was the deep cleft of a pass. The pass wound through the mountain chain, emerged on the breast of a wide glacier. The glacier descended steeply until it was broken into icefalls. From there on snowfields and white plateaux ran down through patches of coniferous forest, into areas of dark-green pigment that denoted the ending of the snow-line. The green gave way to ochrous tints, the broad basin that the modeller had filled with water to represent a lake.

It was there that the eye rested. A rock-mountain reared above the lake. It was distinctive and solitary, not conical but flat along its summit ridge like a table. Its slabs, spurs, chimneys and cracks gave it a vaguely human expression. It seemed to frown down as if at its own reflection in the lake.

Petrie took a pin from his lapel, dropped it from height into the water. Tiny ripples spread, touched the narrow dam that sealed the lake. Beyond the dam the land rose again into high dark shoulders, forming a gorge through which a river ran. The river twisted, always deeply locked within the walls. The gorge opened abruptly on to a plain; and on the plain, extending outward from the natural gateway, was built an immense complex of plant and factory installations. The modeller had worked with enthusiasm. There were domes and futuristic shapes, transformers and turbine sheds, a power-station with tall chimneys on which pinches of cotton-wool were stuck to simulate smoke, a dozen factories with long saw-tooth roofs, gantries, reservoirs to tap the river, railway tracks and rolling-stock, a network of roads, an airfield and a control-tower, villages with row upon row of uniform houses.

Cray said with admiration, 'It's a goddam work of art.'

Farran reached out, ran his fingers across the Karakoram peaks. Their points were like needles against his skin.

'Such delicacy,' Hadji murmured.

Farran nodded. They were fashioned with a curious upward flourish, as if with icing-sugar squeezed and spiralled from a nozzle. Their flanks were gracefully painted in pale tones of blue. But they had no strength. They glowed prettily under the light. He withdrew his hand. These fragile milk-teeth would surely crumble in the blizzard.

Hadji's pointer moved down the glacier and across the snows until it reached the lake. The tip glided up the rock-mountain, over the strange configurations that seemed to form a mouth, two nostrils, deep eye-sockets. He turned. He said softly, 'Does anyone know this mountain?'

He waited. No one spoke.

'It is Jalanath,' Hadji said.

He searched their faces. Then to Arif: 'Tell them, Arif.'

'It is an Indian name,' Arif said. He spoke with a kind of reverence. 'Jalanath. The name of a god. It means Lord of the Waters.' He pointed. 'Some say it has a human face. The face changes according to the soul of the beholder. Beautiful to some, hideous to others.'

71

Petrie sniffed. He said sourly, 'Why do mountains bring out the worst in people? Inflated language. Mystic rot. Idiotic legends. I've said it before, and I'll say it again. A mountain is a mass of rock. No more and no less.' He peered. 'What is it? Male or female?'

Hadji shrugged. 'It is a god.'

'I'm sure it's a girl,' Ricci said, smiling. 'She is admiring herself in the mirror of the water.'

'A girl?' Luc asked. He stared at the mountain. Distaste curled his lips. 'I would not like to wake up in the bed with a hag like that one.'

Petrie rapped impatiently with his pipe. 'Let's get on.'

Hadji reached with the pointer into the heart of the mountains. 'You have made many sorties into the Kara-koram,' he said. 'Many of them as far as the Jilga refuge.' The pointer slid along the frame of the model, paused where a degree of latitude was marked in red. 'But never as deep as this.' He looked at them. 'Can anyone tell me what this indicates?'

'It is the frontier,' Farran said.

Hadji nodded. He took the pointer sideways through the ice-caps. 'At these altitudes you will not find the markings of a boundary. But extend an imaginary line and you will have defined it. Cross that line and you are in Sinkiang.'

Hadji walked down the length of the bench. The turban leaned across the miniature installations. He said, 'To our knowledge the Chinese have built two major nuclear rocket plants. One is at Lop Nor. The other is here (he touched one of the gantries) at Su Tokai.' He passed the pointer back and forth over the installations as if it were a wand. 'It is vast. It is a city of science. It is an arsenal. It is protected by the gorge. It draws its water from the glaciers, stores it in the Lake of Jalanath. It faces out on to a great and uninhabited plain, and this it uses as a testing-ground. It has a population of some five thousand workers, a regiment of the People's Army, a squadron of fighters.' He paused. 'In fact Su Tokai is a target of supreme military importance.'

He straightened, watched their faces for reaction.

'Except,' Kemmerich said in the silence, 'that we are not at war with China.'

Hadji frowned. Petrie said, 'Don't interrupt. Just listen.'

72

Then, sarcastically: 'Later you shall define a state of war for us, when it exists and when it doesn't. Later – but not now.' He tapped bad-temperedly with the pipe. A shred of tobacco shot into the lake. Hadji grimaced, picked it out with his finger, flicked it away. He said, 'Let us recall Maithana.' He dipped the tip of the pointer. 'And let us then reflect that these, the waters of Jalanath, would be released with infinitely greater force. The lake is larger, deeper, higher than the Gohna. The bed of the gorge falls more steeply. And its walls (he touched the green-brown shoulders) are higher and narrower than those of the Alaknanda Valley.'

His voice hushed. He brought together his palms until they almost touched. 'The flood would be compressed. It would leap like water from the narrow neck of a bottle. It would travel at a speed of perhaps forty miles an hour. And then—' He spread his hands over the installations. 'Within three hours it would reach Su Tokai. Everything, that entire complex of planned destructive power, would itself be destroyed. Nothing would remain.'

Hadji dabbed again with the khaki handkerchief, stared at them. Petrie stroked the lapel of his hairy suit. Dorje scraped his feet.

Then Cray said softly, 'So that's it. We are going to blow a dam.'

Hadji shook his head. 'No, Cray. Something much more dramatic.'

He went to the table, put down the pointer. Then, turning, he said, 'Will you sit, please?'

They sat. Arif went behind them to the projector, opened with a key a green metal box, took out some cassettes. Then he went to the light switch, flicked it up. The Armoury was plunged into darkness. They heard his boots clump across the floor, the sounds of his hands working at the projector. It began to whirr. The screen went silver. Some red numerals appeared, then a moving panorama of sunlit snow and purple rock. There was a sense of depth. Sometimes a grotesque shadow with whirling arms danced across the whiteness.

'As you can see,' Arif's voice said behind them, 'these are helicopter films. We are flying due east from the camp.' More mountain architecture flowed. 'We are approaching the short high-altitude valley that you saw on the model.'

A minute passed. The shadow scurried like a crab across a network of ice-streams. An orb of white sun swung suddenly down the top right-hand corner of the screen. 'Did you see that?' Arif said. 'It signified a change of course.' The terrain opened. 'We are now in the valley. It is not really a pass – although we call it that. It is in fact no more than a divide in the massif. It has no importance and for that reason it has no name. But for you it serves a purpose. It leads directly into the Tuzluk glacier.'

A great saddle of rock-strewn snow rode toward them, altering contour with the flight. Farran glanced around him. Silver light flickered on the row of intent faces. The bowl of Petrie's pipe glowed redly in the darkness. The screen went black. A numeral flashed.

'This is an edited film,' Arif explained.

The screen bloomed again into a blue and silver flower. Séracs gleamed like towers of glass.

'At this point,' Arif said, 'we have covered about forty miles. We are flying parallel to the Tibetan border. In a moment you'll see the Tuzluk.'

The glacier appeared. The shadow of the helicopter ran swiftly across its bank, then down the breast of the river of ice. Minutes passed. The film took on a strange, hypnotic quality, the shadow fleeing, the unvarying ice leaping into the eye of the camera. Crimson, now, was staining the silver.

'Sunset,' Arif said. The screen went black again. 'The end of the day. And the end of the helicopter film.'

They heard him fumble with the spool. Hadji's voice came out of darkness. 'We are within one mile of the Chinese frontier. So we could go no farther.'

The projector began to whirr. 'These are stills,' Arif said. 'All of them in Sinkiang territory.' Humour touched his voice. 'They were taken by a man who is sitting not a thousand miles away from us.'

Farran looked sideways at Dorje. Reflected light from the first of the stills glimmered on his features. The bootlace whiskers were gripped in the right side of his mouth. The jaws moved, like those of a man chewing on a twist of tobacco.

'This is the Tuzluk icefall,' Arif said. 'A truly terrible place.' Cascades of ice seemed to pour and curl like sea-waves across the screen. Another still replaced it. This time

74

they could see the gigantic ridges through which the ice was squeezed, the ice overhangs that were poised as blue as steel above the glacis. 'During the day,' Arif said, 'there are continual ice avalanches. It is so dangerous that the Chinese troops never use it.' He laughed softly. 'But for you this has its advantages.'

They left the icefall. Now the screen depicted a succession of smooth snow-pastures. They seemed unbroken, mile upon mile of hills, plateaux and troughs. 'Seventeen miles of marvellous downhill run,' Arif said. Then, significantly: 'A man could make good time here.'

More pictures followed. The snowfields ran into belts of forest and rock pinnacles. Dark green blotches appeared. 'The permanent snowline is around fifteen thousand feet,' Arif said. 'We are now below it.'

The screen went black. Petrie sucked his pipe in the silence. Arif was unmoving. Then he said, 'You are about to see photographs of our objective.'

They waited. Cray and Ardrey leaned forward in their seats. The first of the stills was unimpressive. The frozen waters of the lake lay in a pale green sheet across the foreground. A few birds stood on the ice. Across the lake Jalanath rose in a grey and featureless mass. Snow defined its sloping table of a ridge. Behind it were the white jags of higher peaks. It grew but was distinct from a range of hills and mountains.

Petrie sniffed. 'I can see no face.'

'Wait,' Hadji said.

In the second still the ice had gone. This was summer and the waters lapped on a foreground of scree and boulders. The mountain was in shadow. To the left of the picture they could see where the walls of the gorge pressed together, the dam that sealed it.

Arif held the picture for a time. 'Let me tell you about Jalanath,' he said. 'By Himalayan standards it is not a high mountain. About eighteen thousand feet above sea-level. The lake lies at ten thousand. But the mountain is unique. The rise of eight thousand feet is almost a perpendicular.'

The third still appeared. The dam was nearer. The four sluices were plainly visible. A small concrete tower rose at one end.

'Let's have the next,' Hadji said.

It appeared.

'This is the one,' Hadji said. 'Do you see the face?' He rose, went with the pointer to one side of the screen. The tip moved across the mountain. 'Eyes, nose, mouth – they are all there.'

The fifth picture had been taken from the extreme end of the lake, opposite the dam. In it the mountain showed its profile. The brow rode upward into a thick wig of snow. The central slab that lifted vertically for perhaps two thousand feet formed a straight, almost Grecian nose. Below the cavern of a nostril were the two projecting shelves that were like slightly parted lips. The face seemed to brood above the lake.

'I think you're right, Ricci,' Hadji said. His own profile smiled in silhouette on the screen. 'It is certainly a goddess.' He rapped with the pointer on the face. A tremor ran across the screen. Farran felt the first foreboding. It brushed him like the wing of something passing in the dark. In that second of vibration it had seemed that the mountain shuddered under Hadji's touch.

Hadji turned to face them. He said seriously, 'The next film is very special. It was transmitted from a reconnaissance satellite. Parts of the prints have been magnified.'

He moved away. Jalanath's profile disappeared. They waited. Arif fed spool in the darkness. The screen turned gold. A superscription in dark brown letters travelled slowly across its breadth. It read: ZV WEST HIMALAYAN AXIS.

'The name of the satellite is Zirkon Voyager,' Arif said. Some groups of code appeared; then, on the left of the film, the ladder of tiny white lines and spaced numbers that were the navigational markings. Hadji sat, dropped his pointer, picked it up. In that moment of movement the face of beauty revealed itself on the screen.

Farran felt his throat dry. The peaks of the Karakoram were passing slowly beneath them. They rode upward like ice-blue flames, reached for him, retreated. He stared down from the eye of Zirkon Voyager, lost in the purity of that glacial world.

The ice-cap passed as if on a turning globe. Each man rode with Zircon Voyager on its silent flight. Even Petrie's pipe hung suspended in the dark like a firefly.

Then Arif said quietly, 'It will detect almost anything.

Troop movements. Military installations. Even the size and quality of China's wheat and rice crops.'

Now the satellite was across and beyond the roof of the world. The last of the great ice-caps glimmered and was gone. Purples and browns came out of distance, ran like pigments into the white of glaciers and snows.

Hadji said suddenly, 'This is Jalanath.'

Seen from space the mountain was no more than a broad white cliff-edge, defined by the blue of the lake; a projection of the highlands that rose behind it.

It passed slowly through the base of the screen. Now the gorge made its deep rent in the fabric of the land. The snow had gone. Orange plains descended. The gorge opened. A black hatching made a pattern on the orange.

'Su Tokai,' Hadji murmured.

The screen now was like a desert.

'Observe the size of the testing-grounds,' Arif said.

The film ended. The Armoury went black. Hadji said in the darkness, 'We'll have the enlargements now.'

There was a pause. Then a still of Jalanath appeared. It was the same aerial view, greatly magnified. The summit ridge ran vertically up the screen. The land and its western shore made a border on the left.

Hadji stood, went to the side of the screen. He reached with the pointer, allowed its tip to rest on the snow plateau that lay behind the mountain's ridge. 'Look closely,' he said. The tip travelled slowly upward, always parallel to the ridge, then down again. He said without turning, 'Do you see it? The faint blue shadow that follows the line of the summit ridge?' He waited, shrugged. 'The next picture will demonstrate it clearly.'

The picture appeared. This time the angle of the sun had changed. Light struck obliquely across the mountain. It threw into relief the deep rift in the plateau.

'There you see it,' Hadji said. 'The outward evidence of a massive geological fault.' He ran the pointer up the plateau. Then, turning, he said to Arif, 'Lights, please.'

Arif stopped the projector, went to the switches. The bulbs flared. Petrie flinched. Hadji crossed from the screen to the model. He said, 'The experts tell us that the fissure almost certainly splits the upper body of the mountain.' He smiled slyly. 'They also tell us that with a little encouragement this' – he tapped the mountain's face – 'could be ripped away, dropped like a torn-off mask into the lake below.'

He pointed at the second bench. Arif and Dorje went to one end, Farran and Ardrey to the other. They removed the tarpaulin. Then they sat.

There were three identical objects on the bench, spheroid in shape, made from some granite-grey metal. They were perhaps twice the size of a football. The surfaces were dull, slightly corrugated. There was a large flange at each end, bored with central hole. A metal band girdled their waists, as if at one stage of manufacture there had been an upper and lower shell. Sitting there on the bench, grooved and glinting under the light, they were like huge molluscs.

'They look like oysters,' Hadji said. 'And that is the name we shall use when we refer to them. They are, in fact, miniature H-bombs.'

He sat on the edge of the bench, crossed a leg, watched their faces for reaction. The hut was silent. Wind whined in the stovepipe. Amusement seemed to ripple through his body, reflecting in the dark eyes.

'Gentlemen,' Hadji said, mocking them. 'You are going to climb on the face of a god.'

The tea-kettles came. Now they were moving, cup in hand and smoking nervously, about the hut.

Petrie and Hadji watched from the stove.

Arif said to Farran, 'So now you know.'

'Yes,' Farran said. 'Now we know.' He went to Petrie, stared at him through the steam that curled upward from his cup.

'Well, Farran,' Petrie said. 'I promised you adventure.'

Cray was passing. 'Adventure? It's suicide.'

Farran joined him, accepted a cheroot. Cray took a flask from his pocket, proffered it.

'No.'

Cray tipped whisky into his tea. Dorje came out of the wraiths of tobacco-smoke, bringing his fetid smell. He stood there, pocked cheeks ballooned, swilling the tea around his jaws like a man using a mouth-wash. He swallowed, said to Farran, 'Good, heh?'

'Real good,' Cray said. 'Except for the seven hundred million Chinks.' He offered the flask. 'You want some Scotch?'

Dorje held out his cup and Cray topped it. Dorje laughed, crossed the floor to Arif.

Cray drank, nodded to where Ardrey and Ricci were standing. Their eyes shone. They were elated.

'Just look at them,' Cray said. 'Grinning like apes.'

Farran smiled. 'They'll think about it later. At the moment they're twenty.'

Cray said to Ardrey, 'You know what'll happen if they catch you?'

Ardrey smiled. 'The water torture at the very least.'

'Or the death of a thousand cuts.' This from Ricci.

Both laughed.

Cray shrugged, went to the bench, put down his cup, lifted one of the Oysters.

'That's right, Cray,' Hadji called across the hut. 'Exactly sixty pounds.'

Cray set it down. Kemmerich reached out, stroked its grey armour. His face was very still.

Farran went to the model, stared at it.

'Can it be done?' Luc asked.

'The trip?'

'Yes.'

'I don't know.'

Luc bent across it. 'It looks too easy.'

Petrie came behind them, passed a finger down the snowfields that ran from the Tuzluk glacier. 'In Europe,' he said, 'you'd pay good money for a run like this.'

He went.

Luc said softly, 'One day I am going to slit his tongue.'

Farran touched the lineaments of Jalanath's face.

Hadji said at his elbow. 'The three Oysters will be pinned into the face-bones. On activation—'

The hut went quiet. They were listening.

'On activation the face will fall. Fifty million cubic feet of rock will be swallowed in the lake. An equivalent mass of water will be displaced, hurled in one giant wave across the dam and into the gorge.' He ran his hand down the model, allowed it to hover for a moment over Su Tokai. 'Finish.'

Hadji turned from the model. He said to them, 'Sit down. We'll have the questions now.'

They sat and Hadji said, 'Avoid detail. Keep to what is important.'

Kemmerich said, 'You referred to activation.'

'Yes?'

'In what circumstances will the bombs—'

'Oysters.'

'In what circumstances will the Oysters be activated?'

'No comment. That is a political decision.'

'With respect, that is not an answer.'

'It is the only answer you will get.' Hadji pointed with his beard. 'Yes, Ardrey?'

'When do we go, sir?'

Hadji smiled. 'You can hardly wait, can you?'

'No, sir.'

'There are two factors. The completion of a plan of operation. And the weather.'

'It should be soon,' Farran said. 'The weather is changing.'

'Yes,' Arif agreed. 'It is getting late for high altitude. But still suitable at up to twenty thousand.'

'Twenty thousand?'

'Yes. You will go no higher.'

'And that's good, isn't it?' Hadji said. 'You won't need oxygen. You'll save weight.'

Luc held up a finger.

'Yes, Luc?'

'You mentioned troops. At Su Tokai.'

Hadji nodded.

'Don't they patrol?'

'Of course.'

'As far as the lake?'

Hadji looked at Dorje, and Dorje shook his head.

'Not that far,' Hadji said. 'Why should they? There is only the gorge.'

'But there is the dam,' Farran said. 'They would not leave it unguarded.'

'They might,' Kemmerich said. 'After all, they are not at war.' His voice was cold with disapproval. 'They would not expect an act of sabotage. They would not believe it possible.'

Hadji pursed his lips. Petrie looked up.

Arif said, 'There are three engineers at the dam. And a half-section of troops to guard it. Just five men. They are relieved once monthly from Su Tokai.'

'And at the frontier?' Luc asked.

'Yes, there are mountain troops. One would expect that. But they are stationed on the passes.'

'Surely they patrol?'

'Yes, they patrol. But not over the route selected.'

Petrie said impatiently, 'Come to the point, Luc.'

'The point is this. Will we be armed?'

Hadji hesitated. Then he said, 'Yes. You will be armed.' He thrust with his beard. 'Next question.'

Farran said, 'Is the model to scale?'

'Yes.'

Farran rose, went to the model, studied it. Then, half turning, he said, 'The mountain and the dam face each other from opposite ends of the lake.'

Hadji nodded.

'How long is the lake?'

'About two miles.'

'And the rise of the mountain, you say, is eight thousand feet?'

'Yes.'

Farran studied it again. He said, 'Would you agree that men, watching from the dam, might see movement on the face?'

'If they were searching – yes.'

Farran returned to his seat.

Dorje said, 'On Jalanath there is always movement. It is a place of eagles.'

Farran turned. 'Eagles?'

Dorje grinned, made a soaring motion with his hand. There was a moment in which Farran felt within his stomach the beat of those distant wings.

Hadji said, 'You can climb it from the lake, or descend it from the plateau on the summit. In daytime or at night. It will be your decision.' The beard thrust again. 'Yes, Ricci?'

'The Oysters, sir.'

'Yes?'

'How will they be triggered?'

Hadji looked at Petrie. Petrie nodded. Hadji considered. Then, smiling, he said to Arif, 'You're the expert, Arif.'

Arif said slowly, 'Think of them as electronic locks. Locks that can be turned only by a very special key. This key can be any kind of sound frequency; a voice, Morse, even a bar of music. In this case it will be a coded radio-signal of four groups of numbers—'

'Never mind the details,' Hadji said sharply.

Arif flushed.

Petrie said from the table, 'And only if the Oysters are in season.' He neighed with laughter at his own joke.

Ardrey said, 'About the frontier, sir.'

'Yes?'

'How shall we know when we cross it?'

'When the bastards start firing,' Cray said. 'That's how you know.'

They laughed. Arif said gravely, 'You will see a red line painted on the ice. It is kept bright and free of snow by an old Chinese.'

'With a broom,' Farran said. 'I remember him well.'

'You mean old Fuk U?' This from Cray.

They laughed again and Farran asked, 'Shouldn't the operation have a funny name? All the wartime operations had funny names. Isn't that so, Brigadier?'

Petrie scowled.

Hadji said mildly, 'You've all had your joke. Let's get on, shall we?'

'None of it is a joke,' Kemmerich said. He stood, his face seamed with doubt.

Petrie tapped on the table.

Kemmerich said, 'Su Tokai.'

'Yes?'

'A population of five thousand, I think you said?'

Hadji nodded.

'Plus the military?'

'Yes.'

'How far is Su Tokai from Jalanath?'

'Ninety miles.'

'Ninety miles of gorge and valley?'

'Yes.'

'Surely there are villages?'

'Possibly.'

Arif said quietly: 'Yes, there are villages. Hill people. Shepherds. Some quarries. A few high-crop farms.'

'It adds up, doesn't it?'

'Does it?'

'I think so.' Kemmerich was silent for a moment. Then, coldly, 'How many people will you drown?'

Hadji frowned, tugged his beard.

Cray turned in his seat. 'Chinks,' he said. 'Not people. Chinks.'

'People,' Kemmerich said. 'I'll repeat the question. How many will you drown? Five, eight, ten thousand?'

Petrie tore the feather from his hat-band, began to stab with it at the tweed fibres of his hat. 'I told you,' he said. 'You are committed.'

'No man is committed to killing.'

'He is if he's a soldier.'

'Yes. But my country is not at war. Not with China. Not with anyone.'

'Oh, for Christ,' Cray said wearily.

'You didn't answer,' Kemmerich said. 'Ten thousand?'

Petrie rose. 'A small number,' he said, trembling, 'compared with the Jews you murdered in the last war.'

Farran saw his thin lips twist, knew in that moment that the tweed clothes and the pipe and the pheasant-feather were items of camouflage. Malevolence ran in Petrie's veins like an old infection.

'In the last war,' Kemmerich said quietly, 'I was a boy at school.'

Petrie showed his nicotine teeth. 'You were a German. You are still a German.'

Kemmerich looked around him, ran his fingers through his cropped hair. He seemed uncertain. 'Yes,' he said. 'But I am also—' He stared around him again.

'Well?' Petrie asked with distaste. 'What are you?'

Kemmerich was silent.

'Tell us,' Petrie said.

'I will tell you,' Farran said. He smiled up into Kemmerich's face. 'He is gentle.'

'Gentle?' Cray said. He stood, stared at Farran, then at Kemmerich. 'What sort of a word is that?' He clenched a fist, pounded it into his palm. 'Well, *I'm* not goddam gentle. I promise you that.'

Hadji said to Kemmerich, 'Your conscience is your own affair. But you have a commitment.'

'A commitment,' Petrie said with contempt. Then, brutally: 'Why not come out with it? We got his family out of East Germany. Now we want payment.'

'That's right,' Cray said. 'Payment.' He waved a heavy hand. 'I'd guess that every man in this squad is here to

83

make a payment.' His face had swelled. The scar-tissue around his boxer's eyes was ridged and ugly under the bulbs. 'Payment,' he said again. The word obsessed him. 'Sure, I have to make a payment' – he reached across Ricci's head, gripped Kemmerich's arm – 'just like this one here.' Kemmerich knocked away the hand and Cray's eyes flared. 'Difference is,' Cray said, 'I'm going to enjoy it.' The whisky-voice thickened. 'All this crap about killing Chinks. You know what a Chink is? A Chink is a Red. And a Red isn't hardly fit to live.'

He turned to Hadji. He said earnestly: 'Believe me, Colonel, we're with you all the way.' He glanced again at Kemmerich. ' 'Cept, that is, for this here gentle-Jesus-meek-and-mild. We'll stick those Oysters in the lady's face. And if you got one going spare we'll stick that up her ass as well.'

He laughed and Farran smelled the whisky on his breath. Petrie grimaced. Arif smiled uneasily. Hadji stared. Outside the door one of the sentries hawked, spat into the road.

CHAPTER SIX

In the morning Farran received a signed pass from Hadji. It would admit him at any time to Number Two Armoury. For security reasons, Hadji explained, all plans and preparations must be made therein. No notes or maps or written material relating to the expedition would be taken from the Armoury. Hadji had gone then to the Orderly Room window, staring out at the sweep of brilliant sky.

'We're giving you a helicopter,' he said. 'It'll take you as near to the frontier as we can get you, meet you there on your return. But to use it the weather must be clear as gin. Let's pray that it holds.'

He turned from the window. 'How do you feel about it?' he asked seriously. 'The truth now, Farran.'

Farran smiled. 'Exhilarated.'

'No qualms?'

'A few.'

'Then dismiss them.'

Hadji came from the window. 'We are at war,' he said. 'Have no doubts about it.' He unbuttoned his tunic and shirt, exposed his left chest. There was no pectoral muscle, only a mass of scarred grey flesh.

'From a Chinese shell,' he said. He stroked the twisted lips of the wound. 'I got it four years ago on the Sikkim border.'

He rebuttoned the garments, went again to the window. 'I lost twenty-one men that day,' he said. 'Isn't that war?' The snow-slopes blurred. Images flashed like the shell-bursts of that half-remembered pain; naked crags above the pass and the stone bunkers of the outpost that grew from the snow like old tombs, the absurd four-strand wire fence that defined the border and, fifty yards away, the Chinese soldiers shovelling snow and the sound of the political commissars screaming Hindi through the propaganda loudspeakers until, finally, the hatred drove them through the fence and the hordes came out of the ground like rodents, green figures lurching through the yellow flowers of explosive and the rain of snow, rock and ice, the blood from the chest wound running down his belly and into the crevice of his loins. Twenty-one dead. But we killed three hundred. When the hatred was spent they went back to the shovelling of snow. The little war of Nathu La, he thought. A little pain and dying in the great torrent of India's suffering. Twenty-one. But in that minute a hundred were born on the starving plains.

He turned again from the window. Watching him Farran saw the knowledge in his eyes, knew in that moment that there was more to Hadji than the vanity of words and the green silk turban.

Hadji draped his parka around his shoulders. 'Come,' he said abruptly. 'I'll walk with you to the Armoury.'

Arif was already there. The Oysters were shrouded, the model uncovered. Maps, paper and pens lay on the table. 'We'll sit down quietly,' Arif said, 'and plan.'

Hadji left. Arif frowned up at the glaring bulbs. Then he went to the shutters, opened them, peered out, switched off the lights. Sun struck Jalanath's plaster features. The mountain drew their eyes. After a pause Arif said, 'Listen to me.'

He began to talk. Everything, he insisted, was entirely feasible. At first the mind resisted, because the mind was a coward and had been fed with an old idea of impregnability. Emphatically these were not the European Alps. From these groups – the Pamirs, the Karakoram and the Muztaghs – grew the world's most savage gables. The winds were murderous, the cold more intense, the heights greater, the air thinner, the dangers frightful. When the Indian Army had projected the first of the high mountain-warfare schools men had shaken their heads. The problems were too formidable, they said. Soldiers could not function in those howling places. Yet troops had been trained in mountain-craft, infused with faith in their own capacity to survive, had gone out with watch, map and compass and the blessing of good equipment, burrowed like snow creatures in the frozen eaves of the world's roof – and had returned. It would be like that with Jalanath.

For two years, Arif said, Dorje had ski-trekked the wilderness that lay between Dhalabat and Jalanath, searching for a route that a team of men with sleds could later negotiate. Always he had gone alone, because aloneness was a condition of his being. He had drawn on the chart a slow but lengthening line. Sometimes the line had ended at the ferocious barrier that only the Muztaghs could erect, or it had led perversely to altitudes where only men equipped with oxygen could hope to move. So, undefeated, he had begun again, redrawing the line, this line which could be measured in another way by effort, hunger and pain. He had lost three toes from frostbite, severing them with his own knife when gangrene began. The line on the chart grew longer, crossing the frontier, penetrating deeper into Sinkiang until the ice was behind him and the declining land grew warm. He cut grass like a Mongol nomad on the shores of Jalanath's lake, taking pictures from the cover of the seed-heads. He had squatted like a shepherd among the grazing sheep on the shelves of the gorge, chewing his whiskers and counting the Chinese guards as they glided on the river in their painted launches.

And he had returned with a route.

Later they had sent out special squads of mountain troops. Three secret refuges were built between Dhalabat and the Tuzluk, cached with R/T equipment, fuel and food. These huts were a lifeline, available to the team if bad weather grounded the helicopter and the outward or return journey or both could only be made on foot.

Arif went to the sleds. They had been specially built to accommodate the three Oysters, he explained. And with the addition of tents, radio equipment and climbing gear, arms, ammo and standard Army Compo rations they would be heavy. But they were easy to manoeuvre. And excepting sections of the icefall and the moraine trough (where they would need to be manhandled) the sleds would run smoothly through Dorje's route.

Arif's hand swooped down an imaginary snowfield. Then their eyes met and Farran said with disbelief, 'As easy as that?'

Arif returned to the table. He said seriously, 'Nothing will be easy. But it can be done.' He squeezed Farran's arm. 'Believe me, Farran, it can be done.'

Arif left him alone in the Armoury at four in the afternoon. Notes, calculations, diagrams covered twenty foolscap sheets. Farran riffled through them. Then he put them down, crossed the floor to the model.

The problems were different from any he had known,

With the expeditions there had been a simple conflict: man against mountain. Everything had flowed from that. It had always begun with the choice of men, because the human factor, this careful blending of stamina, skill, character and temperament, was of the first importance. And it had always ended with the logistical problems of establishing and supplying a series of high-altitude, advance camps from the highest of which a few men might reach the summit.

But this adventure of the Oysters had all the desperate qualities of a wartime mission. The team was not of his choosing. They were strong, skilful men with good climbs to their credit. But ability was not enough. The tempers of Ethan Cray and Robert Luc were unpredictable. Kemmerich had deep moral objections. Ardrey was suspect. Each of the team, Cray had suggested, was here to make a payment. What might that indicate? A weakness as yet unrevealed? Some crime to be expiated? Only the vulnerable became pliant in the hands of a creature like Petrie. A thought occurred to him and he went to the table, sorted the papers, wrote an insert on one of them. *For Cray: put a few bottles of whisky in the sleds and in the refuge-huts.*

He returned to the model. He felt the excitement twist inside his bowels. But there was also resentment. Too many questions were unanswered. He had said to Arif over a can of tea, 'There is a flaw in Hadji's argument. If India were really at war she would send an Indian team. She would not need to share the blame.'

Arif did not reply and Farran said, 'To hang those things on the mountain is an act of war.'

'Is it?'

'Merely to take them across the frontier is an act of war.'

'So?'

He sipped his tea. He said softly, 'When will you trigger them?'

Now they were in forbidden areas. He saw the veil fall across Arif's eyes. He said again, 'When will you trigger them?'

Arif was silent.

'When the real war begins?'

Arif shrugged.

'Or before?'

Again the shrug.

'It's before, isn't it? Maybe as soon as they're fixed.'

Discomfort swam like pain in Arif's warm dark eyes.

Farran persisted. 'After all, it would look like a natural disaster.'

Arif looked away. He wanted to escape.

'Arif.'

'Yes,' Arif said with an effort. 'It would look like a natural disaster.'

Farran watched his embarrassment.

Arif said, 'I'm a junior officer, Farran. So I don't know all the answers. Truly.' He glanced at the shrouded weapons. Another emotion, perhaps doubt, touched his eyes; as if the enormity of the act had momentarily become apparent. He said defensively, 'You know how these things begin. Someone gets an idea. He tells someone else. It reaches the intelligence agencies. They make it their own. They love war games, don't they? So they develop it.' Anger rippled in his voice. 'Perhaps the ones who have the power to stop it don't even know about it.'

'That's quite a thought.'

Arif said stubbornly, 'It's a good operation. The risks are big. But so is the prize.'

He had left then, marching stiffly from the Armoury. He came back for a second. 'Don't forget the shutters.'

'I won't.'

Farran went to the table. He pulled the foolscap sheets toward him. Then he turned in his chair, stared across the hut to where Jalanath brooded over the miniature lake. He whispered the name in the silence: 'Jalanath.' Then again: 'Jalanath.' He felt his bowels turn again. The name had a sinister sound; like one of the destroyer-gods of the old Indian mythology. His destiny was now irreversibly linked to that of the mountain. Every path had led to it. He had climbed through the snows of youth and manhood in order to keep an appointment on this melancholy face.

He turned abruptly from the mountain. Consider it logically, he told himself. They cannot leave the warheads there indefinitely. They cannot await the declaration of some distant war of the future. The continuing political risk would be enormous. A man might talk from indiscretion or the effects of drink, or break his oath, or change allegiance, or write his story down and sell it. Or an exercising Chinese Army troop might scale the mountain. So

89

they have to do it now. That is the only conclusion. They will do it when the bombs are fixed. And when the mountain falls and the waters flood and Su Tokai is destroyed the geologists will remember Maithana, that other great catastrophe, and marvel again at the power of nature. And even if Peking suspects there will be no proof.

But the journey from the frontier to the lake? Here also were immense political dangers. Walking to the Armoury he had asked Hadji, 'What if we are caught with the Oysters?'

Hadji searched for one of the English idioms he loved to use. 'In for a penny, in for a pound, Farran. You are armed. You must defend them.'

'And if we can't?'

'That would be an emergency situation. And for that there is a drill.'

It was left to Arif to enlarge. He had taken a fresh sheet of paper, had written by way of heading the one word *Radio*. A normal summit assault, he suggested, would require Very High Frequency walkie-talkie sets for communication between campsites on the mountain, and a short-wave receiver for meterological bulletins. These would consist of minimum lightweight, dry-battery equipment. But the mission to Jalanath was not a sporting climb. It was a secret act in a hostile land. Chinese listening-posts, set like links in a chain from the high snows to the desert plains, would monitor all radio-signals; and for this reason absolute radio silence, except in the most critical situation, must be maintained. In any event the team, unlike the members of a climbing expedition, would not be split. It would move, work, act as a unit. The necessity for walkie-talkie communication did not arise.

But, Arif said, it was vital that HQ Dhalabat be informed of certain events or developments. Thus questions of wireless range and topography arose. VHF waves would not travel around the great natural barrier of the Muztaghs. So lightweight equipment would be inadequate. There was no alternative (a note of apology entered his voice) to the use of a heavy wet-battery transmitter.

Farran stared. 'But the weight, man. All that extra weight.'

'I told you. There is no alternative.'

Farran shook his head. 'I've made a dozen major climbs.

And never with a transmitter. What could it contribute? It would not have have brought me one inch nearer the summit.'

'But you are not making for a summit. You are on a wartime operation.'

'Weight is just as crucial.'

'And so are certain signals. We have to have them, Farran. That means a transmitter.'

Farran smiled sourly. 'I can always drop it down the first crevasse.'

'Yes. But you wouldn't do that. You understand command. You understand orders.'

'Don't be so sure.'

'We're sure enough.'

Arif took his pen, wrote for a time on the foolscap sheet. Then he said, 'There are three situations in which you will break radio silence. You must memorize them and the appropriate coded signal.' He pushed the paper across the table. 'One: when the weapons are pinned successfully to the face of Jalanath you will send by key the signal OYSTER.'

He paused while Farran read. Then: 'Two: if, when en route to Jalanath, and in possession of the weapons, it seems that capture is unavoidable you will send by key the signal PEARL.'

Farran nodded.

'Three: if, when returning from Jalanath, it seems that capture is unavoidable you will send by key the signal SHELL.'

Farran re-read the columns.

Arif said, 'The first signal is self-explanatory.'

'It is indeed. How long will you give us to get clear? Or do we go up with the bombs?'

Arif's eyes melted into dark wounds. 'Naturally we want to learn immediately of your success.'

'Naturally.'

'We'll drink a toast to you in the mess that night, Farran.' His voice warmed. 'By God we will.'

'We'll do the same. In our cosy little snow-house.'

'You'll each get an Indian decoration—'

'How frightfully jolly.'

'—for an unspecified act of courage.'

'Posthumous, of course.'

Arif went silent. He fidgeted with his pen. Then, quietly: 'We know how dangerous it is. We're really very grateful.' He patted Farran's hand, then enclosed it with his fingers. 'The timing of the signal will be your decision. If you want to put a mile or two between yourself and Jalanath—'

'Or a good solid mountain.'

'Exactly. It'll be entirely up to you.'

Farran released his hand.

Arif said, 'The second signal—'

Farran saw embarrassment shade his eyes. Arif said awkwardly, 'In the case of PEARL there is, I'm afraid, an element of personal risk.' He put his tan fingers together like a preacher. 'You'll appreciate the appalling predicament we'd find ourselves in if the Chinese captured the weapons. We've attempted to share the blame, as you put it. But even so—' He hesitated. 'So we've decided to trigger the Oysters on receipt of PEARL. That way we'll destroy the evidence—'

'And us too.'

Arif flushed. 'It's not as bad as it sounds. There'd be no pain. Just – oblivion. It'd be like suddenly standing on the sun.'

'You'll melt the Himalaya. Have you thought of that?'

Arif looked away.

Farran said after a pause, 'Do you really expect me to send that signal?'

'No. Not without an undertaking.'

'An undertaking?'

'Yes. We'd promise not to trigger the bombs until three hours after the signal. The Chinese couldn't examine them expertly in that time. And it'd give you a chance to get away before the things went up.'

'But we might not get away.'

'I'm sure you would.' Arif smiled faintly. 'After all, there's nothing like an H-bomb to concentrate the mind.'

'Will you keep your promise?'

'You have our solemn word.'

'As officers and gentlemen?'

'Yes.'

'I'll think about it.'

'Yes, do. You'll see clearly where your duty lies. If it does come to the worst it's better than Chinese tortures, isn't it?'

'Much better.'

Arif reversed the foolscap sheet, made a further entry. He said, 'If the necessity arises we ourselves will break radio silence to send one important signal. So you'll have to listen at noon each day. That's a strict order, Farran. Noon each day.' He wrote down some letters. 'The signal is AMAR.'

'AMAR.'

'Yes.'

'Is that part of an oyster?'

Arif frowned.

'Like PEARL and SHELL.'

'Oh, I see. No, it isn't a word at all. They are initial letters. They signify "Abandon Mission And Return".'

'That's a very good signal. Don't hesitate to send it.'

'We wouldn't. You see, Farran, political situations are very fluid. Things change quite suddenly. The ones in high places could get cold feet. Or China might wave the olive branch. Something like that. It's imperative we have some means of recalling you. You do see that?'

'Yes. AMAR.'

Arif underlined the letters. Then he took a fresh sheet, wrote down a heading.

Farran read it in reverse. 'Yes,' he said. 'The return. The journey back. We could never carry sufficient supplies for the double trip. Have you considered that?'

'Of course.' Arif tore off an ear of paper, wrote some capitals. 'This,' he said, 'is the name of a village. It is Shindi Kul.' He turned the scrap of paper so that Farran should read the name. 'Say it.'

'Shindi Kul.'

'It's a tiny settlement a few miles from the Jalanath end of the lake. In fact the word Kul means lake. Anyway, you'll make for Shindi and the headman will hide you. From there you'll make the assault on Jalanath. There's a cache of food and fuel, enough to get you home. Understood?'

'Yes.'

'You won't find the name on Dorje's map. If the Chinese got hold of it things'd be pretty awful for the villagers.'

'Death by torture?'

'Or worse. So we've marked the map with a little red oyster shell. You'll know that's Shindi Kul.'

'Will there be a signpost?'

'No. These are primitive communities. They'll do a lot for a little money. You see, Farran, although Sinkiang belongs to China only ten per cent of the people are Chinese. The rest are Moslems, Mongols, Khasaks and others. So there's no real loyalty to Peking. That helps, doesn't it?'

Arif tore the ear of paper into minute pieces. 'One can't be too careful.' He searched under the table for a waste-basket, then put the pieces into his pocket. He looked up. His lips twitched.

'What's funny?'

'Just a thought.'

'Tell me.'

'Well, for all you know they might not be H-bombs at all. Three useless lumps of iron. The whole thing could be an exercise. Just to see if it could be done.' He laughed pleasantly. 'That'd be some joke, wouldn't it?'

'Excruciating.'

Farran left the Armoury at six in the evening. There was a message in the mess.

> MY DEAR FARRAN,
> Why not walk up the hill tomorrow after dinner? We'll give you a drink.
> JOSEPH SHAW

CHAPTER SEVEN

Shaw gave him the drink. They were standing by the window, the night behind them. Shaw raised his glass. Amber light from the four bronze oil-lamps that illuminated the room was reflected on it. The glass tilted and the amber filled his eyes so that they glowed for a moment as yellow as a cat's.

Shaw said, '—and that was forty-five years ago.' He jerked his beard to where the woman sat in the angle of the stone fireplace. Knitting needles tapped. 'Don't seem possible, does it, Kate?' Incredulity touched his voice. 'Forty-five years. I was a young fellow then. Newly ordained. A surgeon's degree. As stuffed full of God as an early Christian martyr. In those days . . .' He swallowed his Cognac. 'In those days up-country you could still see traces of the old Imperial China. Idols and incense, brigands in the hills, street executions, mandarins in sedans with fingernails like talons and perfume balls that they'd put to their noses when the coolies ran by with their pails of night-soil. I can see it still.' The beard jerked again. 'Of course Kate doesn't go back that far. She's younger than me. A good deal younger. When we married the mandarins were all in motor cars.' He set down his glass. His voice sharpened. 'What arrogance! To actually believe that one could bring Christ to people like that – people whose own gods were ancient before the first stone of Bethlehem was laid.' He splashed more Cognac into his glass. 'The sublime arrogance of the Church and its fledgling priests.' He turned his head toward the fireplace, glass poised. 'Once,' he said with sorrow, 'it burned as brightly as those logs.' He peered at the woman's bowed head, as if awaiting consolation.

Kate Shaw said kindly, 'Don't believe him, Captain Farran. He did very well,' She looked up. Tongues of firelight licked in the hollow of her cheek. She put down the garment, sipped delicately at her Sherry. A needle fell. Farran crossed the room, bent to retrieve it. In that moment

95

of bending he saw her ankles. They were ugly and deformed. Cavities and nodules, swellings and sharp points made a pattern under the white of her thick stockings. His eyes went to the two sticks that were propped against her chair. He gave her the needle and she smiled. He saw her fragility. She was like a figure made from porcelain. This frail thing would shatter under a blow. She smiled again. A transparent hand smoothed her flat silver hair. It shone like polished metal. She had a timeless beauty, flawed only by the shapeless ankles. But there was something in her eyes, lurking like the shadows in a well; as if illness, pain or privation had left its imprint.

He went back to Shaw. Outside the sky was paling. He could see the pallor of snow, the ridges emerging like a long black jawbone on the window. Kate Shaw reached for the sticks, gripped the handles, levered herself up from the chair. She stood there for a second, leaning. Her face was blanched from effort. Farran started forward but Shaw murmured gently, 'Leave her be.'

She came slowly across the room, moving the sticks in unison with each careful foot, pausing, moving again. She said, 'If I place them exactly right I can manage. Otherwise—'

'Otherwise,' Shaw said, smiling, 'she'll be over on her bottom.'

Farran heard the tremor in his voice. Turning he saw that Shaw's eyes were bright with tears. The cap of silver hair came nearer. He watched her. There was an unreasoning fear that, falling, the brittle body would shiver into fragments on the stone floor. She reached them and Shaw put his arm around her, kissed the crown of her head. Then he bent, hooked his other arm under the crook of her knees, lifted her, hugged her body against his chest. They looked at him, laughing.

Farran smiled. He said, 'You love each other very much, don't you?'

The remark pleased them. 'That sounded a little wistful,' Shaw said.

He put her down.

She asked, 'Are you married?'

'No.'

'A girl?'

'No.'

'I'll be your girl.'

'Be careful, Farran,' Shaw said. 'Or she'll knit you a jersey.'

She laughed, touched the coarse blue yarn that covered his chest. 'Do you know,' she said, 'that here in Kashmir you cannot buy Kashmir wool? They export it all.'

'It's really hair,' Shaw explained. 'From the bellies of goats. So fine and silky you can pull a Kashmir shawl through a wedding-ring.'

He filled Farran's glass, waved at the room. 'We'll show you our collection,' he said.

Drinking, he had been aware of the opulence of the room; its cabinets, screens, glowing rugs, lacquered tables and objects of art, crowded walls. It had the feel of an oriental museum.

'Not one of the great Chinese collections,' Shaw said with pride. 'But very near it.' He took Farran's arm. 'Come.'

He led Farran across the room. Kate Shaw hobbled behind them.

'It all started with this,' Shaw said. They stopped by an inlaid table. On it were several ritual bronzes, among them a ceremonial axe-head. The axe was secured in a roaring monster mask; and the mask, glittering with turquoise chips, rested in a teak cradle. Shaw touched the blade. 'Do you see this green patination?' Now the voice was reverent. 'It comes from three thousand years of burial in damp soil.' He ran his finger over the fragments of cloth wrappings that were stuck to the mask. 'It was a gift. I was serving in Ningpo at the time. I'd saved the eye of one of the wealthy magistrates and, quite properly, he wanted to show his gratitude. He had a house full of valuable stuff. He told me to take whatever I fancied. I don't know why but I chose the axe-head. He was so surprised he hissed like a snake. He turned as cold as ice and said, "The object it priceless. You either have knowledge – or you have an instinct." He made no move so I said, "Surely it's worth an eye?" He nodded and I took it.' Shaw smiled. 'It isn't priceless. But in London today it'd make four thousand guineas.'

'That's how it began,' Kate Shaw said.

Shaw nodded. 'An object here, an object there. I had an

instinct all right.' He pointed at Farran's feet. 'That rug you're standing on—'

Farran looked down.

'Five centuries ago that lay on the earth floor of a Turkestan tent.' He bent, grasped a corner of the rug, twisted it so that the pile was exposed. 'Equivalent to the very best Persian.' He straightened. 'I'd value it at two thousand. Not a penny less.'

'And increasing every day,' Farran said.

'Yes. That's the beauty of it.'

Shaw bent again, produced a steel comb, passed it through the fringes of the rug so that they lay untangled on the floor. He said, crouching, 'In the beginning it was all for the Mission. It was my offering. I wanted to beautify it.'

'Like the treasure in a church,' Kate Shaw said.

'Yes. But the collection grew. I loved each piece as a child loves a toy. And when they posted us to Tihwa I couldn't bear to part with it.' Shaw stood. He laughed. 'You see, Farran, I'd become a collector. And collectors have no morals.' His face sobered. 'Here in this room you see our savings. We have nothing else.' He scratched his beard with the teeth of the comb. 'I'm an old man now. I'll work till I die. But Kate's a cripple.' He squeezed her shoulders. 'She'll need money. The collection will provide it. Do you understand?'

The shutters rattled. 'Wind's getting up,' Shaw said. He opened a drawer. 'Cigar?'

Farran accepted. They lit up. Shaw added an inch of Cognac to his glass. He watched Farran through the curling smoke. 'I can read your thoughts,' he said. He laughed again. 'I was never one of your emaciated priests, Farran. I always had taste. I liked good things. I lived well.' He held the Cognac under his nose, savouring its bouquet. 'How can a man hear God if he's listening to the rumblings in his stomach?'

In the hour that followed Shaw showed him the collection. He was fiercely proud. Each piece was described, dated, placed in a historical context, and given a valuation. There were cauldrons and wine-vessels, vases and jade, hand-painted silk banners and gilt-bronze Buddhas, grotesques and ancient Manichean manuscripts. Shaw lifted a bronze dragon, turned its head towards the lamps. 'You see the fiery light in its jaws?' he asked. 'It comes from twenty small rubies. Clever, isn't it?' He set it down, led Farran to a table on which stood a dozen miniatures.

'Tang tomb-figures,' Shaw said. He picked one up, stroked its glass robes. 'On its own it'd make no more than seventy pounds.' His voice became exultant. 'But this is a set.' He put it down with infinite care. 'And sold as a set they'd make real money.'

Many of the pieces were linked to the events and faces of a distant past. Shaw searched in the greying alleys of his mind, evoking pictures of a China that had gone. He had the evangelist's gift of words. There were sunlit tea-gardens, wistaria and lilac, soft dialects that lapped as gentle as river-water, old barbarities that still lay impaled in the memory like slivers of ice.

'In China,' he said, 'one learned about death. When I think of it – that endless stream of souls passing into darkness.'

Kate Shaw turned her head. Farran saw the pain in her eyes.

Shaw shrugged. He said wearily, 'Darkness or light. Who can say?'

He led them to the farther end of the great stone-and-timber room. Oil paintings and water-colours covered the wall.

Kate Shaw smiled. 'We wouldn't get much for these.'

'Yours?'

She nodded.

Farran examined them. The scenes were Chinese. There were girls in poppy-fields, dragon-roofed temples, shaggy Mongol ponies breasting chi-chi grass, tranquil water with slender boats from which cormorants fished, a pleasant landscape with a foreground of blue poppies and black clematis. They were pretty. They showed a graceful talent. But they had no power.

'This is a view of the Gobi Desert,' Kate Shaw said.

Farran studied it. A line of camels carried panniers of sultanas across a tawny backdrop.

'The sand is the colour of lions,' she said. 'I've tried to capture that.'

The painting had stillness but no mystery, no sense of arid space. He delved for the facile words of praise.

'It's nice,' he said.

'But it shouldn't be,' Shaw said gently. 'I keep telling her that.' He touched one of the camels. 'This amiable creature would never bite your kneecap off.' His finger moved across the canvas. 'The deserts of Sinkiang are the biggest on earth.' The finger tapped. 'One might enjoy a picnic here. But one would never die of thirst.'

Farran moved a pace. The big central canvas was a mountain panorama.

'The Heavenly Mountains,' she said.

He felt his pulses race. Ice-caps rose above a ridge of pines. The style was instantly recognizable. The peaks were painted with the distinctive flourish he had noted on the model in Number Two Armoury; as if the brush, loaded with white pigment, had been spiralled upward to a point. Like the peaks in the model the flanks were delicately coloured in pale tones of blue. He continued to stare. He heard Shaw's voice say behind him, '—and the same with the ice mountains. She sees only beauty. When she paints them they elude her. Try to see them differently, I tell her. There is no life up there. Imagine them in darkness. Try to hear the wind. Try—' The voice stopped abruptly. Then: 'Why do you stare? Are they familiar?'

'Yes.'

Shaw was smiling. 'A climb?'

'A model.'

The smile died. Shaw frowned, examining the painting for a time, nodded slowly in understanding. Kate Shaw looked down at her feet like a child caught in a furtive act. In the silence they heard the wind grieving in the eaves, the sound of a bell ringing distantly in the monastery. A log shifted. Then the door opened and Dr Azfar came softly into the room.

He stood there without speaking, the nervous fingers driving down the skirts of his surgical coat. Shaw nodded and said, 'I'll come.' He stared at Farran. Irony gleamed for a moment in his eyes. Then he turned, followed Azfar from the room.

Kate Shaw said, 'Will you put another log on?'

Farran went to the fireplace, bent across the pile of split pine. He heard her feet shuffling behind him. He said with sarcasm, 'It was a gorgeous model.' He settled a log. The pine bark flared and with it his anger. He wanted to punish her for her deceit. 'But it's bloody useless.' He chose

100

another log. 'All that lovely snow-white snow, the pretty little valleys we're going to ski through.' He threw the log on to the fire. Sparks showered. He turned. 'Do you really believe you can cross the Himalaya like a ski-tour?'

'I don't know.'

'You don't know? But you built the model, didn't you? The lovely hand-painted useless bitch of a model?' He saw the hurt withering her face. He could not stop. 'Turn left, turn right – and before you know it you'll be in China.' Heat struck against his calves. He moved toward her. 'God,' he said, smiling with contempt. 'I loved the cotton-wool on the factory chimneys.'

She touched her cheek, then her neck. It was as fragile as a flower-stalk.

'Why?' he asked.

'They asked me to do it. And I did it.'

'Do you know why they need it?'

'Yes.'

'You actually know what we're going to do?'

'Yes.'

'Do you realize what will happen?'

'Yes.'

'All those people in the valleys, in Su Tokai?'

'Yes.'

'Even the Red Army are God's creatures.'

'Yes.'

'And there might be some Christians among them.'

'There might.'

'Doesn't it worry you?'

'Yes.'

'Then why? Give me a reason.'

He saw the sticks tremble under her weight. 'Why?' he said again.

'I belong to Joe. I follow him.'

'Whither thou goest I will go?'

'Something like that.'

'But that's crap. A missionary would do only what is right.'

She turned her head distractedly. Whorls of amber light slid across her silver hair.

'Was he really a missionary?'

'The best.'

'The best?'

'Yes.'

'What does that mean? Lots of converts?'

'Partly.'

'Did he get a bonus on the conversions?'

She turned from him so that he saw her profile. It was like that of a young girl.

'Why not?' he asked. 'He puts a price on everything else, doesn't he?'

He moved toward the door.

'Farran.'

He stopped.

'Joe was a good man. They loved him. He'd talk to them about Christ and it was like switching a light on in their hearts.'

Farran nodded. 'And then he'd reach for the nearest Ming vase.'

He opened the door.

She said to his back. 'Do you know what it takes to qualify in medicine? To get ordained? To learn to speak and write in Mandarin? And when you've done those simple things to pour away the years of your life in service in a foreign land?' He heard her voice tremble. 'To *give* until there's nothing left?'

'He's got the collection.'

'Why must a priest be poor? Why must he die with nothing?'

'The eye of the needle. Remember?'

He stood there with his fingers on the handle. Then he turned. She was hunched over the sticks, her knuckles yellow-white. 'You're angry now,' she said. 'But it'll pass.' Her voice was weak, as if the effort of speech had sapped her. 'Come back then. I like you, Farran.'

He felt the anger drain in that moment. It was too easy to hurt this grave and fragile woman. He said, 'Why is he here? What is he involved in?'

She shook her head, began to hobble toward the fire-light. It flickered on her face. Wetness glinted on her cheek. 'Better ask him,' she said. She sat, searched for her wool. 'Better ask him.'

When Farran left the wind had risen. There was snow in it. He stood by the hospital gate, staring down into the valley. The lights of the camp glowed in the night. Below the camp was the smaller constellation of the village. He zipped his parka to the throat, pulled down his bonnet. Then he turned left along the path that skirted the hospital.

At the rear the ground fell sharply into a deep gully, rose again into pine-clad slopes. In the faint starlight he could see the ugly grey swathes where the timber had been cut for fuel. He passed the gate that led to the tiny grave-yard, stopped where the lateral wall divided the hospital and the monastery. The wall sealed the path, continued down the slope to form a barrier of jagged wooden stakes. The end was lost in blackness.

Above the wall was the tiered roof of the temple. Another roof, very long and humped with age, adjoined it. This, he judged, might be a dormitory for monks or novices. Might: the word lodged in his mind. He had never seen a monk or a novice; not in the village of Dhalabat or on the paths and roads that radiated from it, not a robe or shaved head or a begging bowl. There were flocks or herds on the summer pastures of the lower ground, barley crops and fruits, but no monk was ever seen to tend them. He had heard the temple bell, an occasional muttering of praying voices. But that was all.

He studied the wall. It was perhaps ten feet high, built of stone, then rendered smooth. The fence would be easier. He edged carefully down the slope, holding on to the stakes. The scree moved under his boots. Stones leapt into the gully. He reached the end. There was a moment in which he hung from the terminal stake above the blackness of the void. Then he was around it, pulling himself from stake to stake toward that lip that defined the path.

He reached the path. It ran to the right, into shadow. A six-foot brick wall separated it from the monastery. He could see the temple roof, the eaves of the humped roof, a wash of yellow light that was reflected upward from the unseen windows.

He listened. There was no sound except the sighing of the wind. The brick wall was easily climbed. He lay for a second along its crest, then dropped down on the inner side.

In front of him, across the flagstoned area, was the temple. To his right the lights of the dormitory glowed through opaque glass. He crossed the area. A stone Buddha sat by the temple entrance. The door opened. Farran moved to the flank, into shadow. Two Indian

soldiers came out. Light spilled. The door closed. They
descended the steps, shouldered their carbines, marched
down the path into darkness.

The sound of the boots died. Farran hesitated. Then he
walked under the carved eaves of the temple toward its
rear. Snow was falling.

There were steps at the rear, a stone platform, a large
lighted window. On the platform were a number of wooden
cases with army stencils. He mounted the steps, went to
the window, looked in.

Oil-lamps burned. There were desks, tables, cabinets, a
long table of ancient black wood at which three Indian
non-coms were eating. A civilian clerk in a puggaree was
sorting papers. There were gaps around the window-jambs.
Farran could hear a murmur of Urdu from the table. A
cook came in with a kettle of tea, put it on the table, went
out again. The clerk looked at his watch, said something
to the non-coms, laughed, crossed the room to the party
wall that adjoined the hospital. Against the wall was a desk,
and on the desk a tape-recorder. One of the soldiers stood,
joined the clerk. The clerk depressed a button. There was
a moment of silence. Then the three clear notes of a
novice-bell came from the recorder. The soldier clapped
his hands with pleasure. The bell rang again. A sonorous
chant filled the temple, died away. The soldier touched the
buttons, grinned. It was like a toy. The priest's voice rose, the
voices chanted. The clerk frowned, pushed away the soldier.
Authority must be asserted. The soldier returned to the
table. The chant faded.

Farran descended the steps, walked back under the eaves
to the front of the temple. Now the Buddha wore a cap of
snow. He turned left down the path that fronted the dormitory. He could hear voices, the hum of a generator. The
dormitory formed an L with the smaller building that
housed the generator. Farran stopped. From the angle
made by the buildings rose an antenna. It was very high.
It gleamed on the night sky like a steel needle.

He walked around the flank. It faced onto a large inner
courtyard. More buildings surrounded the courtyard.
Through the whirling snow he could see an Indian Army
truck with a Signals emblem painted on its body, an iron
gateway that led from the courtyard, a sentry by the pillar.

Three soldiers stood by the truck, two of them lashing canvas.

He left the cover of the generator house. The soldiers turned, stared, saluted. He returned it. Then he walked boldly to where the dormitory block faced the courtyard.

He climbed the four worn steps, opened the door, entered. It was an antechamber. A paraffin stove burned. Facing him were double doors. A table was aligned to the right-hand wall. A havildar with a bright green sash was seated at it. He half rose.

Farran smiled and said, 'Oyster.' He crossed the chamber, pushed open the doors, stepped into the dormitory.

He stood there with his back to the doors. The room was long and low. It was filled with men and equipment. It had indeed been a monks' dormitory. On either side of the room were the shallow stone daises each of which had at one time supported a straw pallet. But now they served a different purpose. Each pair was joined by wood planking to provide a platform. Transmitters and receivers and other radio machinery sat on the platforms. There were three big screens on which satellite films painted their beautiful moving pictures. Men with clipboards watched, made notes. Voices murmured into radio telephones. Somewhere a Morse key tapped. Shaw's blue jersey came from behind a partition, was stamped in silhouette on one of the screens. Farran saw his hand reach for a dial. The film stopped. The fingers played. The film reversed, was frozen now into a still of snow, rocks and blue-green water. Shaw bent to a smaller screen, began to depress buttons. A segment of the landscape, greatly magnified, appeared. An Indian lieutenant came from a desk, stared over Shaw's shoulder.

Farran crossed the room so that he stood behind them. They did not turn. Shaw was manipulating dials. The picture quartered, then expanded into details of scrub and mountain strata.

The lieutenant pointed. Shaw touched a button. An object leapt into prominence. It was grey, symmetrical, cut across its face by a horizontal slit.

Shaw said carefully, 'It is new. It is concrete. It is of course a pillbox.'

The lieutenant made a note.

Shaw said without looking up, 'Take a look, Farran.'

The lieutenant turned, stared. Farran bent. Shaw, he realized, had seen his reflection on the glass of the screen.

Shaw said softly, 'This is a message from the Voyager. Do you know that name?'

'Yes.'

'He is the perfect spy. He cannot be caught. Or questioned. Or destroyed. He cannot betray. He sees. He reports. His information is exact. And nothing can escape his eye.' Shaw laughed, stood. 'Believe me, Farran, they can't scratch their noses without we know it.'

The lieutenant returned to his desk. Farran watched the activity of the room.

'Here in this ancient place,' Shaw said quietly, 'India watches her enemy – and waits.'

Shaw led him to the room behind the partition, closed the door. It was an office. There was another exit door, an icicled window with a view of the temple, a desk, a table that was stacked with Chinese newspapers. Adjacent to the desk was a powerful radio transmitter and a Morse key.

There were two framed photographs on the wall above the desk. One was a portrait of Kate Shaw. The other depicted the graveyard in the monastery garden. The child's stone was in the foreground. A sprig of saxifrage had been placed on the upper frame so that its white panicles drooped above the grave.

'A moment,' Shaw said. He left the office.

Farran went to the desk, studied the woman's portrait. The face was much younger. It glowed with vitality. The eyes were merry. The hair was black.

'She was lovely then,' Shaw said behind him.

Farran turned.

Shaw stood in the doorway. He held a teleprint in his hand. He went to the desk, opened a drawer, took out a large manila envelope. He proffered it. 'These pictures are more recent,' he said.

Farran drew out the contents. They were two X-ray photographs.

'Hold them to the light.'

Farran obeyed. There were a left ankle and a right ankle. The bones had no definition. They were an impacted blur.

'You don't have to be an orthopaedist to see the damage,' Shaw said.

Farran stared at them. Shaw stood silently. Something flowed from the pictures into his hands like the sense of some old unspeakable pain. He turned, the question on his lips.

Shaw shook his head. 'Don't ask me. After all these years I still cannot talk about it. Except to say that men did this to her. Yellow men. Deliberately and without pity.'

Farran put down the pictures on the desk. Then he slid them into the envelope. Kate Shaw's face smiled from the wall. The gravestones leaned under the white flower. He reached out, touched the Morse key and, turning, saw in Shaw's eyes a darkness he had not seen before. He knew in that instant, intuitively, that these things were connected; the mementos of grief, the transmitter, the key.

He nodded and said, 'You'll be the one to send the signal. You'll trigger the bombs.'

Shaw did not answer. He went to the desk, returned the envelope to the drawer. Then he said: 'Don't try to judge me, Farran. I am not a fanatic. I have no hatred – only reproach. But I will do what I can against the barbarians. Do you understand?'

Wind drove against the window. Farran turned his head, listened. An icicle broke, fell like a stiletto.

'Don't worry about the weather,' Shaw said. He gave Farran the teleprint. 'It's the long-range forecast.'

Farran read it.

'As clear as crystal,' Shaw said with pleasure. 'Conditions couldn't be better.' He rubbed his spotted hands. 'You'll go tomorrow, Farran.' Now he was smiling. 'You'll go tomorrow.'

CHAPTER EIGHT

They went at noon, a small convoy of two Weasels and a covered truck. The truck led. It contained the sleds, the Oysters, the stores and the equipment. The first of the tractors was driven by Arif. Farran sat beside him. In the rear seats were Ardrey and Ricci. Behind them in the second tractor were Cray, Luc and Kemmerich.

There had been no final briefing, only the verbal orders from Hadji and a precautionary item in the Orders of the Day that required Captain R. M. V. Farran's squad (Beta Company) to hold itself in readiness for expeditionary training.

The road climbed west, spiralling through the banked snow until the air grew colder and the last of the green-brown patches was drowned in whiteness. This was the terrain of perpetual snow.

Farran said, 'What happened to Mrs. Shaw?'

'Happened?'

'Her legs.'

Arif shrugged. 'That was years ago.'

'Yes. But what happened?'

'The Reds expelled them. Did you know that?'

'Yes.'

'They knew about Shaw's antiques. So they forbade him to take them. They could each take one piece of hand-luggage. But that was all.'

The road dipped into the rim of a broad white bowl.

'But Shaw got them through,' Arif said. 'God knows how. The stuff was sent into Kashmir the day before their own departure. But the Reds found out. They stopped the Shaws a mile from the pass. And they punished him.'

'Him?'

'Through her. They smashed every bone in her ankles. Then they let them go.'

Farran stared from the Weasel. The whiteness blurred. Imagination sent a flood of weakness through his legs.

'He's had quite a cross to bear,' Arif said. 'And he's borne it very manfully.'

Farran looked at him. But there was no cynicism in Arif's face.

Arif smiled and said, 'It's a perfect day. Let's forget the horrors, shall we?'

The road ran down steeply from the rim.

'There it is,' Ardrey said.

Farran heard the excitement in his voice. Below them in the centre of the bowl was a helicopter, a truck, a little group of men.

Hadji and Joseph Shaw were there, Dorje, the helicopter pilot, the truck-driver, Petrie in a tweed overcoat that matched his tweed suit and tweed hat, four Indian non-coms.

The convoy stopped. Arif and the squad climbed from the Weasels. The covered truck reversed until its rear cut the shadow of the rotors. No one spoke. The squad and the non-coms began to transfer gear from the truck into the belly of the big Puma helicopter. The pilot climbed into the Puma, grunted, pointed, ordered, checked the distribution of weight. The three Oysters, each of them slung in a green nylon snood, were the last items to be stowed.

Farran crossed the snow to where Hadji, Shaw and Petrie were talking. Arif followed. Dorje broke apart. Breath broke in clouds. Petrie stamped. Shaw beat his hands together.

'We should have had a band,' Farran said. 'A big military band.'

They smiled. Now that the time had come they had no words. Petrie pulled out his pipe, sucked it.

Hadji said, 'I prepared a speech. But I think I'll leave it.'

They smiled again. Wind, very slight and trapped in the snow bowl, brought the scent of Dorje's coat.

Farran went to him. He stared into the deep mongol eyes. Dorje had protected them. Dorje's strength was a tower and a refuge. Dorje was indestructible.

'Come with us,' Farran said. He heard something in his voice, a note of strain. Behind Dorje's bonnet were the endless peaks, this wilderness where they had to go. 'We need you.' But Dorje shook his head, rejecting him. The whiskers vibrated like wire.

Farran turned from him.

Arif said severely, 'You haven't paid your mess bill.'

They frowned, nodded. They were glad of anything, even a small misdemeanour.

'We'll deduct it from his pay,' Petrie said. He filled his pipe and Shaw pointed to the truck and said, 'Kate's in there.'

Farran walked across the snow to the truck. She crouched in a blanket, her face a white oval in a hood of fur. He stood there without speaking. He felt his throat swell with emotion. This woman's legs for a vase or an axe-head, her pain for a bit of jade.

She leaned toward him. He kissed her temple. The hood smelled fragrant, as if it had lain in a drawer against a lavender-bag.

'Take care,' she whispered.

He left her, returned to the group. He said to Shaw, 'She's too bloody good for you.'

'I agree.'

The Puma's motors exploded into life. The rotor made a slow revolution. Hadji put his hand on his turban like a woman protecting her hat in a high wind. Cray and Audrey got into the helicopter.

Shaw said, 'What are you waiting for? A blessing?'

The words came faintly against the noise of the motors. Farran did not move. Shaw shrugged and said, 'All right. For what it's worth – God be with you.'

Farran turned, began the walk to the Puma.

'Farran.'

He stopped, not turning.

Shaw's voice came again. 'Farran.'

He turned. He could not be sure but it seemed that Shaw's lips trembled in his beard.

The lips framed words. 'I meant it.'

Farran turned again. The rotor made patterns on the glaring snow. He reached with his hand and Ricci pulled him into the Puma.

When the Puma lifted the blades threw a whirlpool of wind and snow. Petrie's hat was whipped from his head, leapt like a live thing across the bowl. They watched him pursue it. The figure grew tiny, overbalanced, fell heavily on its rump. Ethan Cray roared with laughter. The Puma

110

turned. Men, truck and Weasels vanished from sight. Cray wiped his eyes. 'Did you see that?'

Farran did not answer. There had been no dignity in the leaving. The moment had been turned into farce. He felt a surge of resentment; against Petrie and the hat, against Hadji and the undelivered speech. Why should I need a ceremony? he asked himself.

Now they were cocooned in noise. Light danced inside the aluminium shell, was reflected on the white of their combat suits. Below them the shadow of the Puma scuttled on the snow. The Puma changed course. The rock walls opened. This was the high-altitude valley they had seen on the helicopter film. Farran stared across the pilot's shoulder into distance. The infinite patterns of rock, snow and ice advanced, slipped beneath them. The day glowed with colour. The light was brilliant. The land came at them, toppling like a painted china plate. The beauty of it dried his mouth.

The Puma flew low and fast through the valley. East, across the valley wall, were the mountains of Tibet. The Puma slowed. The pilot pointed. A square of stone and timber was perched in the lee of a tower of rock. This was the first of the secret refuges. The faces in the helicopter nodded, smiled. Farran checked his map. The hut was accurately marked, a tiny square in Indian ink.

The Puma gathered speed. Farran studied the valley floor. In places it was no more than a cleft. Ice-streams writhed like green veins. Snow made enormous bridges. But it was negotiable by men on foot. And if the weather came down and the helicopter was grounded this unused pass and its three refuge huts provided a feasible return route: it led direct from the Tuzluk to the regions of the Dhalabat base.

He looked at his watch, then at the map.

'Thirty miles,' Cray said. 'I reckon we done thirty miles.'

'Thirty-five,' the pilot said. He pointed again. The second hut appeared. It lay on a ledge, protected from the snow-fall by a rock overhang.

'It's good to see it,' Kemmerich said seriously. 'Good to know it's there.'

They watched it, this place where a spark of life might be sustained. The hut grew small, was lost to sight. The Puma banked into the curve of the pass. The sun struck behind them. Now the shadow of the Puma raced ahead. It leapt, grew, contracted. It flew like a thing pursued. They stared, mesmerized. Then the Puma banked again. The Tuzluk massif came slowly out of distance. It divided. Through the perspex they saw the gleam of the river of ice.

The pilot put down the Puma on the bank of the glacier. Above it and built into the body of a rock buttress was the third refuge.

They climbed from the helicopter, began to unload. The pilot remained in his seat, the rotor turning. He was clearly afraid. He watched the valley, the massif, the sky. He pointed to a scarf of mist. 'Please hurry.'

When the gear and the stores were unloaded the pilot checked the security of the doors, reknotted his neck bandana. There was a moment in which the olive face looked down on them with a kind of compassion. Then the Puma rose, hovered, made a tight half-circle above the glacier, flew into the sun. They watched it go, a fragile insect on the glaring bulb of light. Now the sky was empty. They listened. The motors died, resurged, died again. They did not move or speak. The Puma was gone. They stood there in the silence of the glacier, alone with the sense of abandonment.

Farran turned, gestured at the hut. 'Let's take a look.'

They followed him.

The hut was like any other refuge. There was a wooden table and chairs, bunk-beds against the walls, a stove and a Primus, fuel. There was also a radio transmitter. Ricci opened one of the cupboards. The shelves were stocked with tinned foods, evaporated milk, soup concentrates, some bags of cereals. Cray smiled with pleasure. Two bottles of Johnnie Walker stood beside the cans.

Farran watched them. Already they were assessing the comforts of the hut. Ardrey lifted a blanket, stroked its texture. Cray prodded one of the mattresses. Luc closed the door.

Cray turned. 'I been thinking—'

'I know,' Farran said. 'But we have to move.'

'We could brew up,' Ardrey said.

'No.'

'Wouldn't take long.'

'I said no.'

Only Kemmerich was silent.

'Look, Farran,' Luc said. 'There is only four hours of daylight. We have to load the sleds—'

'Christ, yes—'

'—and that'll take time. Then we have to pitch the tents before dark.'

'Wouldn't hardly be worth it,' Cray said.

Ricci stared from the window at the wastes of snow. 'Better stay here,' he said. 'Make an early start tomorrow.'

Farran pulled on his mittens. He said coldly: 'You finished?'

He saw their faces harden. 'Outside,' he said.

They did not move. Kemmerich opened the door.

'Out.'

They went with regret.

Ricci closed the door.

'Bolt it,' Farran said.

Ricci bolted it.

Cray spat with disgust.

'I'd like to stay,' Farran said kindly. 'But we can't waste a minute. If the weather breaks even an hour could be vital.'

He studied the sky. Sun burned his face. 'We'll cross the frontier today,' he said.

He led them down to the glacier bank.

It needed forty minutes to load the sleds. The heaviest single items were the Oysters and the transceiver. Two of the Oysters were placed in one sled, the transceiver and the third Oyster in the other. Then the rations, the tents, the climbing gear, the ammo, the sleeping-bags and sundry stores were evenly distributed. The sleds were covered by tarpaulins and cross-strapped. Skis and ski-poles and the six pairs of racquettes were left unstowed. Each man carried a pack, and across each pack and slung diagonally was an Armalite AR-18 rifle with a full magazine.

Three men would manipulate each sled. In the front and central to the runners was an aluminium prow with a hand-grip. In the rear and rising from the runners like handlebars were the aluminium extensions with which two men would push, restrain or otherwise control the sled. The runners were of waxed and hardened wood, each of them six inches in breadth.

Farran lifted his binoculars. Blue-green waves of ice broke across the lenses. The glacier was sixteen miles long. Dorje's route ran direct down the breast and into the icefall. He could not see the icefall, only the flow of the glacier and the distant curve where it was squeezed between the shoulders of Tuzluk and Kengshe.

He studied the surface. There were snowdrifts, undulations, places where it glittered in sun like a shattered mirror. But it was relatively smooth.

He turned to them and said, 'Skis.'

They secured the ski-poles and the racquettes under the tarpaulin straps. Then they clipped on the *langlaufen*. Bending to the skis and lacing the straps about his ankles Farran felt the blood pulse in his head, a wave of breathlessness. He knew these signs.

He said to Luc, 'They told us twenty thousand. But it's higher than that.'

The Belgian nodded.

Farran stared downstream at the turrets of black rock, at the glaring ice. A breeze came off the glacier, as cold as death. Disquiet brushed him. This was the first deception. What else had been minimized?

Now they were stamping with the skis to check the bindings. The sounds skated, beat in the rock-caverns like the wings of bats, died. Farran went to the leading sled, aligned his skis between the front runners to the right of the prow, hooked his left forearm under and over it so that the metal pressed against his ribs. Cray and Luc moved to the rear. Ardrey and Ricci went with Kemmerich to the second sled. The German positioned himself at the prow.

Farran pulled down his ear-flaps. Beyond the glacier range upon range was lost in violet hazes. The disquiet came again. He stood there rooted in the snow, oppressed by the enormity of this frozen land.

Cray gave his whisky-laugh. 'We shoulda brought dog-teams.'

Farran looked behind him. They were waiting.

Cray murmured, 'Let's go, White Fang.' He jerked at the sled, freeing the runners.

The sled moved.

At base, on the day before embarking, they had had four

114

hours' practice with the sleds. The sleds had been lightly weighted. They had evolved a simple drill. They had proved that three men could guide, run with and arrest a loaded sled.

But this practice was on chosen snow-slopes. Now, moving with the sled down the gradient of the river of ice, moving slowly and the runners softly roaring and the ice-crystals crushing like broken glass and enveloped in the white flare of the glacier light, Farran knew they must learn again.

Already the weight of the sled pressed ominously behind him. He felt the front crossbar nudge against his spine in the area below his pack. He pulled against the prow so that the intervening space was restored. The sled gathered speed. He leaned back against its pressure. The bar struck his spine and he cried out from the sudden pain. He stemmed his skis but, now, he could not shift his weight forward on to the edges. He held out his right arm parallel to his body in the predetermined signal. 'Check it!' he shouted. He looked behind him. Cray and Luc began to stem, thrusting the inverted Vs of their skis into the powdered ice. The sled lurched to the right toward the bank. Cray shouted. Farran swung his weight against the prow. The sled turned sharply to the left. Kemmerich's black-goggled face, tilted across the prow of the second sled, leapt across his vision. The sleds collided, drove for the bank, stopped in the mass of curdled snow. Farran felt the tips of his skis run like spears into the base of the bank, the sudden shock when the skis stopped and flung him forward into the wall of snow.

He pressed with his palms, releasing his face and body from the snow. Pain throbbed in his nose. They came from the sleds, staring. Ardrey said anxiously, 'You all right?' He took off his glove, touched his nostrils. Blood was frozen on his face in twin streams. 'All right,' he said, nodding. He looked down at the skis. He felt a momentary fear. Standard skis, secured at the heels, would have snapped his ankles.

He said to them, nasally through blood, 'This is ice, not snow. We have to go slowly.' He spat blood. It froze in mid-air, struck the ice with a metallic tap. 'We'll try again. But not together.' Then to Kemmerich: 'You keep a hundred feet between us, d'you hear?'

This time they took the sled very slowly down the left channel of the glacier where the snow lay in shallow drifts. The snow gave purchase to the runners. Cray and Luc used their weight like a drag so that the sled should not gain momentum, skis stemmed, forearms braced against the downward pull. The runners began again their muted roar. Farran watched the glacial slope. It came at him in long white tongues out of the brilliant orb of light in which they moved. Tuzluk's shoulder turned above them. Higher on the slope Kemmerich's sled was running easily in a spray of snow.

Now the wind of motion burned his face. The sled seemed to cut through thicknesses of white-hot light. Below him his skis ran slightly parted, the rear ends between the runners. The sled bounced and he saw the right ski slide, shaving the edge of the right runner. Fear rose. Danger was a few inches away. If a ski was trapped beneath a runner . . . he shook his head against this image of a leg twisting in its socket, brought together his skis so that the ankles locked. I must not stem the skis, he told himself: in no circumstances must I stem them.

He pulled at the prow so that the sled ran for the crown of the glacier. He felt immediately its instability. It began to skid, turning its bows toward the right glacier bank. Then, on the periphery of vision, he saw Cray's body move out sideways from the sled, correcting the lateral slide. The bows came round. 'That's good,' he shouted. 'Try it again.'

He turned the sled for the left-hand bank. The rear runners slid. This time Luc moved outward from the rear, leaning in counterweight to the slide. The sled regained the fall-line. Now it was running faster. New vistas opened. Tuzluk and Kengshe were changing contour as the glacier turned. They began to weave in a series of long curves down the glacier, he using the prow like the helm of a boat and Luc or Cray moving in response and the sled no longer ponderous but sensitive and alive on the white river. He looked back once and Kemmerich too was weaving smoothly through the curving line.

They crossed the frontier, this frontier which had no definition, in the region of the tenth mile of the downhill

116

glacier run. Then, an hour before sunset, they reached the icefall.

They pitched the six-man tent in the cover of a rock outcrop and, while the light was good, unloaded from the sleds the pressure-cooker, sufficient fuel and rations, pans for melting snow, mattresses and sleeping-bags. Cray hung a hurricane lamp from the ridgepole. Then Farran led them down the glacier.

They knew from Dorje's map that the west wall of Kengshe forced the glacier into an abrupt change in direction, that it made a swing through an angle of ninety degrees and, flowing downward across the angled slope of the underlying bed of rock, was spilled across a lip. This was the theory of all icefalls. All this was on Dorje's map.

But they were unprepared for what they saw.

The icefall was immense. It plunged like a frozen sea toward the distant lower gorge. It was split by chasms. It poured over cliffs. It curled in giant waves. They felt its terrifying power. Standing on the lip above the great cascade they were puny. They watched the red of the sunset run like a dye through this silent yet moving sea, and did not speak.

With darkness the wind rose. They could hear it below them in the icefall. There was menace in the sound. The icefall was in their minds and would not be dismissed.

Farran said, 'We knew it would be bad.'

'But not this bad.'

'Arif said so. I remember his words. A truly terrible place. That's what he said.'

'That bloody Arif.'

Cray unscrewed his flask, drank some Scotch.

Ardrey asked, 'How many bottles do you have, Ethan?'

'Enough.'

'Enough,' Luc said, 'because he never offers it.'

Cray turned, frowning. 'You want some?'

'Keep it.'

'Go on. Have some.'

'No.'

Cray proffered the flask around the tent. 'Anyone is welcome.'

They shook their heads.

Cray pushed the flask under Luc's nose. 'Take a shot.'

'No.'

'Then why say what you said?'

Luc pushed away the flask.

'Why say a lousy thing like that?'

Farran saw the veins pulse in Cray's face. At these altitudes, he knew, tempers were never far away. Cold, wind, anxiety, thin air rubbed the emotions raw. 'Drop it,' he told them. 'It doesn't matter.'

'But it does matter.'

'I said drop it.'

'Oh, for God's sake,' Ardrey said. He reached out, snatched the flask from Cray's hand, drank, coughed, wiped a trickle of Scotch from his chin, drank again. 'There,' he said.

He returned the flask. Cray stared at it, at Ardrey, at the flask again. His cheeks flushed. 'But you don't like whisky,' he said. 'You hate the stuff.'

'That's right.'

Cray trembled. 'Then why drink it?' He shook the flask. Then, shouting: 'Why the hell waste it?'

Wind boomed in the icefall. The sound was deep, like waves pounding in a cave.

'Listen to that,' Kemmerich said softly. He put down the Armalite rifle and the oil-rag, cocked an ear.

The sound rose in pitch, began to shriek in the icefall like a mad thing trapped. Wind struck the tent. The lamp swung, throwing a moving aureole of light on the nylon walls.

Ricci stared up at the lamp. 'D'you know what I'm thinking?'

'That's a stupid question,' Cray said. He sealed the flask. He was still nervous. 'How should we know what a man is thinking?'

'I am thinking,' Ricci said, 'of a disturbing thing. Of a little yellow box glowing away in the darkness.'

'The tent?'

'Yes.'

Farran shook his head. 'Who is there to see it?'

'A patrol.'

'Up here?'

'Could be.'

Cray said mockingly. 'These devilish Chinese are everywhere.'

118

'Not up here they're not.'

'But it's possible, surely?' Ardrey said.

'Not a chance. The Red Army guards the passes. But that's all.'

Cray laughed again. The anger had gone. 'We'd know if they were out there.'

'How?'

'We'd see *their* little yellow box, wouldn't we?'

Now they were smiling. The tent was warm; warm from the cooker, from their own body-heat, from the insulation of the tent's nylon lining.

'We have one thing in our favour,' Ricci said.

'What's that?'

'They don't know we've declared war on them.'

Ardrey laughed. 'Six men against the People's Army?'

'A little unequal,' Cray agreed.

'Except for the Oysters.'

'That's true,' Ricci said. He put his boots inside his sleeping-bag, stretched out beside them. 'We have superior fire-power. Three beautiful umpteen-megaton H-bombs—'

'—which we cannot fire.'

'You don't fire an H-bomb. You trigger it.'

Something crashed in the icefall.

'Christ!' Cray said.

They listened. The echo rumbled in the ice-caves.

'In an icefall,' Kemmerich said calmly, 'ice is always falling. That ought to be obvious.'

The echo died.

'It sounded as big as a house,' Ardrey said.

'It probably was.'

Farran saw the alarm in Ardrey's face. He said, 'The ice is moving. At the rate of perhaps two feet in every day. So something has to give.'

'It can happen at any time,' Kemmerich said. 'But the most dangerous moment is at dawn when the sun first touches the ice. If the ice is unstable it will detach.'

Now the anxiety had surfaced again.

Farran said seriously, 'You can thank God for the Tuzluk icefall. I know it's bad. But that's our insurance. That's why Dorje chose it.'

Again the crash. The echo ran in a series of deep detonations until it was lost in wind.

'It's bad all right.'

119

'Real bad.'

Wind buffeted the tent. The lamp swung. Cray turned his face up to the moving whorls of mellow light. He said, 'About the bombs, Farran.'

Farran waited.

'You say this old bird Shaw will send the signal?'

'Yes.'

'How?'

'By Morse.'

'You sure?'

'Pretty sure.'

'They could bounce it off the satellite,' Luc said. 'That would be the scientific way.'

'How about that, Farran?'

'No. It'll be by key.' He saw in that moment Kate Shaw's suffering face. 'A finger on a key. A personal message from Joseph Shaw.'

At one hour after daybreak they stowed and lashed the sleds, retaining for the descent the ropes, the hand-winch, crampons for the boots. Then they took the sleds to the lip of the icefall.

Farran glassed it. Mist filled the beds of the gorges. There was a residue of darkness that would not dissolve until the sun was high. He moved the lenses very slowly down the icefall.

The cascade fell through two thousand feet of shelves and cliffs. Half-way down, where the walls moved inward to compress the fall, there were deep ice-troughs. These troughs had been scooped out on either side of the fall, he knew, by the intense sun-heat that was radiated from the black Karakoram rock. They glistened like glass. They ran with the curve of the icefall to where the glacier levelled into a broad ice plateau.

Beyond and below the plateau were the two white streams that formed the confluence of the Tuzluk and Kengshe glaciers, the single river that ran from it. He could not see the snout of the glacier, only the mist and shadow of distance where it was lost.

He held the glasses for a moment on this depth of purple shadow. Then he returned them, bringing them slowly up toward the brink on which they stood. Blue ice hung poised on the ridges above the fall. There were hanging glaciers, boulders, slabs, towers; ice architecture in a thousand massive forms.

He slipped the binoculars into the case. Then he turned to them. 'It's just a staircase,' he said. 'A giant staircase.' He picked up one of the nylon ropes, threw it to Cray. 'We'll take it step by step.'

By sunset they were no more than five hundred feet down the icefall. They had been successful with only one of the sleds. The other remained perched on the lip above them. This was the season of afternoon snow and they pitched the tent in a flurry of driving flakes. The wind was harsh, the cold intense. Already the sun was quartered behind Kengshe's summit ridge. Below them the night was filling the gorges like a tide.

Cray said, 'It's a bad place, Farran.'

'Do we have a choice?'

Here where the icefall narrowed, the tent pitched with caution at the centre and the rock-walls rising on either side, they were under the blue ice of the hanging glaciers. The glaciers jutted out in cliffs of ice. They clung at incredible angles. Cray pointed. Ardrey came from the sled with a can of kerosene, stared through the line of the finger.

'Looks ready to go,' Cray said softly.

They watched the poised ice.

'I'm sure it's moving,' Ardrey said.

Farran heard the strain in his voice. He said, 'It'll hold.' This one, he thought, could sweep the glacier at any moment. The wind was raw. Ice-crystals came sharp as needles into his throat. He felt them prick his lungs, the sudden suspension of breath. He patted Ardrey's arm. He said, 'Himalayan ice sticks like hell. Did you know that?'

In the tent, the food eaten and the lamp swaying, he prayed the ice would stick. It was there, above them in the night. It was there, wrenched by the wind. It was in their thoughts, curtains of ice falling down the mind, ice moving, cathedrals of ice coming from the darkness to build a tomb across them. Already the first temperature changes were taking place, the water freezing in the cracks, expanding, breaking the shackles that stuck those great convoluted masses to the rock. At first it would be like distant gunfire. Then it would roar and the night would explode into sound and the avalanche would impel against them its first suffocating wind.

'D'you know what we forgot?' Cray said.

Cray's voice restored him.

'What?'

'Arif's signal.'

'God, yes.'

'At noon,' Ardrey said, 'we were hanging by our balls on a precipice. How could we listen?'

'Maybe there was nothing.'

Kemmerich turned painfully on his mattress. 'In any case,' he said, 'the radio is in the sled up top.'

The German's voice was thinned from exhaustion. Farran could see the waves of tiredness breaking on his face, half closing the eyelids, weakening the mouth. He had taken nothing except half a meat-bar and a pint of orange-juice and melted snow. He had not washed and the sweats of those hours in the heat of the icefall sheened his cheeks.

'It's been a hard day,' Farran said.

'Yeah,' Cray said with hatred. 'Those sleds.'

They had learned to hate the sleds. At first Farran had assigned three men to a sled. Each sled would be lowered by ropes down the stairs of the icefall. At the end of the day, he'd estimated, they would be off the icefall and ready for the long run down.

But in practice it had not been like that. The sleds had swung, bounced, turned on the ice-walls. So he had split the teams; one man, below, with the sled, to guide and stabilize, two men to lower. But now the dead weight of the sleds proved too much for the strength of two men. The first of the sleds ran easily from the grasp of Ardrey and Ricci, slid fifty feet into a mass of crenellated ice, over-turned. A strap had broken, and some of the contents spilled.

They reloaded and relashed the sled. Then, because the position of the sled was of no value to the descent, they winched it back to the lip. There they secured the sled between two ice boulders, and all six men were assigned to the second sled.

But now the cliffs of the icefall had become precipitous. The packs were too heavy and cumbersome, especially for the two men who, spiked by crampons to the ice, had been deputed to stabilize the bows of the sled. So they removed the packs, aligned them on a ledge. Ten minutes later the sled swung like a pendulum and one of the ropes was snagged in the protruding head of an ice-axe and three of the packs were swept into the ravine.

It took two hours for Kemmerich, Ardrey and Ricci to retrieve the packs. In the meantime Farran, Cray and Luc attempted again the lowering of the second sled. This they achieved by removing the two Oysters. The Oysters, still in their green snoods, were placed on a shelf. By noon, with patience and the use of Cray's enormous muscular power, they had gained two hundred feet of descent. They were rejoined by Kemmerich, Ardrey and Ricci. At this point six men and one sled were sited two hundred feet down the icefall; and six packs, two Oysters and one laden sled were positioned above them. All this was ludicrous. They knew this; that effort, altitude and the sun-heat of the glacier had disoriented them.

They rested. Then they climbed the ice walls to where the packs were, shouldered them, brought them down and arranged them around the sled. Then, again, they climbed the ice walls to retrieve the Oysters. There was nothing except the nylon snoods in which to carry the Oysters; and since the nature of the gradient of the ice made this impossible they descended to the sled. The Oysters, they decided, could be loaded into empty plywood pack-frames, or lowered on ropes.

They chose the ropes because the use of frames involved the unpacking of two of them and they could not face this simple effort. Then they climbed the ice walls for the third time, knotted the ropes in the snoods. Only two men were necessary for the manipulation of one Oyster. So Farran and Luc descended to the sled.

The first Oyster was successfully lowered. The second twisted in Luc's hands, fell heavily on to the sled. They heard the splintering of glass and by the time Cray and the others had climbed down the ice-walls an amber stain spreading on the ice.

Cray went to the sled, stared down at the stain. Then he crouched, removed his mitten and nylon inner glove, rubbed his finger on the stain, put the finger in his mouth. They saw his face redden with anger. 'My Scotch,' he said.

He stood, wheeled on Luc. Farran got between them. Cray's voice gusted into his neck. 'He bust my bottle!'

Farran thrust with his elbow into the American's rib-cage, pushed with his hand.

Cray shouted, 'How many bottles you bust?'

Luc did not move and Farran said, 'It was an accident.'

Cray began to shake. His mouth was enspittled. He could not speak. He went to the stain, stared down at it.

Farran pointed to the mitten and the glove. 'Put them on.'

Cray obeyed.

They spent the remainder of the day on the next three hundred feet of ice. Heat rebounded off the rock-walls. They were immersed in it. It coiled like a red filament in the brain. It stood in waves on the rock. They moved sweating down the shimmering stairs. Below them the gorges, the glaciers and the blue-white wilderness reeled in mist.

When the snow came they were grateful. It made a curtain to the sun, and the sun floated like a white bulb of fire behind it. They opened their mouths, taking the heavy flakes as if they were wafers on the tongue.

But now, in the tent in the night and the ice poised above them, they were ready to quarrel. Clay stared sullenly at the lamp. Johnnie Walker marched across his mind. He lay there with his sense of outrage and Luc, knowing this, said, 'We should discuss a matter of weight.'

'Weight?'

'Yes.'

'We've spent the day discussing weight,' Farran said. The sleds would not leave them. 'Give it a rest.'

'Weight,' Luc said. 'Unnecessary weight.'

Cray turned. 'Like what?'

'Like bottles of Scotch.'

'Oh, Gawd,' Ardrey said wearily, 'we are back on the Scotch again.'

'Let's forget it,' Ricci murmured. He smiled at Luc. 'Please?'

'Is it fair?' Luc asked slowly. 'Is it fair that one man should indulge his tastes at the expense of others? Consider the weight of a crate of whisky—'

'Listen,' Ardrey said abruptly. He held up a hand.

They listened. Wind made its booming noise in the caverns. It rose in pitch, screamed for a time, abated. In that hiatus of sound they heard the rending of ice, a rumble, a concussion as if something of immense size had fallen. They felt the tremor. Sweat was beaded on Ardrey's temples. Cray's hands clenched.

The echoes died. Wind resurged. Ardrey let fall his hand.

'A crate of whisky,' Cray said with contempt. 'I should be so lucky.' He unscrewed his flask, drank.

They watched him.

'Take a good long swig,' Luc said. 'The more you drink the less we have to carry.'

Cray's fingers trembled on the flask.

'Is it fair?' Luc asked again. 'A dozen bottles—'

'Six—'

'All right, six—'

'Less the one you broke.'

Luc shrugged. 'Six bottles. Five bottles. What does it matter? It is weight.' He turned to Farran. 'Did you approve it?'

'Yes.'

'Why?'

'You know why.'

'We all have needs.' Luc's voice had become sharper. 'I would have liked a book or two. Perhaps a few more tins of steak-and-kidney.' He was silent for a time. Then: 'I think we should discard these bottles.'

'Think again,' Cray said.

Farran saw his eyes flare. He held out a hand. 'I'd like a tot,' he said.

Cray passed him the flask. He drank, returned it.

'Is that your answer?' Luc said.

'Yes.'

The dark lips smiled. 'Orders? Out here?'

'Especially out here.'

Luc stared. Then he shrugged, searching his pack, took out his razor-case. He opened it, selected Wednesday's razor. Then, cross-legged on his mattress, he began to shave. He always shaved dry, without a mirror, stretching the skin over his gaunt jaw-bones, feeling for bristle, cutting with tiny meticulous movements of the blade. They could see the contents of the case, the six matched razors in their compartments, the eighth, larger razor that was clipped into the lid.

'Me,' Cray said, 'I'm growing a beard.' He lighted a

cheroot. 'We're all growing beards. In fact, Luc, you're the only man that's shaving.'

'So?'

'So it's extra weight. Like my Scotch.'

Farran heard the accent of provocation. Light glinted on the razors. He was suddenly afraid for Cray. He said quietly. 'You know the rule. We don't smoke in the tent.'

'Three puffs?'

Farran nodded.

Cray drew deeply on the cheroot three times, holding the smoke in his lungs, expelled it slowly. Then he shifted the reindeer skins that covered the floor, exposed an inch of ice, gently stubbed out the cheroot. He returned it to its packet. Then he reached out, lifted the leather razor-case, weighed it in his palm. 'At least a pound, I'd say.'

The razor paused. 'Put it down.'

Cray smiled.

'Put it down.'

The blade moved from Luc's chin. Now it was poised above Cray's hand. Farran could see the dark bristles like iron filings on its edge. Images came; that night in the Pingal refuge, the playing-cards in Cray's hand, the shovel that had cut down savagely into the knuckles.

He said in warning, 'Cray.'

Cray did not move.

The blade turned, reflecting light. Yellow lozenges danced in the corner of the tent. Then the lozenges moved to Cray's eyes, illuminating them. Farran saw something in their depths; not aggressiveness, nor challenge, but the shadow of fear. Cray was like a child reaching for a flame, recoiling from its heat, reaching out again because the danger could not be resisted.

Luc whispered, 'Put it down.'

In that moment they heard the rumbling. It was very near. It was like a train in the night, projecting sound, vibrating. Wind struck the tent. Fragments skated down the icefall like stones flung from a hand. The sound became a roar. It encased them. The floor trembled. The air was sucked from the tent. They began to pant. Ardrey turned on his face, covered his ears with his hands. Kemmerich came from the stupors of exhaustion, stared up at the hurricane lamp like a man in prayer. Then the sound diminished. The avalanche passed. They listened to the echoes moving in volleys through the icefall, into the shuddering night. A solitary stone followed the echoes. They heard it tap-tap-tap until the sound was lost in darkness.

Farran reached out, took the razor-case from Cray's hand, set it down. Then he touched Ardrey's shoulder. He said gently, 'It's all right. It's gone.' But Ardrey did not move. Farran leaned across, drew the hands slowly from the ears.

Later, the tent dark and the glacial light luminous on the walls and the stench of the reindeer skins heavy in the tent, he came from sleep. Something had changed. He knew this instinctively. He could not immediately define the change. The vestige of a dream was there; some force that had grasped his mattress and turned it on the ice. He put out his hand, raking his fingers over the skins that were spread on the floor. His pulses raced. The fingers found a jagged lip, a void in which the skins were hanging, another lip. He stared through the darkness at the floor. He could see the depression in the skins where the crevasse had opened.

Sweat poured. Heat suffused his face. Beneath him, it seemed, the world was splitting. He lay there, listened to the wind and the breathing of the five sleeping men until the first flush of daylight touched the tent.

In the morning they recovered the sled from the brink and brought both sleds to a point that was seven hundred feet down the icefall. They listened to the transceiver between five minutes before and five after noon. There was no signal from base. They ate some of the Compo rations, brewed tea, and at thirty minutes past noon began again the descent.

By sunset of that second day on the icefall they were half-way between the brink and the ice plateau. They secured the sleds, pitched the tents. Then Farran went alone to where the ice fell abruptly from the ridge. Below him the cascade poured until, one thousand feet beneath his feet, its end was lost in shadow. He watched the shadow creep. The plateau glimmered, as smooth as a pearl. Then it was gone. Boots crunched behind him and Cray's voice said, 'We have to get off this icefall, Farran.'

There was urgency in the voice. Farran turned. The sunset light washed across Cray's face, accenting the scars and flattened bones.

'Been two days now,' Cray said accusingly.

'Yes.'

'And still only half-way down.'

Farran nodded.

'That'll make four days on the icefall.'

'At this rate, yes.'

Cray stared down the fall. Ice towers reached like tallow candles from the shadow. He said, 'How many days did you allow?'

'One.'

Cray turned from the fall. 'But, Christ, man, we're eating food.'

'You want to stop eating?'

'I want to get down. Before the weather breaks. Before the chow goes. Before someone busts his lousy neck.'

Cray went to one of the ice tunnels, began to urinate. He said without turning, 'Have you thought of that?'

'What?'

'That situation. An accident.'

'I try not to.'

'It could happen.'

'Yes.'

'Kemmerich is bushed.'

'I know.'

'Tired men get hurt. Easily.'

Cray returned. He stared again at the icefall, at the glaciers and the gorge, at the darkness that was rising like a swamp. He shook his head, shivered. Farran knew that the pressures of the wilderness were building. Everything was too vast, too savage. Life out here was a weak tongue of flame, easily extinguished.

'Or sickness,' Cray said. 'A man could fall sick.'

He waited, as if for reassurance.

Farran said, 'Things can happen. But let's meet them when they come.'

Cray nodded. But the anxiety remained. 'Those sleds,' he said. 'We could make them lighter.'

'How?'

Cray hesitated. Then: 'We have three Oysters and a transmitter.'

'Well?'

'That's where the weight is.' He began to stab at the ice with his boot, making patterns with the crampons. 'How many H-bombs you figure we need to blow up the mountain?'

Farran laughed.

'I mean it.'

'Better ask Einstein.'

Cray scowled. 'I often wonder about you, Farran. You make jokes about things that aren't funny.' He spat across the ridge, listened for the tap of the frozen globule. Then he said slowly, 'Chances are two bombs would do it. Agreed?'

'Yes.'

'We could ditch one Oyster and the transmitter. That'd save better than one hundred pounds in weight.'

Farran did not answer. He walked a pace along the ridge, stared at the peaks that were serrated on the thin rim of sun.

Cray came behind him. The whisky-voice said, 'Can you honestly say you haven't thought of that?'

'I thought of it.'

'Well, then?'

'No.'

'Why not?'

He was silent.

'Why not?'

'Orders.'

'From a load of fucking Indos?'

He saw the faces of Dorje, Hadji and Arif in that moment. Below him was the desolate land where Dorje had come alone. Alone up here: there was terror in the thought. He said quietly, 'Yes. From a load of fucking Indos.'

Cray moved to his side, spat again. The saliva caught the sun, fell like a red bead. Somewhere a voice was singing. They listened. It was Ricci. The voice rose. It was pleasant and melodious.

Cray smiled. 'He's a happy bastard.'

'Yes.'

'Wild too. As wild as hell.' Cray opened his parka, drew out his flask. 'That's why he's here,' he said. 'Did you know that?'

'Yes.'

'I mean that's the only reason.' Cray shrugged. 'Some of us – we been in trouble. But not Ricci. He's as pure as snow. He's also rich and as crazy as a loon. Ski-jumps, bobs, motor-races – you name anything a man can bust his neck at and Ricci's done it.'

He offered the flask and Farran drank from it.

'You're getting the flavour,' Cray said sourly.

Farran returned the flask. He watched the Scotch ripple in Cray's throat. He said softly, 'What kind of trouble?'

'Me?'

'Yes.'

'Didn't Hadji tell you?'

'No.'

Ricci's voice rose again. Cray smiled, pocketed the flask. 'What kind of trouble?'

'These.' Cray held up his fists. He said proudly, 'I'm an Army Champion, Farran.' He lunged and a mittened fist leapt across Farran's shoulder.

'You mean you hurt someone?'

Cray nodded.

'In a ring?'

'In a cell.'

The sun went below Kengshe's ridge. The ice turned grey.

'As you know,' Cray said, 'I'm also an Army MP. And Army MPs sometimes find some very nasty things down in the dungeons. Like Reds.'

Wind came, disjointing Ricci's voice.

Cray said slowly, 'I knew this fella was there. He was on my mind. This shit of a Red, down in the cell, all snug and safe whilst other fellas was being shot up in the Nam. It all built up till I couldn't sit there a moment longer. I stood up. I went downstairs. I unlocked his cell. And I beat him so bad I nearly busted a gut.'

'How bad?'

'As bad as could be.'

Cray bent, picked up an ice-pebble, flung it down the icefall. Then he turned. 'So you see, Farran, I have some charges stacked against me. Serious charges. You remember that. 'Cause when you send that signal, that little word OYSTER, they're going to tear those charges up.'

He stood there, big and pugnacious on the lip of the ice cliff. Farran nodded. They heard Ardrey's voice shout distantly, 'Tea up!' A metal pan fell, clattered on the ice.

They turned. There was an aureole of pink light behind the peaks, cast upward by the unseen sun.

'It'll be a fine day tomorrow,' Farran said. 'We'll make good time.'

But he had not believed this. Behind Cray's head the wind was tearing fleeces of snow from Tuzluk's summit. Cloud was massing. And later in the tent they heard the gale in the icefall and smelled the mist behind the odour of the Primus and knew with certainty that the weather was changing.

Now, in his sleeping-bag and on the edge of sleep, Farran listened to the gale and the breaking ice, to the voices in the tent. The voices were distant. Yet he could hear the disquiet in them. They came from the springs of fear; words that might drown the sounds of the icefall or distract from the awareness of the mist and the cornices of hanging ice. The voices were swift and garrulous. They were components of the amber lamplight that swayed behind the membranes of his eyelids. He could also hear the snick of Thursday's razor as it moved across the Belgian's jaws, the faint hiss of the pressure-stove, Kemmerich's cough. Poor bloody Kem. It had been a bad day, a terrible day in which they had clawed their way down that cleft of imprisoned glare until the sweat had washed the sun-cream from their faces, until the sleds had defeated them and Kemmerich, panting in the dry cold air, had fallen to his knees and stained the ice with the slivers of tissue that were the sloughed-off epithelial lining of his throat.

Ardrey was saying, '—but I wouldn't have the nerve. Not for a ski-jump.'

'It isn't nerve. It's training.'

'Imagine it.' This was Cray. 'Imagine taking off like that. Like a bird.'

Ricci laughed.

'I tried it once,' Kemmerich said. The voice was weak. 'But I think I was too old. To be a jumper you have to be young and very stupid.'

The words died in a paroxysm of coughing. Farran heard him unwrap one of his antibiotic tablets.

'You shouldn't talk,' Cray said kindly.

Wind roared in the tunnels of the icefall, struck the tent.

'What's this one?' Ardrey asked.

'The Cresta.'

Farran listened. This was the third or fourth photograph, pictures of other places and other times, familiar snaps grown grubby and broken at the edges that they would re-examine as if there were something new to be discovered. They would delve into packs and wallets, add to the little pile on the blanket by the stove.

'And this one?'

'Same. The Cresta.'

Only Luc would remain aloof, guarding the past, spending words as if they were coins of value.

'I once went down in a bob,' Cray said. He laughed. 'But never again. It scared the shit out of me.'

Farran heard his fingers fumble on the photograph, the faint tap as it joined the pile. If he opened his eyes he would see the details of the picture, the red bobsleigh at the foot of the run, the banner that advertised Kneissl skis, the group that was gathered around the bob and Ricci, silver trophy in hand, smiling from under his bright red helmet.

Kemmerich coughed, sipped water, coughed again. Then there was another sound, metallic yet smooth. This too was recognizable. The magazine had been withdrawn from one of the Armalites. Kemmerich, the good soldier, was about to oil his rifle.

'You'll rub that thing away,' Cray said.

The razor scraped. Ice fell somewhere on the western wall. The tremors came. The steel wire that secured the tent began to sing in a high key. Little gusts of freezing air moved inside the tent. They listened. The cannonades of sound died in the night.

Then Kemmerich said, 'There is a matter to discuss.'

'You should discuss sleep.'

'That's right, Kem. You're pretty tired.'

'It won't wait,' Kemmerich said. The voice had become a whisper. 'We must discuss it now.'

There was a silence. Then Cray said, 'Okay. What shall we discuss? Women?'

'No.' A finger tapped on something solid. 'This.'

This? Farran opened his eyes. Kemmerich's finger was tapping on the butt of the Armalite. He looked into the German's face, at the muff of grey beard, at the cheeks that were red and raw where the sun had stripped the skin from them like paper.

'God willing,' Kemmerich whispered, 'we shall soon get down to the lower snows. Then there is the possibility that we shall meet with Chinese troops.' He lifted the rifle. 'The question is – do we use it?'

The razor stopped. Luc turned.

'One thing's for sure,' Cray said softly, 'we're not going to throw fucking snowballs at them.'

Kemmerich stared. 'With you,' he whispered, 'it's all fucking this and fucking that. Why don't you clean out your mouth?'

Farran saw the vein on Cray's temple engorge with blood. He sat upright, put his hand on Cray's fist. The fist strained against his palm. Then it relaxed. He withdrew his hand and Cray reached across the blankets, took the rifle from Kemmerich's fingers.

Cray said evenly, 'Time was when you Krauts wouldn't have worried about shooting up a few Chinese Chinks. You'd have gassed the lot before breakfast.' He ran his finger up the barrel of the Armalite, examined the smear of gun-oil on its tip. 'You clean it. You oil it. You polish it. You love the feel of it. But you're afraid of it.' He looked up. 'And you know why? Because you're a new breed of Kraut. You're stuffed full of guilt. And so you should be. Trouble is you spend so long repenting that the guts have fallen clean out of you.' He tossed the rifle into Kemmerich's lap.

They were silent for a time. Cray drank some Scotch.

Farran said, 'Let's get this clear. We are talking about a situation – the killing of Chinese troops in our own defence. But what is the object of our mission? To drown Su Tokai, to drown Chinese.' He shrugged. 'What is the difference?'

'I'll tell you,' Luc said. He explored his face for uncut bristle, blew on the razor-blade, returned the razor to the open case. 'The difference is that someone else will send that signal. We'll all be long gone and we'll never see the water hit them. But aim a gun and fire it, take a life' – he smiled cruelly – 'that's personal. That's different.'

Luc stared at them, turning his face slowly under the lamp so that they saw its dark and wolfish features. Above him the tent bellied with the weight of snow. He asked, 'Which of you has seen combat?'

They were silent.

Luc nodded. He looked down at the pile of snapshots, shook his head with contempt.

He said softly, 'I'll show you a photograph.'

He reached into his pack, took out a wallet. Then, opening it, he produced a photograph. He held it under the light for a moment. Then he placed it on the snapshots like a man playing a winning card.

They bent forward. No one touched it. It depicted the front half of an army truck. A palm-frond hung in the right foreground. There was a distant line of bush and thorn trees. Three black bodies lay on the ground in the middle distance. A pi-dog, paw upraised, sniffed at the feet. A man stood by the wheel of the truck. It was Robert Luc. He wore the beret, silver-winged emblem and camouflage smock of the Belgian paras. His cheeks were hollow, his eyes sunken. He was as famished and predatory as the pi-dog.

'Congo,' Luc said. Then to Farran, 'Go on. Pick it up.'

Farran picked it up, turned it toward the light. Details emerged, the shadow of a gun, a tear in the smock. A canvas belt was buckled around the smock. Loops of wire or string were threaded through the belt, and a number of small shell-like objects hung from the loops. He knew that Luc was watching him. He saw Luc's hand go to the case, take out the large razor from the clips in the upper lid. Then the blade moved through light until it came to rest on the picture. It slid downward, glinting with oil. The edge stopped above the little withered objects.

He waited but Luc did not speak. The blade was unmoving on the picture. He looked up into Luc's face and the sharp lips framed a single word, 'Ears.'

The tent was silent. He could hear Kemmerich swallowing carefully into his lacerated throat. The blade withdrew. A hand took the photograph from his fingers.

Luc said, 'It answers all the questions, doesn't it? You begin with scruples. But you also begin with an enemy. You end by cutting trophies from his flesh.'

He rose, took the shovel, opened the sleeve of the tent, went out into the night.

Farran left the tent before sunrise. Fear immediately touched him. Mist hung like a pall on the icefall. It choked in the throat. He could not see Tuzluk or Kengshe, only the dark knees of rock that supported them.

He fixed crampons to his boots. Then, taking an ice-axe,

134

he made his way laterally along the icefall to where the wall of Kengshe would be. It came out of mist. Below him was the descending trough of ice that heat had channelled between the glacier and the rock. But there was no way down. It was strewn with the debris of avalanches. Towers and cottages of ice were stuck like teeth in the bed.

He left the trough, returned to the tent. Cray came out, stared at the mist, shook his head. At this point the tent was perhaps two hundred yards from Tuzluk. Farran did not speak or stop.

When he reached the wall of Tuzluk the mist was already luminous with the first light of dawn. It had begun to billow in wind, revealing the sky as if through a rent, closing again. He watched the light strengthen, watched it creep like milk in the trough that separated the mountain from the fall.

The ice trough slowly formed. It began to glisten. It twisted with the turn of the rock wall. It was very steep. In places it was cambered. It fell through terrifying ramps and scarps toward the white china plate that was the distant ice plateau. But it was free from debris. From this point on the walls of Tuzluk did not sweep it. There were a few isolated boulders that would melt when the sun rose, a great edifice of ice that was lodged in the centre of the second bend like a broken molar. But that was all.

He went back to the tent. They were standing there, staring at the mist. They were sullen with worry. He pointed at Ricci and said 'Come with me.'

When they reached the beginning of the trough they stood for a moment in the graveyard stench of the mist. Ricci stared around him, at the rock, at the trough, at the plateau that gleamed far below like an unreachable haven.

Farran said, 'Do you have the photographs?'

Ricci was puzzled. 'The photographs?'

Farran nodded.

Ricci hesitated. Then he took out his pigskin billfold, opened it, held it out. 'Which one?'

There were four snapshots in the billfold. Farran plucked one out. 'This.'

Ricci took it. Farran tapped the red nose of the bobsleigh. Then, without speaking, he pointed down the trough.

'You can't mean it,' Ricci said.

'I mean it.'

'A sled? Like a bob?' Ricci was incredulous. He stared down the trough. 'Down that?'

'Yes.'

Ricci returned the picture to the billfold. They heard Kemmerich coughing behind the walls of mist.

'It's getting worse,' Farran said. 'And the food is going. We'll die if we're trapped up here.'

Ricci stared again at the trough. His lips twitched. He began to laugh.

'Do I get a silver cup?' he asked.

When the sleds were positioned one behind the other above the trough Ricci walked slowly around them. He checked the straps and the distribution of weight. He went to the front of the leading sled, stood between the runners, pushed against the prow, shook his head. Then he left the prow, took the ski-pole and measured its length against the height of the sled.

They watched him. During that hour in which they had eaten breakfast and stacked the sleds it had seemed that the sun would suck the mist from the icefall. For a time the mist had risen, and they had seen the plateau and the converging ice-streams and even the snows beyond the gorge. But now the temperature had fallen. It was intensely cold. They could not see the sun, and the mist, as grey as steel, made a low roof above their heads.

Ricci stared at the first of the sleds, at the trough that dipped for a thousand feet below him, at the sled again. Then he shrugged, took both ski-poles, climbed onto the sled so that he lay face downward and parallel to its runners. He looked behind him.

'Secure my feet,' he said.

They fixed his boots under the rear straps. Ricci nodded. Then, slipping his hands up through the loops of the poles, he thrust with the points of the poles first left then right. The sled moved under the thrusts. He nodded again, smiled at Farran.

Farran looked around him. He saw the imprint of doubt in their faces. His own doubts resurged. The risks were too great. The sleds would smash into fragments on the buttresses of rock and ice, hurtle into chasms. They would lose the food, the tents, the fuel, perish in the Himalayan night. He opened his mouth to speak, framing the order that

136

would bring Ricci down from his perch on the sled. In that moment he saw their faces turn yellow as the light went. The mist was falling across them. He tasted its pungent flavour. Already the plateau and the ice-streams were gone from sight. He felt the terror of the icefall in that moment. The words pounded in his brain – *we have to get down, we have to get down, we have to get down.*

'Fix your skis,' he told them. 'We'll go together. The whole bloody lot. Shit or bust.'

He climbed on to the second sled, gripped his ski-poles. Ardrey unbuckled the rear strap, rebuckled it across his ankles. Kemmerich went to the rear of Ricci's sled. He saw Cray move behind him.

Kemmerich bent, leaned with his weight. The sled began to move. Across the prow he saw it dip into the gradient, heard the hiss of its runners.

'Now,' he said.

Cray leaned.

'Bon voyage,' Cray said.

He pushed.

The sled ran easily toward Ricci's tail. The cleated soles of the boots came nearer. There was a second in which the prows lifted, were poised on the rippled hump above the trough.

Then they swooped.

Farran felt the ponderous weight of the sled leap like a thing released. He saw the rear of Ricci's sled slew to the left, then to the right, the swift correcting thrust of the metal poles. His own prow swung and, stabbing with his left pole, he restored the sled to the fall-line. They gathered speed. The runners roared. Ricci's boots fled before him. He could see the shaking mass of Ricci's pack, the poles like lances of metal light in the twin waves of powder snow that curled from the bows. Now they were bounding through a tunnel of mist and ice and sullen yellow light, through thicknesses of mist that the sleds ripped like veils from the trough. The walls fused into a blur of rock, ice and snow. He could not see the details of the trough, only the rear of the sled, the shaking pack, the showering snow. Keep on its tail, he told himself. That is all you can do. Keep on its tail. Trust in Ricci. He began to synchronize his thrusts with the thrusts of the poles in front. Oh, God, don't let it get faster! The trough dipped. The sleds went faster. The runners screamed. The sled struck something, leapt, descended. Blood shot across the root of his tongue. He opened his mouth and the freezing rush of air shot like a flame into his throat and lungs. He cried out with pain and the crystals of flying ice from Ricci's sled rattled against his teeth. A sleeve of sky whipped across his vision. He saw below him the rink of diamond light that was the plateau. Now the sled was spinning. Peaks fell down the sky. The sun whirled like a torch. Ricci's sled came out of the glare, struck. The sleds reared. A man's body was flung black across the sun. Someone was shouting. He began to slide. Ice rasped his cheeks. He stopped.

He got to his feet. The sled was on its side. The other was rammed in the glacier bank. Ricci lay on his face. The straps from the capsized sled trailed on the ice and an ear of the tarpaulin flapped in wind.

Ricci stood. Four black shapes came very fast out of the trough and on to the plateau, skimmed in toward the sled, stopped. They stood there, leaning on their poles, panting in the thin air. No one spoke. They stared at the sleds, at the wall of mist where the icefall rose, at the trough, at each other. They began to laugh. The laughter echoed in the halls of ice that hemmed the plateau. Cray turned to the icefall, stuck two derisive fingers into the air and shouted, 'We beat you, you cow! We beat you!' Even Robert Luc was laughing. Ricci sat down on the capsized sled, wiped the tears of laughter from his eyes.

After they had relashed the sleds they took them to the edge of the plateau. The wind had dropped and it was very quiet. Below them were the glacier streams that ran from the icefall, snowfields, the haze of distance where the land declined.

Somewhere in that haze was Jalanath.

CHAPTER NINE

In the communications room of the Monastery of Thyang-jun three men stood by the larger of the three satellite transmission screens. They were Hadji, Petrie and Shaw. They watched intently. Zirkon Voyager, somewhere in orbit above the Karakoram, had begun to paint its message. The pictures rose in vivid colours across the glass.

'Five days now,' Petrie said. 'And still no signal.' He turned to Hadji. 'Are you worried?'

'No.'

'Then you should be. What about food?'

Hadji shrugged. 'They'll have finished the Compo. Now they'll be on assault rations.'

'Which is?'

'Two pounds per man per day.'

'Don't sound much.'

'It's enough.'

'You cut it too damn fine.'

'There was bad weather over the Tuzluk,' Shaw said. 'That could explain it.' He bent across the screen.

'What's up?'

'This.' Shaw pointed. He pressed a button and the picture was immobilized on the smaller screen. A havildar came forward and Shaw said to him, 'Give me a tighter scale.'

The havildar manipulated dials. A magnified section appeared.

'Again,' Shaw said.

The area widened.

'Just here,' Shaw said. He touched a grey object that sat squarely in a mass of rock and ice.

They bent forward.

'Another pillbox,' Shaw said. His face was sober. 'And bang across their route.'

Farran studied the pillbox through the binoculars. There was a horizontal slit in the concrete from which a gun might command the snow valley. Behind the pillbox was a timber hut on a concrete base. A radio antenna grew from the roof. The sun was low and the red of it touched the metal of the antenna.

He lowered the binoculars. 'Not a sign of life,' he said.

'Maybe it isn't manned,' Cray said.

'It's manned,' Luc said. He pointed. 'Look.'

Four figures were coming through the flushed snows to the east of the pillbox. They wore racquettes and they trudged with rhythmic steps across the slope. At that distance they were miniature. They grew larger. They carried rifles and marched with ski-poles. They reached the hut, removed the racquettes, began to dig out the impacted ice with the spikes of the poles.

Farran raised the binoculars. The soldiers appeared on the lenses. They had flat Mongolian faces. They wore grey-green padded tunics, peaked cloth caps with red stars sewn above the peak.

'Are they yellow?' Cray asked.

'Not really.'

Farran passed him the binoculars. The soldiers went into the hut. Then one came out, filled a bucket with snow, went back in.

This, then, was the enemy?

They pitched the tent behind the shallow wall of the valley. Then, the supper eaten and they drinking tea, Luc said, 'How much food is left, Farran?'

'Not much.'

'Be exact.'

'One day.'

Cray put down his can. 'One day? Is that all?'

'Yes.'

They were silent.

Then Luc said softly, 'Well, what are you going to do?'

Farran spread Dorje's map.

'We cannot eat a map,' Luc said.

Farran moved his finger down the route. He tapped on the little red oyster shell that was drawn on it.

Luc stared. 'What is it?' The voice thinned with sarcasm. 'A Chinese restaurant?'

'It's Shindi Kul.'

'The village?'

'Yes.'

'The marvellous village where we are going to get food and shelter and a helping hand?'

'Yes.'

Luc grimaced and Cray said nervously, 'I never believed in that village.' He gulped his tea. 'Is it really there?'

'It's there,' Farran said. 'Five miles down. We'll get there tomorrow.'

'But we can't be certain.'

'Why not?' He tapped again on the map. 'Everything else has been true. The route. The landmarks. The navigation. Why should it lie now?'

'The altitudes were wrong.'

'And I don't see that bloody pillbox on it.'

'That's right, Farran.'

He shook his head. 'We have to rely on Dorje. The route in and the route out. We have to trust him.'

He leaned over, began to pump the pressure-stove. They watched him.

Luc said, 'There's food in that pillbox, Farran.'

'There are also four soldiers.'

Luc smiled.

'Four is easy,' Cray said.

Farran looked up from the stove.

'Easy,' Cray said again.

Luc nodded.

He stared at them. Now they were in alliance. Even the faces were close.

He said, 'We'd have to kill them.'

Their faces nodded.

Kemmerich looked down at his hands.

Farran said, 'You saw the radio antenna. That means they're in contact. If they don't report more soldiers will come.'

'No problem,' Luc said. 'We'd dispose of the bodies.'

'That's right,' Cray said. He spread his hands. 'Why, in a country like this most anything could happen. They coulda got lost, frozen, fallen down a crack. Something like that.'

They waited. The stove hissed in the silence.

Farran said, 'We can't take the risk. This isn't a raid. It's a secret mission. We fix the bombs. Softly. Undetected. And when the mountain falls it'll be a natural disaster.'

141

'It'll be a natural disaster,' Cray said coldly, 'if we run out of food.'

'We won't run out. There'll be food at Shindi Kul.'

He saw the tension leave Kemmerich's hands.

'Is that your decision?' Luc asked.

'Yes.'

That night he rocked uneasily between sleep and wakefulness. His blood was heated with some nameless and transient infection. Images leaned out of dreams, brought him sweating into the dark of the tent. Then sleep came: and, now, endless tides of water thundered through a gorge and red clouds towered in the skies and a mandarin with rat-tail whiskers bent over the body of a woman. The woman had a fragile neck and silver hair and she made no sound when the mandarin took a silver hammer and, with exquisite care, broke the bones of each tethered ankle, not even a sound when Shaw, too, leaned across her and, picking out the fragments, dropped them one by one into the urns and vases of his collection.

Coming from the dream and wet with sweat he listened to the breathing in the tent. This sound of breathing was always a sound of the mountain past. It evoked a hundred huts where, perched on some rib of rock and wedged with friends and strangers on the big communal bunk, he had slept, twisted, listened, smelling the boots and the wool and the wet clothes that were hung on lines below the roof.

Remember the Cabine de Valsorey? It was built on the south face of the Grand Combin, and it marked the half-way point on the Haute Route ski-tour that ran between Chamonix and Zermatt. There were more than forty people in the hut that night. He had lain in the angle of the hut next to the Welsh school-teacher. She had been prim and cold on the trip from Le Tour to the Grand Combin. But in the night of the cabin they had both awakened and she had thrust her buttocks into his lap and, touching her, he had felt the rivers of passion that ran within her. He had screwed her from behind and when she cried out with the pleasure of it her cry was only one more sound in the other sounds of the breathing hut. The next day he'd skied and climbed very badly and he'd resolved never again to sleep with Welsh school-teachers in mountain huts.

When they reached Zermatt he drank a Cognac with

142

Bozon the guide. Later, after dark, he went alone through the village and across the bridge to the little cemetery. This, for him, was a kind of shrine. It contained the graves of many dead climbers, men whose broken bodies had been brought down for burial from the Matterhorn and other peaks. On many of the graves there were ice-axes. They had been placed there at the time of the burial. No one had touched these axes. They had lain there through the years until, now, they were rusted and rotted and specked with fungus. After a tour or a climb he liked to come to the graveyard, or graveyards like it, and say a prayer of thanksgiving for the deliverance from danger of himself and his companions. Standing there he could always feel the presence of the young men who had kept their separate appointments. Sometimes the stones and their inscriptions gleamed in alpine starlight.

The stones and their inscriptions. The stones split with age, crumbled, reformed. He had slipped again into the dream. The cemetery retreated and now, within the angle of two ancient walls, there was a group of four headstones. Each had a stone surround and an area of soil from which yellow and purple flowers grew. Time and weather had greened three of the headstones. The fourth was smaller and paler, the grave of a child. Behind the stones and the wall were the triple roofs of a temple. The wall dissolved, became a picture-frame. A sprig of white flowers rested on the frame, drooped toward the child's headstone. He could not read the inscriptions on the stones. He wanted to read them but they were indistinct. A name and a date. It was imperative that he read them. Four stones. Four names. Four dates. Now he was striving, tearing at the veils that blurred the stones. *I have to read them, have to, have to, have to . . .*

Farran awoke. He sat up, stared into the darkness of the tent. Sweat ran. The headstones stood like teeth. Then they went. He heard the breathing of the sleeping men. Behind the breathing, in the recesses of memory, Arif's voice said faintly, 'The key can be any kind of sound frequency. In this case it will be a coded radio-signal of four groups of numbers.'

Farran lay back in the sleeping-bag. Wind grieved outside the tent. He knew in that moment that the key to the Oysters had revealed itself.

When Farran awoke again there was a pallor of grey light in the tent. He turned on his side, then raised himself on his elbow. Cray and Luc had gone. It was a rule that the first man to awaken should start the stove. But the stove was cold.

He got up, opened the sleeve of the tent, looked out. Snow had fallen in the night and he could see the prints of boots. The prints led from the tent, making a twisting spoor in the direction of the valley.

He turned, stared down at the two empty sleeping-bags, at the kit that lay behind them. The Armalites were gone. Luc's pack was unbuckled and a corner of the razor-case protruded from it. On impulse he bent, drew the case from the pack, opened it.

The big razor was missing.

When they reached the pillbox Luc and Cray were standing in the sun. A cheroot hung from Cray's lips. Tinned food was piled in the snow.

No one spoke. Farran went into the pillbox. There were three cases of ammunition, one unmounted heavy weapon. But that was all.

He left the pillbox. Kemmerich, Ardrey and Ricci were waiting. He shook his head, lead them toward the hut.

One of the Chinese lay by the entrance. The face was buried in snow. Farran stepped over him, went into the hut. It was warm inside. A kerosene stove hissed. There was a line of drying socks. There was also a smell of blood. The three Chinese lay on the floor. They were dead. Two of them were bruised about the face and head. Each of them had a slashed throat. He heard Ardrey retch behind him. He bent across the bodies. The faces were young and smooth. He felt his own need to vomit, and turned away. Turning he saw the transceiver in the corner of the hut and the red glass eye that had begun to wink in the centre of it.

They listened. The call-sign came. Kemmerich went to the transceiver, stared. The brief rhythm was repeated for a time. Then it stopped.

Outside the hut Farran turned the body of the soldier. The throat gaped. This face too was unlined and youthful. He touched the cheek and there was no bristle to rasp against his finger. Ricci's shadow fell across his face and he said without looking up, 'They were only boys.' He felt the pity dry his mouth, swelling like a pain. He said, trembling, 'Boys. Just boys.' Rage filled him. He could see Luc crouching in the snow, cleaning the razor in it, flicking from the blade little crusts of bloodied snow.

He left the soldier, walked swiftly toward Luc, put the instep of his boot hard into the Belgian's head. The rage blurred his eyes. He saw Luc roll, then the arc of Cray's fist as it swung out of the sun. The blow flung him like a skittle. The peaks reeled. He tasted snow. He felt Cray lift him, another blow. The snow rose like a white shelf, struck him. Then Cray's fingers were clawed in his hair and his head was jerked backward and there was a moment in which the skin of his throat was bared and taut and Luc's dark face, as feral as a hungry cat, loomed across him. Something glinted in the sun.

Then he heard the shot.

The sound beat echoes out of the rock walls. His vision cleared. Luc's arm was poised above him. The blade of the razor was a sliver of metal fire. Kemmerich's rifle moved until it was aligned on Luc's chest. Cray's whisky-breath broke in clouds above his head. In that second of immobility, the razor poised and the rifle still, they heard the call-sign.

They listened. It came from the hut in rapid pulses of dot-and-dash. There was urgency in the rhythm. It came again and again, demanding reply. The sound, this enemy hand on a distant key, restored them. The blade retreated. The hand released his hair. The rifle lowered.

Farran got to his feet. He picked up his sun-glasses and bonnet, put them on. The signal had not stopped. He listened again.

He said. 'We have got to get out of here. Quickly!'

They buried the bodies of the four soldiers in a snow-bank. They also buried their rifles, packs, racquettes and ski-poles. They returned to the hut and obliterated the bloodstains on the concrete floor by pouring kerosene on them. Then they carried the cans of food up and across the traverse of the valley wall to where the tent was.

They struck camp, stowed the sleds, fixed their racquettes.

The sun was strong and the mist was lifting. Already they could see, distantly below them, dark swathes where the snow had gone, the first stands of timber.

145

Shindi Kul exhibited its sores of poverty in the centre of a skein of streams. The mountains fed the streams and the streams fed the lake. The snow-water was grey and fast. The village lay two miles from the southern tip of the lake. They had first seen the village (but not the lake or Jalanath) from the edge of the conifers. From there on down the snow gave way to pastures of drowned grass. The sleds ran well on the wet grass. This was sheep country and the flocks ran in dirty brown waves before the prows.

There were many sheep in the village, in pens, in the streams. There were also many people; men and women with faces that were as brown and seamed as old leather, children with thin legs and festering sores. Only the sheep made noise. The people had learned silence from the vast spaces around them, from the weight of poverty. They stared, nodded, touched the sleds, and were quiet. The headman led them through the village. There were derelict huts with noisome caverns underneath where the sheep had lived out the winter, mounds of rotting melon rinds in which rats moved, little piles of chopped roots and sheep-dung that were used as fuel. Plagues of flies made garlands in the air. Excreta eddied in the streams.

'I don't like this place,' Cray said.

'You don't have to,' Farran said. He pointed to the rising ground through which the streams ran. 'We'll pitch the tent up there where the water's pure.'

Cray nodded with relief. A child with sunken eyes and a sheepskin coat slipped its hand into his palm. He bent, lifted the child to his shoulders. The legs around his neck were like stalks. 'Poor little bastard,' he said.

Inside one of the huts was a stock of canned meat and canned fruit, strips of pemmican, some sacks of tsampa and lentils, drums of fuel. Farran picked up one of the cans. It was instantly recognizable. It wore the same coloured label as the cans they had stolen from the pillbox hut. There was also a blue stencil across the label. This too he had seen before. He touched the Chinese characters. 'It's army stuff.' he said.

He replaced the can. Arif had not deceived them. The food was here, more than enough to get them back across the frontier. But disquiet had brushed him.

He said to Cray: 'About the cans you took—'

'What about them?'

'Did you leave any in the hut?'

'No.'

'You took the lot?'

Cray nodded.

'Then we've made a mistake.' He looked up into the child's staring black eyes. 'Whoever comes will query why there's no food.'

Luc shrugged. 'So they ran out.'

'They wouldn't do that. Not up there.'

The child kicked its legs.

'What is it?' Kemmerich asked, smiling. 'A boy or a girl?'

'Christ knows.'

Cray put the child down. It ran out into the sun.

Farran followed. He stared past the headman's wadded coat to the slopes and the crest of trees. Above the treeline were the snows. Somewhere in that whiteness the red eye winked and the radio called in the silence of the hut. Perhaps the investigating patrol was already there.

The patrol came very fast into the snow valley. They skied in perfect harmony, exactly spaced, the line of eight men black and sinuous on the whiteness. They carried on their backs a pack, a rifle, the separate parts of a machine-gun. They were led by the equivalent of a sergeant. This was a section of the 2nd Mountain Division of the People's Army. They had spent two years in the high altitudes. They had become hard and fierce, impervious to cold and silence.

When they reached the pillbox they removed their skis, built them into two pyramids. They went into the pillbox, then into the hut. The sergeant went to the transceiver, made his preliminary report of arrival to the communications base of the Sector. Then he examined the hut.

There were drying socks on the line, shirts and woollens in the lockers. The blankets were folded in the regulation manner and the pillows placed on top. But there was a photograph and some letters under one of the pillows, and a wrist-watch under another. Obviously the men had not deserted.

The sergeant sat down on one of the bunks, took a document from his pocket. It listed the names and records of the men in the pillbox detail. They were militia of the first grade: youths in the third tour of their military training. They were boys – but not without experience. The weather had been good, the post was within easy reach of two other mountain posts, and each of the militiamen was able to navigate on simple compass bearings. So they were unlikely to be lost.

The sergeant stood, put away the document. An accident was always a possibility. A breaking snow-bridge, a fall into a deep crevasse – such things were possible. And yet a pocket of unease lay in his mind. He walked around the silent hut, stared at the floor, the bunks, the stove, the food cupboard.

He opened the cupboard. There were sacks of roasted barley and vegetables, salt and tea, clarified butter, biscuits. But something was surely missing. He frowned. There were no cans. Several dockets lay to the left of one of the shelves. He picked them up. The dockets were copies of army supply notes. Each of them was signed by the hut leader. The uppermost docket was dated the previous day. It indicated that there had been, among other things, a helicopter delivery of canned meat, fish and fruit. The coding (2 x 4) informed him that the food represented two weeks' rations for four men.

The sergeant left the hut. The snow was well trampled, cut by skis and patterned by snowshoes. It afforded no clues. He spoke to the soldiers and they began to make wide circles around the hut and the pillbox, searching in the troughs and flats of the snow. One of the soldiers called, pointed to a snow-bank.

The bank was broken and crumpled. It bore rectangular marks like those made by the blade of a spade. Two of the soldiers returned to the hut for spades. Within five minutes they had uncovered the bodies of the four militiamen.

The sergeant was a primitive man. He had no compassion. But he was sensitive to challenge and to insult. He began to shake with rage. For years there had been infiltrations by the Indian Army; across the Sikkim–Tibet border, sometimes from the Indian zone of Kashmir. The rage grew. Sheets of blood fell down his brain. He wanted to kill. But the fury abated. The bodies came into focus. He bent across them.

The throats were cut. Was this a soldier's method? He shook his head. Sometimes, perhaps, for reasons of stealth.

But the knife was a hillman's weapon. Everyone knew this. The hillmen: these nomads who wandered high with their tick-ridden sheep when the summer came, down again with the winter cold, who carried knives in their boots, who craved ox-meat and the succulent things that were canned in the cities. There had been some recent thefts from army posts. And a few of the shepherds had ben caught and punished. The rage re-entered him. Now, it seemed, they were prepared to murder for their bellies.

He went back into the hut, transmitted a long and detailed message. He waited, and when the reply SEEK AND PUNISH came he nodded with satisfaction. Killing was not an art exclusive to the shepherds.

The sergeant left the hut, gave an order. The four dead militiamen were taken from the cold and placed on the floor of the pillbox where the cold would preserve them. Then the four drums of kerosene (which an enthusiastic man might need for the firing of a village) were distributed among the men of the patrol. He sealed the pillbox and the hut, gave another order. They fixed their skis.

The patrol moved off into the valley.

The disquiet had not left him and Farran searched for a camp site that would lie concealed and away from Shindi Kul and the route they had trekked down from the Chinese post. They pitched the tent high above the village within the cover of a grove of trees. After they had bathed in the streams and eaten they went down again into the village. Farran pointed to the great ranges that overshadowed them and, taking the headman's arm, said, 'Jalanath.'

The headman nodded, repeated the name with a different intonation. Then he led them through the press of sheep, handcarts, people and dogs that filled the road between the huts and barns.

Two miles of scrub and rocky slopes separated the village from the lake. Trees and undergrowth fringed the southern shore. Water gleamed behind the thin grey trunks. They emerged from shadow into sunlight.

Their eyes lifted.

Jalanath reared above them. So close, so perpendicular was the mountain that they could not see its features. It rose foreshortened from the water and was lost in cloud. They felt its presence. In this great amphitheatre of rock and mountain it drew and held the eye and was solitary. It laid its profiled shadow on the lake. In the silence they heard the wind moving in the reeds that edged the shore, a faint bird-call.

The bird came out of haze, drawing their eyes from the mountain to the lake. Opposite, at the northern tip, was the dam. Two miles of water reduced it to a wafer of white concrete. They could see at one end its white tower, some outbuildings on the flanking shores, a little jetty, two craft.

'Boats,' Cray said with surprise.

Behind the dam was the gorge. The walls rose high, forming a throat of purple shadow. Below the dam and within the depth of shadow would be the river.

They watched but there was no movement, only the shimmer of heat and the fleets of black, white-beaked ducks that made ripples on the water.

It needed thirty minutes to reach a point half-way around the western shore of the lake. They had kept to cover, walking in single file through the insect-singing grass, emerging again where the grass grew high and the seed-heads brushed the face. They broke from the grass and onto a bank of rock that was concealed by boulders from the dam.

Across the lake was Jalanath.

The sun was low and the first pink colour charged the light. It struck across the mountain, revealing the details of its face. The cloud had gone and they could see its curved summit and white wig of snow. A range of higher peaks rose behind it. The colour deepened in the shelves that were the mountain's lips. The face seemed to smile. It was serene.

'She's pretty,' Ricci said.

'Yes, pretty.'

Farran did not speak. The word was too trivial for this thing of beauty. He watched the face become radiant in the sunset light.

'Like a painted whore,' Luc said with distaste.

'That's right.' Cray said. 'And as ugly as sin.'

Now there was movement on the face. Birds swooped and soared. At that distance they were as tiny as beads, not recognizable forms but disturbances of shadow. *A place of eagles,* Dorje had said. Bird-cry echoed in the crags. The sound was forlorn.

Farran listened. Then he took some paper and a ballpoint from his pocket. He drew a diagram of the mountain, filled in the features of a human face.

'Let's do some work,' he said.

After two hours of descent along the line of the snow valley the sergeant stopped the patrol. They had found no trail. There had been no snowfall since the killing of the militiamen. There should be prints, tracks, some sign of the shepherds. Yet there was nothing.

It took five hours on racquettes to make the return climb to the pillbox. The sun was sinking when he reached it. The sergeant was in an evil temper and he slapped the faces of two of the men without proper cause.

They re-opened the barrack hut, started the stove and prepared for the night. Then the sergeant left the hut, went alone to the flank of the pillbox. From here he could see the valley and its shallow wall. He had assumed that the shepherds would choose the shortest distance down to the snow-line, that is through the valley. But they were cunning.

He walked on his racquettes down the slope and into the cleft of the valley. Then he turned, trudged up the gradient. As he marched he watched the valley wall. After a hundred metres he found where the snow of the wall was broken, deeply indented by boots. He followed the imprints to the crest of the wall.

He stood there for a time. Below him and making a diagonal to the run of the valley were the rocks and trenches of a possible route down to the pastures under the snow-line, down in fact to the villages around the lake. He walked a dozen paces. Then he crouched, narrowed his eyes so that he should see the ground in sharp relief.

The snow was hard and wind had scoured the surface. He could see the pattern of racquettes. He placed his own racquette on one of the imprints. The shapes were different. He nodded, crouched again. There were curving lines running through the imprints, broad and parallel like the runners of a sled.

He straightened. This then was the route. In the morning they would follow it. Wind was coming off the snow,

151

driving crystals into his hard dark face. Above him, on the high snows, the sun was red.

Now the sun was red. It tinted the paper. Farran tapped the diagram and said, 'The lady's mouth. I put it at three thousand feet.'

They nodded.

'Yeah,' Cray said. 'Three thousand.'

Farran marked it. Then he took the binoculars slowly up toward the immense caverns that formed the nostrils.

'And the nostrils?' he asked.

'Four,' Ardrey said.

'Maybe a little less.'

Farran moved the binoculars up the slab that was Jalanath's nose. He reached the eye-orbits.

'Six thousand,' Cray said. 'But don't bother. We'd never make it – not with sixty pounds of Oyster.'

'I agree,' Luc said. 'If we could rig a mile of line, take our time, spend a night on the face—' He shrugged.

'It's not on, Farran.'

Farran glassed the summit. It was really a great precipice, he thought. The lake was ten thousand feet above the sea level, the summit eighteen. The world had formed and the cataclysm had gouged out the mountain's natural base. Then the glaciers had filled the bowl so that eight thousand feet of rock overhung the water. He brought the binoculars down the face. Eagles crossed the lenses. He reached the slope of scree and boulders that rose from the reed-green shore. Then he lowered the binoculars, marked on the diagram the heights of the nostrils and eyes.

In that moment they heard the engine.

The sound puttered somewhere on the lake. It came from the direction of the dam. It grew louder. They left the bank, retreated into the cover of the grass. Crouching they could see an area of the lake through the parted wands.

They waited. The bows of a launch glided into the picture that was framed by the wands. Four soldiers with lemon faces and automatic rifles sat behind the cabin. The red stars on their caps were vivid in the dying light. A stern-flag fluttered. Then there was only water, ducks bobbing on the ripples.

The sun had gone when they reached the village. They

152

went with the headman to the hut where the stores were cached. There they chose the canned food and fuel they would require for the return journey, took it outside the hut. About one half the number of cans, the pemmican, tsampa and lentils remained inside.

Farran pointed to it, then at the headman, smiled. He saw gratitude for the gift gleam in the man's slant eyes.

Later, in the camp above the village, they built a fire. There was no danger in this. The fire was not conspicuous for, around and above them on the slopes, the cooking-fires of many shepherd camps burned in the darkness. They had brought their sleeping-bags from the tent, arranged them around the fire. Tonight they would sleep under the sky.

After they had eaten Farran spread Dorje's map in the firelight, took the diagram from his pocket. The climb or climbs on the face of Jalanath and the escape route must be co-ordinated, he told them. Both the outward and the return journeys had been planned on one fundamental condition – that a team of men with sleds start from a point higher than the objective. Thus gravity became a partner in a gradual descent. From Tuzluk to Jalanath they had lost ten thousand feet in height. But here on the lake the positions were reversed. They had to get significantly higher than the head of the Tuzluk glacier; and to this end (he drew his finger up the map) they must make their way from the level of the lake up through a depression in the mountain chain of which Jalanath was in fact a frontal cliff. The depression was marked on the old survey maps as Lebmann's Col. It ran behind and at a tangent to Jalanath and rose to an altitude of twenty-three thousand feet. Here were the glaciers of the twin peaks of Khurdo: they ran direct into the Tuzluk.

Farran looked up from the map. Their faces were intent, un-still in the play of firelight. But Lebmann's Col, he told them, could be reached by an alternative route. It could be reached easily from the summit of Jalanath. Plainly this was something they must use to their advantage. Consider the facts, he invited. The mountain was only two miles from the dam. And anyone scanning it through a telescope or field-glasses must surely see the presence of climbers on its face. The second danger was from the patrol-boats. There were probably two daily circuits of the lake. The boat would pass very close to the base of the mountain. The soldiers' function was to guard the dam. They would have no special reason to study the mountain. But anything was possible; an upward glance, falling stones, a reflection on metal, some movement that was different to the patterns of flight made by the eagles. Discovery meant descent and capture unless – and this was the priceless value of Dorje's other route – the climbers could continue up the face to the summit.

He saw the objection begin to frame itself on Luc's lips. He raised a finger and Luc was silent. Obviously if there was to be no descent then food and equipment must be available on the summit. This presupposed that one of the sleds be taken previously up Lebmann's Col. A mile and a half of steep but gradual incline – with sufficient men it was entirely possible.

Farran dropped some kindling on the fire, watched the sparks rise like fireflies on the wind. Then he picked up the diagram of Jalanath. He touched the mouth. The two parallel shelves formed a deep and horizontal fissure that was at least one thousand feet in length. Two Oysters placed therein, one at either end of the mouth, would when detonated provide the basal force needed to exploit the mountain's structural fault. Ideally the third Oyster should then be fixed and detonated in one of the eye-sockets. But this, they agreed, was unreachable. It would therefore be placed in the left nostril or, to put it less delicately, stuck up the lady's nose.

They had smiled at that. This then was the plan, he told them. There would be two separate climbs. Tomorrow at sunrise five men would climb the lower face, fix the first two Oysters. One man would remain to guard the stores and equipment and to listen at noon on the transceiver for a possible HQ signal. On the following day four men would take one sled (which was sufficient for the return) up Lebmann's Col. At the same time two men, the strongest of them, would fix the remaining Oyster. These two men would complete the climb up the face to the summit. The team would be reunited on the plateau or below it.

Farran put down the diagram.

'Let's talk about it,' he said.

They talked until the fire was low. Farran stood, went to the pile of hewn wood, took some logs and rebuilt the fire. It was past midnight but he was unready for sleep. He could feel the tension in his stomach. The wind made shapes in the fire, forming and dissolving them behind the greater shape of Jalanath. The mountain now was drawn indelibly on his mind. It dominated. And yet there was no terror in it. Why then the unease? It was guilt, of course. They had come to the mountain not with respect or love or humility; but as destroyers.

He turned restlessly on the sleeping-bag, turned again. He heard Ardrey murmur, 'Why can't they just blow the dam? Comes to the same thing.'

'Not really.'

'Why not?'

'Because,' Luc said, 'the dam is merely a regulator. Blow it and you take perhaps fifty feet off the level of the water. But drop the mountain in it—'

'—and you throw the whole goddam lake at them,' Cray said.

He unscrewed his flask, drank. He began to laugh. Whisky sprayed the fire. He said, coughing, 'It will be one hell of a beautiful splash.'

He gave the flask to Luc. Luc sipped, returned it. Then Cray offered a cheroot and Luc accepted. Farran saw the new affinity that had grown between them. They had shared in the killing at the pillbox, and were set apart.

The voices retreated. Farran twisted again, stared up at the sky and the scud of cloud that was moving on the moon. Then, turning, he took a charred stick from the edge of the fire, began to stab nervously into the ashes. Then he turned the diagram into the red reflection, drew three matchstick men on Jalanath's summit, a mushroom cloud exploding above it, some more matchstick men sitting in a boat. The tension was building. He reversed the sheet of paper, stared at it, drew four oblong shapes, each with a curved top.

'Hairpins?' Cray asked.

'Gravestones.'

'Ours?'

He shook his head, sketched a border of flowers at the foot of each of the stones.

'Beautiful,' Cray said. 'But it's still only a guess.'

'No. It's more than a guess.'

He thickened the outlines of the stones. One, that of the child, had been smaller than the others. He ran his pen over the first of the outlines, reduced it in size.

'It's not a bad theory,' Luc said. 'The code would never have to be written down. But it would be there – recorded in another way.'

'It's more than a guess,' Farran said again. 'More than a theory.' He held the pen poised above the child's headstone. Shaw's voice spoke faintly within him, reproaching God: *On Christmas Day we might surely have expected a gift, don't you think?* He wrote the words *Christmas Day* across the stone.

'Shaw's kid?' Cray asked.

'Yes. And the year was 1954.'

He hesitated. Then he wrote lower on the stone the numerals 25.12.1954.

'It's a lovely game,' Ricci said, smiling. 'Can we all play?'

'Why not?' He put a matchstick man on the second headstone.

'Who's that?'

'A missionary.'

'Then he'll need a collar.'

He drew a dog-collar around the neck of the matchstick man.

'And when did he knock on the pearly gates?' Ardrey asked.

'It was the year of the cholera. The great epidemic.'

'Which was?'

'1892.'

He wrote it down on the stone.

'And now you're beat,' Cray said.

'No. I can complete it.'

'You can?'

He nodded, completed the date so that it read 17.9.1892.

'You sure of that?'

'Yes.'

'Go top of the class, Farran.'

Farran smiled. 'It's the day and month of my own anniversary. That's why I remember.'

'Have a cheroot.'

Farran took it, lighted it with a twig from the fire.

'So we have two gravestones out of four,' Ardrey said.

'One half the deadly code.'

'Fine,' Luc said. 'Fine. Now we can blow up half the mountain.'

Kemmerich stood. 'It's a stupid game,' he said. He zipped his parka, walked off into the darkness.

They watched him go.

Luc said seriously, 'I think he's finished.'

'One thing's for sure,' Cray said. 'He'll never make that climb. Do you know that, Farran?'

'Yes.'

'Right from the start he was too damn old.'

They were silent.

Then Ricci said, 'Where were we?'

Farran drew a matchstick figure on the third headstone.

'Who's that?'

'Millicent.'

'Millicent?'

'The preacher's wife.'

Cray peered at it. 'Don't look like a woman to me.'

Farran drew two enormous breasts on the figure.

'Lucky old Reverend,' Ardrey said.

Farran smiled. 'This one's easy,' he said. 'She caught the bug off Holy Joe and died exactly one week later.'

'What a waste,' Cray said. 'What a waste of them lovely tits.'

Farran wrote on the stone the numerals 24.9.1892.

'Three out of four,' Luc said. 'Not bad going.'

'But the next one's hard,' Farran said. 'I can't remember it – only what was said.' He stared into the fire, superimposing on its palpitating heart the monastery garden and its mossy stones. Then he nodded, smiled.

'Something's stirring,' Cray said.

Farran drew the final matchstick figure. He made it very erect, with one upraised arm. He put a big bugle in the hand. 'He was a soldier,' he said. 'Like us.'

'But what's that?'

'A bugle.'

'A bugle?'

'Yes.'

'Is the bugle important?'

'Yes. It has to do with the funny things they used to write on tombstones.'

'Do make us laugh.'

'Well, in this particular year—'

'—which you can't remember.'

'—the little man who writes funny things on tombstones had got around to the Himalaya.'

'And what did he write?'

'*Answered the Last Bugle.*'

'On the soldier's stone?'

'Yes.'

Cray stared at the paper. 'It's a very fine bugle. But I'll settle for Millicent's tits.'

'In your condition, Ethan,' Ardrey said, 'you'd settle for anyone's tits.'

'True, true.'

'The point is,' Farran said, 'that our soldier died around the time of the Indian Mutiny.'

'Shaw said that?'

'Yes.'

'Then we have the year,' Ardrey said. '1857.'

Farran wrote it down.

'Clever lad,' Cray said.

Ardrey said, 'At the Academy—'

'You mean Sandhurst?'

Ardrey nodded. 'At Sandhurst they were very keen on Empire Military History. Especially the bits where the sahibs fired cannon at the sepoys. The Mutiny is engraved on my heart. I can tell you everything. Even the colour of the Viceroy's socks.'

'Just tell me when it started.'

'It flared up. Here and there. Over a period.'

'Delhi. When did it reach Delhi?'

'That's easy. Delhi was the important date.'

Farran waited.

'Eleventh of May.'

Farran wrote it.

'That's it,' Luc said. 'Now we can blow up the mountain.'

Farran shook his head.

'No?' Cray asked.

'No.'

Ardrey said stubbornly, 'The date is right.'

'Yes. But there was more to it than that. Something Shaw said.'

'About the date?'

158

'About the soldier. He was a Captain in the Lancers. He was a mystery. What was he doing in Dhalabat, miles from his regiment? Was it connected with the Mutiny?' Now Shaw's voice was echoing in his mind.

'Light is dawning,' Cray said.

'The Mutiny had reached Delhi ten days before his death. That's what Shaw said.' He felt confusion well suddenly into his mind. Perhaps it was the cholera that had reached Delhi and not the Mutiny. Perhaps it had happened ten days after and not before.

'Well?' Luc asked.

The mists of doubt cleared in that second. 'I'm sure I'm right,' he said.

Farran scratched out the date. Then he wrote across the headstone: 21.5.1857.

'May I see it?' Ricci asked.

He gave Ricci the paper.

Ricci studied it. Then he said, 'Assume this is the code. Assume the dates are right.' He returned the paper. 'But do you have them in the correct order?'

'That's right,' Ardrey said. 'Four groups of numbers. Imagine the permutations.'

'How about that, Farran?'

Farran smoothed the paper. 'I'll make one alteration,' he said.

He put his pen through the small tombstone that was first in the line, redrew it so that it was fourth and last. He wrote in the date.

'Why?' Cray asked.

'The missionary, his wife, the captain, the child. That was the order. Why should they vary it?'

He stood. He said with certainty, 'That's how it'll be.'

He stuffed the paper in his pocket. They were watching him.

He smiled. 'Just a game,' he said.

He left them.

He had known where Kemmerich would go.

He followed the line of the ridge until the timber thinned and he could see water and the lights of the dam. Kemmerich was standing in silhouette where the ridge jutted above the lake. He was staring at the mountain.

Farran joined him. They did not speak. Cloud obscured

159

the moon. Jalanath was a dark mass and only the snows of the summit and the peaks beyond it had pallor. Then the cloud passed and light bathed the face and the snows went white. The face was lustrous, as soft in the night as that of a sleeping woman. They felt its unbearable melancholy.

Kemmerich said, 'You could put your hand out and stroke her cheek.'

Farran heard the pain in his voice. He felt his own guilt resurge. The light left the mountain. Soon the bombs would cling to it like leeches. Wind was bending the reeds. He began to shiver.

CHAPTER TEN

At an hour before sunrise Farran, Cray, Luc, Ardrey and Ricci left the camp above the village. They carried the two Oysters in their nylon snoods, packframes, some nylon line, pitons and snap-links, hammers, two Armalites and ammunition, a little food and orange-juice.

Kemmerich remained. He would rest, wash garments, guard the camp and the third Oyster, listen at noonday for a possible HQ signal.

They did not pass the village. When they reached the shore of the lake the sun had not yet touched the water and the shadow of Jalanath lay across it.

At the same time—

—in the high snows the sergeant and the seven men of the mountain patrol left the pillbox, climbed the wall of the snow valley to the crest. There had been no snowfall in the night and the sled and racquette tracks, faintly broken by the wind, were still drawn on the surface.

They fixed racquettes, began the long trek down.

When they began the climb the lights on the dam were visible through the early mists. The lake was very still and the reeds stood in the mist like spears.

There was a plan.

Robert Luc would lead, test a simple route up the face.

Cray and Farran would each carry an Oyster in a packframe; and Ardrey and Ricci would belay them over the difficult pitches.

At first they would form a single rope. Then, when they neared the fissure that was Jalanath's mouth, they would separate. An Oyster would be secured through its flanges at the two extremes of the mouth.

Farran watched Luc move up the first fifty feet of the face, slow as a sloth, each hold tested and retested, the boots feeling in the cracks. Here, looking up from the root of the mountain, there were no features; only the rise of the wet black rock and the distant eagles falling through the mist like stones.

After two hours' trek the sergeant stopped the patrol. Plainly the shepherds had paused here. There were ruts where the sleds had rested, trampled snow, a melted yellow depression in the snow where a man had urinated. And there was something else.

It glinted in sun. It lay in a snowbank off the trail. It reflected light, yet was too bright for ice. The sergeant went to it, bent. It was a glass bottle. He picked it up.

He brushed snow off the label, studied it. It was a diagonal label in red and gold. It bore words and numbers that were not oriental. There was also a small gold label at the base of the bottle. It depicted a walking man. The man wore a high yellow hat, a red coat with long tails, tight white trousers and shining black boots. He carried a walking-stick.

The sergeant frowned. He had never seen such a bottle. He showed it to the members of the patrol and they examined it without interest and shrugged and returned it. A bottle was a bottle.

The sergeant put it to his nose. It smelled of rawness. There was still a little liquid in the bottle. He drank it. It was like *rakshi*, the spirit that was distilled in Nepal from rice. But it was not as fiery. Its flavour lay pleasantly on the tongue.

But the bottle, its labels and its western characters had left a question in his mind. It was not part of the pattern. He opened his jacket, slipped the bottle inside, re-fastened it. He licked his lips, savouring the taste of the spirit.

It was the first time he had tasted Johnnie Walker.

Now the mists were gone from Jalanath. Already, at one thousand feet, the weight of the Oyster had sapped the strength from his legs. Sweat ran. The ice of the night had melted and water streamed down from the rock above him. Farran turned his face up into it, allowed the water to spray across his lips.

He looked at his watch. It was ten minutes after eleven.

At ten minutes after eleven a truck drove down the main

road of the School of Snow and Mountain Warfare at Dhalabat, stopped outside the Orderly Room.

A man got out, beat his hands together, stamped his feet. He was an American and his name was Mervyn Baer. He was also a senior officer of the Central Intelligence Agency. He had had a tiring journey; from CIA Headquarters in Langley, Virginia (where there had been an unpleasant interview with the Director of the Plans and Operations Division) to London (where there had been another unpleasant interview with the CIA Station Head and the Deputy Head of the British Secret Intelligence Service); from London to the elegant apartment of the resident CIA agent in Delhi; from Delhi to Srinagar; and from Srinagar to the military airstrip at Lakh. At Lakh he had received a hot drink and a Letter of Authorization from an Indian with very good credentials; and from Lakh he had been driven in a truck up into the mountains to Dhalabat.

In Hadji's office he shook hands, stared at the green silk turban, sat.

'A drink?' Hadji asked.

'Scotch.'

Hadji poured, gave it to him.

Baer sipped. 'If there is any ice . . .?'

The turban shook. An olive finger pointed to the window and the frieze of giant peaks. 'I can send a man up for some.'

Baer heard the mockery in the voice. He felt ill at ease. He stared around the room. 'It's pretty dark in here.'

'Then remove your glasses.'

Baer flushed. He knew he was very tired. He removed his sun-glasses. The room glared. His eyes were sore with fatigue. He put the glasses back on. A tweed hat sat on the corner of the desk. There was a coloured feather in the band. He said, 'I see Petrie's here.'

Petrie entered and Baer said, 'We've met before, Brigadier.' Petrie's fingers closed for a moment over his knuckles. He flexed his fingers. He hated soldierly grips. 'You may not remember me . . .'

Petrie stared at the sun-glasses. 'Perhaps you were in disguise.'

Goddam British, Baer thought. Do they think they still own India? He removed the glasses, put them in his pocket. Then he took from the same pocket a number of docu-

163

ments. He placed them in front of Hadji, enumerating them as he did so. 'From Washington. From London. From Delhi.'

Hadji studied them. Then he looked at Baer, at the long-lashed eyes that were as blue and demure as a doll's in his ruin of a face; as if innocence lived side by side with stealth. He passed the papers to Petrie.

Baer said, 'Do you accept my credentials?'

Hadji nodded.

'What I have to say concerns the President.'

Petrie looked up from the papers. 'Which President?'

Baer stared. 'Of the United States of America.'

Hadji nodded again. Why do they always use that phrase, he asked himself, as if it had some kind of cosmic significance? He said, 'What is your business, Mr Baer?'

'Oysters.'

Petrie sucked his empty pipe.

Baer said, 'Has the mission yet reported?'

'No.'

'No signal of any kind?'

'None.'

'So they haven't yet succeeded?'

'Not yet.'

Baer trembled with relief. The nightmare was dissolving.

'But they will,' Petrie said. 'They're first-class chaps. They'll do it.'

'You better pray they don't.'

'Why?'

'Because there will shortly be an announcement.'

'An announcement?'

'From Washington. To the world.'

Baer drank some whisky.

'Come on, man,' Petrie said irritably. 'Out with it.'

'The President,' Baer said with disbelief, 'is going to visit Peking.'

'Oh, my God,' Hadji said.

Petrie blew a long hollow note on his pipe.

'You can't hardly believe it, can you?' Baer said, 'Right through the bamboo curtain – or whatever you call it. State visit. All luvvy-duvvy with the Yellow Peril.' He held out his glass. 'Can I have another Scotch?'

'We'll all have one.'

They drank, standing.

'This is very serious,' Petrie said.

'Serious? It's a crisis.'

Hadji looked at his watch.

Baer said, 'None of the Heads of State knows about the operation.' He spread his hands in appeal. 'Why should they? Secret is secret. And what they don't know about they don't lose no sleep over. But this time—' He shook his head. The anxiety was returning. 'This time I think we all went a little bit too far. Suppose, just suppose the Chinese find those things. Or even worse—' He shook his head again: the mental picture was too terrible to contemplate. 'Suppose,' he whispered, 'the Chinese find out when the President is actually in China?'

'It would – embarrass him,' Petrie said.

'*Embarrass* him.' Baer stared. Goddam British. He said nervously, 'I don't think the department would survive it.'

He finished his drink. He said to Hadji, 'Now, Colonel, can you recall these men?'

'Of course.'

'Then please do it.'

Hadji looked again at his watch. 'They'll listen in at noon. We have thirty minutes.'

In Hadji's staff-car, on the hill road that led up to the monastery, Baer said, 'I'm not a religious man. But I prayed all the way here. Prayed I'd be in time.'

He looked sideways at Petrie. He wanted to talk, to share his relief. But Petrie did not answer. The car jolted, and the tweed hat fell from Petrie's knees to the floor.

Baer picked it up, placed it upside-down on Petrie's lap. He could see the initials AJP on the inner band. He wanted to talk. He touched the initials and said, 'Is that wise? In our profession?'

Petrie smiled thinly. 'It's a precaution. Against theft.' He turned the hat upright. 'I once had a hat stolen—'

Baer nodded.

'—from an American hotel.'

Baer stared at the monastery.

Goddam British.

In the Communications Room Baer stood with Petrie and watched the satellite pictures and the traffic of clerks and non-coms. Hadji had gone into an inner room.

'It's five to twelve,' Baer said.

The door to the inner room opened. Hadji beckoned.

They entered. There were desks and a transmitter, a bearded man in a blue jersey.

'This is Dr Shaw,' Hadji said. 'I've explained the situation.'

Shaw nodded coldly.

Baer said with surprise, 'English?'

'Yes.'

Baer felt his bewilderment mount. He looked at Petrie, then at Shaw. Were they still in occupation? There was emotion in the bearded face. This was a man on the verge of tears or anger, he thought.

Shaw sat down heavily in front of the transmitter.

Hadji explained, 'The signal is AMAR. It means Abandon Mission And Return.' He touched Shaw's shoulder. 'Send it please.'

Shaw did not move.

Hadji saw his eyes go to the wall above the desk, the picture of the graveyard and the single flower that drooped on the frame. He said to Shaw, gently, 'I know how you feel. I wish we could have done it. But we have no choice.'

Shaw did not move.

Hadji said with menace, 'Send it.'

Shaw adjusted the frequency. His hand went slowly to the key.

Kemmerich, alone in the camp, received the signal AMAR at one minute before noon. Relief flooded him. The mountain and the people in the gorge and at Su Tokai were saved. But there were complications. Farran and the others were already on Jalanath. By nightfall the two Oysters would be fixed. How much information should he send? There were listening posts in the area, and any transmissions beyond the coded signals increased the danger.

He looked at his watch. The line of communication was always open from five minutes to twelve until five minutes after twelve. He needed time to think.

He decided in the first place to send a simple acknowledgement.

In Shaw's office they waited in silence. Baer licked his drying lips. The signal came. XXX it read.

Baer asked, 'Is that—?'

'Yes,' Hadji said. The rosebud lips smiled. 'Acknowledged and understood. You can relax.'

Baer felt the weakness run through his legs. He wanted to cry, laugh, shake their hands, buy them a drink. He wiped his wet eyes. He offered up a silent prayer of thanksgiving. Then he said aloud, 'Thank God.'

He stood. He wanted to confess his fears. 'I was afraid,' he told them. 'Afraid they might—' He shook his head, denying the awful picture that had, momentarily, imprinted itself on his mind. 'Afraid those men might already be climbing that damn mountain.'

Now, at two thousand feet, Farran could see the lake spread like a blue handkerchief below him, the jaws of the gorge running into mist behind the dam. He looked up the face. Robert Luc was high above him. Cray and Ricci were pinned on the chimney that led to the lower lip.

Hadji stared down at Shaw's bowed head. He said, 'I'm sorry, Joseph. Truly sorry.'

Shaw heard them leave. The door closed. He sat in silence. Then he opened the Radio Log. He wrote in the Transmission column: *1159 Hours* AMAR; and in the Received column: *1201 Hours* XXX.

Kemmerich went to the edge of the trees. He could see below him the haze of smoke that came from the cooking-fires in the village.

He returned to the transceiver. He had made his decision. He would have to risk it. He sent his call-sign and then the message: AMAR CONFIRMED BUT OYSTERS ALREADY FIXED. ADVISE US IF TO LEAVE OR RECOVER.

Shaw wrote the message on his Signals pad. Excitement rose. Oysters fixed! He stared at the pad, at the photograph and the tiny headstone, at the clock, at the pad again. Emotion shook him. He sent: LEAVE OYSTERS FIXED AND RETURN.

He waited until he received XXX. He sat for a time in the quiet of the office. Then, without recording the last two messages and the final acknowledgement, he closed the

Radio Log. He tore the perforated slip from the pad, ripped it into pieces, dropped them into the waste-basket.

At one hour after noon they reached Jalanath's mouth. Farran could see above him the sloping slab of the lower lip, the rope that crossed it, Luc and Ardrey already in the fissure. He knew his strength had gone. The rope went taut and they brought him slowly up the slab and into the fissure. Lying on his back and heaving into the rock floor he felt them remove the Oyster and its frame from his back. Behind the waves of exhaustion he could hear a distant hammering; and knew that, at the extreme of the mouth, Cray and Ricci had begun to secure their Oyster.

He saw the question in Ardrey's eyes and he said, 'Yes. Do it now.'

He watched them manipulate the Oyster into the depth of the fissure. Luc took his hammer and drove a piton through each of the holes in the flanges and into the rock. Then, retaining the snood in which the Oyster rested, he tied the nylon mesh to the pitons.

Farran stood. The lip was wide enough and high enough for a man to walk without danger. He went to the Oyster, looked down at it. It was difficult to believe that this ugly sphere of iron contained a marvel of technology, the power to move a mountain. He felt the guilt re-enter, now as tangible as sickness. He turned away, went to the edge of the lip.

It was a scene of beauty, a beauty to which Jalanath was related. The lake was set like a jewel in the ring of mountains and, from height, the dam was as fragile as a sliver of whale bone. There was a froth of white water where the streams fed the lake, a darkness in the centre that told of depth. He felt its peace; and, for a moment, the old sense of fulfilment. Then it vanished. Already the mountain was fouled. Looking down he could see where it would fall, how the lake, poisoned by radiation, would be flung across the dam and into the gorge beyond.

He turned. Ardrey was taking food and orange-juice from the packframe. 'Ten minutes,' Farran said. 'Then down.'

Farran knew at the beginning of the descent that his legs were not controlled. They had adjusted to the dead weight

168

of the Oyster and now, freed of it, could not co-ordinate with the new lightness of his body. There was no ice or wetness on the rock and the holds were good. But he slipped twice on the first two hundred feet.

He stopped. Perhaps the instability would pass. Above him Luc and Ricci were moving down the face. Cray, the strongest of them, was paying out rope. Ardrey smiled up at him. The boy's blond beard gleamed in sun. They began to move again. Below was the fall of the mountain, seeming to reflect splinters of black light. The lake and its hem of reeds shimmered like a butterfly's wing. He could see the dam, a white spume above the sluices, the little jetty and the two moored patrol-boats.

At two thousand five hundred feet above the lake Ardrey reached the strata that ran, very smooth and dangerous, across the grain of the mountain. Farran watched him search for a hold. He called down the face, 'Take it very easy.' He belayed the rope around a spur. Ardrey's coloured bonnet moved slowly down the strata. It obscured the dam. Then the bonnet went lower and the dam reappeared. Farran thought he saw movement at the base of the tower but he could not be sure. Anxiety touched him. Would some guard or engineer saunter on to the terrace of the dam, lift his face into the sun, bend to a telescope and idly scan the water and the shores? A slight upward lift and Jalanath would smile on the lens. He began to sweat.

Now Ardrey was on the brink of an overhang. Farran released the rope from the spur, signalled to Luc, began his own descent. There were very few holds; a number of shallow cracks in which a boot or the finger-tips might find support. But that was all. Heat came off the rock. He could smell its musky scent. He watched Luc pay out rope until it lay looped and loose on the slab. He looked below. Ardrey was flat on the overhang, his boots wedged against the crenellated ridge of rock that grew along the brink. Ardrey winked at him. He looked away. But something had changed, some minute alteration in the pattern. He looked down again, past the bonnet to the lake and then to the dam. *Only one patrol-boat was moored to the jetty.*

Sweat started from his pores. A sudden pulse of weakness ran through the muscles of his legs. Where was the boat? He clung unmoving to the rock.

Luc's voice said impatiently above him, 'Go on then.'

169

The voice was remote. A cloud crossed the sun and the shadow of it passed over the surface of the lake. But there was no other movement, no sign of the boat. The anxiety mounted. Here on this sun-glaring face they were utterly exposed. We have to go faster, he told himself. We have to get off this mountain. He called down the face: 'Alan.'

Ardrey looked up.

'Stay where you are. We'll abseil.'

On the overhang he watched Ardrey hammer two pitons into a deep horizontal crack. The blows threw echoes down the mountain wall. Ardrey uncoiled his bandolier of rope, doubled it, then attached it to the anchorage of the pitons. Luc was coming sloth-like down the face.

Farran took the two ends of the rope and, leaning out across the overhang, cast them down the rock face. Five hundred feet below them was the shelf that, seen from distance, defined Jalanath's chin. Below the shelf and partially obscured by the jutting wall was the lake. It lay there blue, somnolent and empty. The boat had not appeared.

Luc joined them on the overhang. Farran saw his eyes go to the dam and its single patrol-boat.

'We better hurry,' Luc said.

Ardrey waited and Farran nodded and said, 'Off you go.'

Ardrey took the doubled rope in his left hand, stood astride it so that, facing the anchor, the rope passed between his legs and behind his right thigh. He ran the rope across the front of his body and over the left shoulder. Then he gripped the hanging rope with his right hand so that he might control the speed of his descent. He paused, stared down the mountain through the wisps of passing cloud, lowered himself over the brink of the overhang.

Farran watched him abseil down the face, the slender body straight and controlled, the rope sliding smoothly through his hands and the legs meeting and leaving the rock in a series of springs. The bonnet plunged and swung above the void like a falling multicoloured flower. Farran felt the nausea invade his stomach. He looked away, then down again. One hundred and fifty feet below Ardrey had reached a ledge, was disengaging from the rope.

He hesitated. He knew that he was still unstable. He saw Luc's eyes assessing him. He said sharply, 'You next.'

The dark lips smiled. Luc positioned himself, arranged

the rope, checked the anchorage. Farran watched him go with caution down the wall.

Farran reached the shelf of Jalanath's chin in three fast abseils. The shelf, two thousand feet above the lake, was narrow and broken where the rope hung. He stood there for a moment crouched against the rock, the rope supporting him like a harness beneath his crotch. He was reluctant to leave it. To his left Ardrey was taking pitons from his pocket. To his right Luc stood balanced against the slope of the wall. Immediately above him Ricci waited for the disengaging of the rope.

Farran looked down the face. The doubled rope, knotted at the end as a precaution, hung twenty feet below the shelf. It swung gently above the blueness of the lake. Nothing moved on the water. Ardrey began to hammer in the first of the pitons. The impacts struck like pistol-shots in the rock-walls. But now there was another sound.

'Hold it,' Farran said.

Ardrey lowered the hammer. They listened. A sound, as faint as the murmur of a distant bee, rose from somewhere on the lake. Farran felt his mouth dry. He said to Ardrey, 'It's a boat.' Then to Luc: 'Do you hear it?'

In that moment he saw the eagle.

It fell out of the sun. Its shadow beat on the shelf. Then it was gone. He listened. He could not hear the wings. Then the bird came again in a long curving trajectory, skimming the rock a yard above his head. This time the weakness flowed from head to toe. He closed his eyes, pressed his cheek to the rock. The wings beat like a pulse inside his brain. Somewhere outside the red membrane of his eyelids the bird, this old and secret enemy, swooped and soared. It had always been like this, the approach of a single bird, the bird hovering unsupported on purple voids, accenting depth, instilling terror. 'Make it go,' he whispered to the rock. He waited. The shelf was silent. The wings had gone. He opened his eyes.

The bird stood ragged-winged on the sun. Its shadow touched him. He stared. In that second all the angles changed. New perspectives reeled across his vision. The vertigo rose like sickness. Bile filled his mouth. The sun went white and the sky streamed in rivers of hot blue wax. He began to slide. 'I'm going!' he screamed.

He went; fast, open-mouthed and yelling down the shelf.

Pain rasped his shins. Something met his boots, yielded for a second like a buffer, broke away. Then he was over the brink. The rope ran hot against his fingers. He locked them. Heat and pain seared the flesh. He braced himself. When the jerk came and the knot of the abseil rope rode up against his spine the pain leapt and his eyes spurted tears. He held to the rope, eyes shut, swinging in a pain-filled redness above the lake.

Ardrey looked down. Farran swung and turned on the end of the rope, as inert as a hanged man. 'Farran,' he called. 'Farran.' There was no response. Then the white oval of a face turned up to him, rocking against the hazes of the lake. Stones skated down the slab and, now, Robert Luc was beside him.

'Help me,' Ardrey said. 'Help me get him up.'

Luc did not move. His head was cocked on one side. He was listening.

'Luc.'

They heard the engine of the patrol-boat. The sound was nearer.

Luc whispered: 'They'll see him.'

The boat appeared. They could see the V of white water at its bows. It was as tiny as a toy on a pool. But it was growing larger.

Luc said urgently, 'We have to drop him.' He drew his sheath-knife. 'We have no choice.'

He bent to the rope. The knife poised. Ardrey gripped his wrist. They began to sway, faces near, teeth bared, locked on the shelf. The engine-noise grew louder. The blade grated on the rope, left it, touched again. Ardrey brought the wrist toward him. They strained again. Now they could see the distant speck of colour that was the patrol-boat's flag, the ripples arrowing on the lake. Luc wrenched away his wrist. Ardrey saw the savagery in his eyes. The knife thrust toward his face. He put up his hands in defence and the blade made two swift arcs of light. He cried out with pain. Blood spurted from the slashed palms. He leaned across the rope so that his body covered it, waited for the knife.

Then Luc relaxed. 'Keep very still,' he said. The boat approached. They watched it pass beneath them, turn with the curve of the shore, head for the green hem of reeds on the opposite side. The putter of the engine grew faint.

Luc sheathed the knife. The spittle of effort glistened on his chin. He wiped it. The lips twisted. 'Call it a draw,' he said.

They bent to the rope, began to haul.

The sun was low when they reached the base of Jalanath. The evening mist was already on the lake. They bathed and bandaged Ardrey's hands. Then they walked around the shore to where the slopes rose abruptly to the camp.

The sun went.

The sun went. The sergeant pointed and the patrol, spread fanwise on the hillside and rifles at the ready, began to move. The herdsmen and the flocks ran before them, down the hill in a brown and bleating mass. Below were the cooking-fires of Shindi Kul.

In the village they made a systematic search. In two years this was the lowest altitude to which they had descended. The sergeant hated the village, its stench and its impurity, ordure on the boots instead of snow. He wanted to destroy it. And when they discovered the canned food and the army stencils, this evidence of theft and murder, they set about their task with enthusiasm.

They closed the alleys between the huts, sealed the exits with bales and hand-carts. Then they shepherded the shepherds and the sheep, the dogs, men, women and children into the central clearing and the single road. Then they swamped the huts with kerosene. And when the kerosene was gone they took the big communal vat of lamp-oil and flung it over the sheep and the people and the bales of wool.

When Farran and the team entered the camp there was a good fire, and washed clothes hung on lines in its reflection. Tea was brewing. He went to Kemmerich and saw at once the change in the German's face.

'How are you, Kem?' he asked.

Kemmerich smiled broadly.

'You found some money?' Cray asked.

'Better than that.'

Kemmerich pointed to a slip of paper on the transceiver.

Farran picked it up, held it into the firelight. He read the message, nodded, gave the slip to Cray.

'Poetry.' Cray said. 'Sheer poetry.'

He gave the slip to Luc, and Luc read the messages aloud.

'Did you hear that?' Farran said to Ardrey. 'We can go home now.' He heard the tremor in his voice. Home was Dhalabat, billiards and brandy in the mess, the warmth of Arif's smile, a place where there was no fear, no eagles, no Chinese. He looked away from the fire and into the dusk. Something had ended on Jalanath.

'But why leave the Oysters?' Ricci asked. He shrugged. 'So long as they are there—'

'—they're a risk,' Luc said, nodding. He poured tea. 'But not as big a risk as to make another climb.'

'Christ, no.'

'We were nearly caught today.'

'I coulda dropped a stone right into that lousy boat.'

Farran watched them. They were smiling, nervous with relief.

'Let's celebrate,' Cray said. He splashed whisky into each of the cans, stirred it into the tea. He offered a can to Ardrey and Ardrey made a face, held up his bandaged hands.

'Hurt?' Farran asked.

'Yes.'

Farran put the can to Ardrey's lips, then again. Ardrey smiled with gratitude. Farran left him, went to the stores. He took some antiseptic, antibiotic tablets, bandages and a roll of adhesive plaster, a clean cloth. Then he filled a basin with hot water, returned to Ardrey.

'Sit down,' he said.

Ardrey sat.

Farran watched him swallow tea and tablets. Then he knelt, began to unwind the bandages. Across the crook of Ardrey's arm he saw Robert Luc squat by the fire, open his pack, take out a leather strop, a honing block and the razor-case. The Belgian plunged his sheath-knife into the soil, wiped it, began to hone its double blade. Farran stood, went to the fire, dropped the soiled bandages into the flames. He stood there for a moment, staring down at the crown of Luc's head and the blade that turned and flashed in the firelight. Then he went back to Ardrey, knelt again, examined the hands. There were long slashes in each of the palms. On one of the hands the skin between thumb and index-finger was deeply divided. He felt his anger rise. He could hear the rhythmic hiss of the blade on the hone.

He bathed the wounds, washing away the crusts of congealed blood. Then he poured antiseptic into them. Then, cutting the adhesive plaster into short lengths, he stuck the strips across the palms so that the lips of the slashes would be drawn and held together.

Cray's shadow fell across him. He looked up. Cray stared silently at the hands, then at Luc and the hissing knife. Farran felt the tension in him. He unwrapped a bandage but Cray did not move or speak.

Farran said to Ardrey, 'You were very brave today.' Then to Cray, 'Did you see what he did?'

'I saw him.'

'And I saw him too,' Ricci said. He came to the fire, smiled with affection, ruffled Ardrey's hair.

Farran began to bandage. He said to Ardrey, softly, 'It'll be all right now.'

'Yes.'

'Do you know what I mean?'

'Yes.'

Farran looked into the boy's face. A victory for Ardrey, he thought; and a failure for me. He stared down into the basin of stained water, knowing in that moment that he would never climb again. He completed the bandaging, stood.

'They'll do fine,' he said.

He took the basin to the fringe of the clearing, flung the water into the underbrush. When he turned he saw that Cray had moved around the fire, was standing directly above the Belgian's bowed head.

The blade flowed and hissed on the hone.

'Sharp enough?' Cray asked.

Luc did not answer.

'Sharp enough to cut a man?'

Luc continued to hone.

Cray held out his hands so that the palms went red in firelight. 'Cut them,' he said. 'Go on. Cut them.'

Luc put down the hone, tested the point and the cutting-edges of the blade against his finger.

'Looks pretty sharp, Luc.'

175

Luc sheathed the knife. Then he secured the leather strop to the packframe, took the large razor from its case, began to sharpen it.

Cray lowered his hands. The fingers clenched and unclenched. When he spoke his voice was thick with anger. 'I've beat a few men in my time,' he said. 'But only with these.' He hooked the air with his fists. 'I never used steel on a man. I never got pleasure outa cutting someone up.'

He waited. The razor moved rhythmically on the strop. Reflections from the metal danced on Luc's impassive face.

'A razor,' Cray said with contempt. 'What kind of an alley-rat can use a thing like that?' He moved nearer. 'You may be the fastest shave alive, Luc. But I tell you this. There's nothing in the world that's faster than a fighter's fist.' He hooked the air again. 'Why, a man's fist can be faster than a striking snake.' He began to lunge, hook, uppercut. The fists made rapid patterns around Luc's unmoving head. 'And I can prove it.'

The razor stopped.

'You got eleven notches in that thing,' Cray said. 'Why don't you try for another?'

Luc stood. He straightened his parka so that it sat neatly on his body. Then he walked two paces from the fire, turned. Cray followed. Now they were facing. Cray put out an arm, measured the distance between their chests. Luc stood there silently, his right arm hanging and the razor a glint of metal against his thigh. Cray's fists hung unmoving at his sides.

'Ready?' Cray asked.

Luc nodded.

Now the clearing was silent. Wind fanned the fire and kindling fell. Leaves rustled. Cray moistened his lips with a quick dart of the tongue. Farran heard the spittle in Ardrey's throat. Cray did not move. Farran saw the apprehension in his eyes. He felt a sudden fear for Cray. He opened his mouth to speak.

In that instant they heard the rifle-fire.

It came from the village. There was a cry, a silence, then more bursts of automatic fire.

'Douse the fire,' Farran said.

They poured their cans onto the fire, then the contents of the tea-kettle. They stood there in the darkness. An ember flared and Cray stamped it out. They waited. The leaves

176

dripped water in the silence. Then, suddenly, a ball of flame, as yellow as a sunflower, leapt on the sky. It grew until the sky was an aureole of light and the trees stood in silhouette. Now they could hear cries, bleating, the long staccatos of a machine-gun. More fireballs shot on the sky.

Farran led them through the trees. They stopped at the fringe. Shindi Kul burned below them. Wind fed the flames and the huts exploded and the timbers fell. Human shapes ran in frenzy through the fire. They saw the peaked caps and bandoliers of soldiers. Beyond the flames was a pile of packs, skis and racquettes. They watched until the village became a single incandescent heart of fire. Sheep rolled on the hillside in the night like burning coals.

When the punishment was completed and nothing of the village remained the sergeant led the patrol toward the lake. The nearest military post was located at the dam and it was his duty to report.

Farran and the team watched them go. Then they went down the slope.

The village glowed and smoke billowed on the sky. They walked through the debris. Nothing lived. In the clearing the carcases of men and sheep were welded by heat into one inseparable mass. As they walked, through the odours of fleece and flesh, through the smoke and over the spark-showering earth, their anger grew. Cray and Kemmerich were crying.

'Why?' Cray said. His voice was piteous. He rubbed his smoke-sore eyes. 'Why should they do a thing like this?' He began to stamp around the debris, beating his right fist into his left hand. 'Why? Can you tell me that?'

Luc stared around him with empty eyes. He had seen it before; dead villages where the thatch was palm and the flesh was black.

'I guess we brought it down on them,' Luc said.

Cray turned. 'How could that be?'

'I don't know. But why else should soldiers come?'

Farran nodded and Cray said, 'Do you agree with that?'

'Yes.'

Shadow ran. A dog, prick-eared and shaggy, came out of darkness. It loped toward the charred mounds in the clearing, began to sniff.

'They might come back,' Ricci said.

'I'd like that,' Cray said. 'I'd like that fine.' Smoke came on the wind. He began to cough. 'I'd kill the yellow bastards.' Anger shook him. He flexed his fingers. 'Kill them.' The word fed his anger. He walked into the debris, kicked and kicked with his heavy boots until the embers flew and the sparks leapt on wind. He returned to them. He said thickly, 'We let it happen, Farran.'

'We had no choice.'

'Oh yes we did. We had guns. We coulda stopped them.'

'No.'

'We coulda tried.'

'That's right,' Ardrey said. He held his bandaged hands against his chest so that they would not throb. 'We stood there and let it happen.'

Now the dog was howling. The sound went into the night like a lament.

'They'll come back,' Ricci said. 'I know it.'

'How can you know?'

'Because they're mountain troops.' Ricci pointed into the night where the high snows were. 'They'll go back there – where they belong.'

'Eight men,' Cray said. 'We could take them easy.'

The dog stopped howling. A timber frame collapsed. Flame ran. They felt its breath of heat.

Farran said to them, 'Is that what you want?'

'Yes.'

'You, Luc? What about you?'

Luc nodded.

'Kem?'

He saw the conflict in the German's face. Kemmerich hesitated, stared at the mounds. Then he said quietly, 'Yes. I want that.'

Farran looked at them. The faces had changed. They flickered in the glow, ugly with the need for vengeance. But he could feel his own deep protest.

'One day,' Cray urged. 'That's all we ask.'

Farran said, 'So we wait?'

'Yes.'

'Watch the lake and hope they'll come?'

'Yes.'

'And when they come we shoot them up?'

They nodded.

178

'All that risk for eight men?'

He saw their resentment.

Cray pointed at the dead. 'We owe them, Farran.'

He did not answer. He looked around him; at the skeletal huts, at the sheep with melted eyes.

'Don't we?' Cray asked softly.

'Yes,' Farran said. 'We owe them.' He put a hand in his pocket. 'But I can give you something better.'

He produced a folded sheet of paper, opened it. It was the diagram of Jalanath. He reversed the paper, held it up so that they should see it.

Firelight revealed the drawings of the four headstones and their scribbled dates.

CHAPTER ELEVEN

At one hour before first light the sled they would use for the trek up Lebmann's Col and down to the Tuzluk was stowed and lashed. The second, discarded sled was concealed in the underbrush.

Luc and Cray stood apart by the camp-fire. Already the loaded packframes had been hefted to their backs. Cray's pack contained the Oyster and some climbing gear. Luc carried assault rations and the last of the self-heating cans, the two nylon shelters they would need for a night on the face, two pairs of racquettes for use on the summit snows. Both wore a coil of line that was looped across the shoulder and chest.

Farran stamped out the fire.

'See you, old chap,' Cray said.

They went into the greyness.

It was still dark when they took the sled past the remains of Shindi Kul. But there was greyness coming in the east and the charred timbers stood against it like the ribs of gutted ships. They could smell its acrid scent and when the dawn wind came a hundred eyes of redness glowed. There were many dead and living sheep on the hillsides.

The sled ran well on the thick wet pasture. They could see where the hills divided and the timbered cleft that led to Lebmann's Col.

Luc and Cray made good time on Jalanath. The lines from the previous day's climb had been left on the difficult pitches; and by mid-morning they were half-way to the mountain's lips.

By mid-morning they had pulled the sled above the tree-line. Farran glassed the land above them. There were slopes of scree and barren ground where progress would be slow. But the first rise of the Col lay in the shadow of the mountain chain and because of this there was a sleeve of permanent snow. He pointed to it. They bent again to the traces.

Luc and Cray reached the lips at noon. They removed the packframes. Sun struck into the fissure. They sat in its warmth and drank diluted orange-juice. Then they each ate an assault-ration.

When they had rested they examined the pitch above them. One thousand feet of rock formed the upper lip. They could see the great indentation that was the left nostril. Here they would fix the third Oyster. But the lip was smooth.

'She'll take time,' Cray said.

He went to the edge. The mist had gone from the lake. It shimmered like blue silk. Both the patrol-boats were moored at the jetty. Beyond the dam the walls of the gorge ran into distance until the cleft was no more than a sinuous black line. Then the line was lost in hills and the hills were lost in haze. Behind the haze, he thought, is Su Tokai and the deserts of Sinkiang. He shook his head, marvelling at the strangeness of his situation. Then he took out his flask, unscrewed it and drank some whisky. He offered the flask and Luc drank from it, returned it.

Cray wiped the top, took another drink. He held the whisky under his tongue, enjoying the flavour, swallowed.

He said, 'Thank God for Johnnie Walker.'

In the barrack-room at the flank of the dam the sergeant of the mountain patrol stared at the bottle. It stood on a table by the window and the sun illuminated the colours of the label, the figure of the walking man in the red coat and the high yellow hat. The figure strode perpetually across the sergeant's mind. He was a savage and he could not rationalize his thoughts or make logical deductions. But he resented the bottle and its ridiculous walker. Some instinct was at work and he could not throw away the bottle or forget it. The officer-in-charge had not yet arrived on his weekly visit from Su Tokai. But the sergeant had made an enquiry; and one of the engineers (a man who was used to the bars of Chungking) had told him that the bottle would, when full, contain Scottish wine. It was a Western drink and it was sold all over the world and it was drunk, among other places, in Indian Army

181

messes. At this point in his muddled thought-processes the yellow hat was replaced by a turban. Indians marched across the roof of the world, descended to Sinkiang.

The sergeant rose, left the barrack-room, went out onto the flanking wall of the dam. There was also another question to which he had no answer. Where were the sleds? He had followed the tracks but there had been no sleds in the village. He stared for a time at the lake, its shores, its towering walls, at the mountain with the features of a human face. He decided not to wait for the arrival of the officer-in-charge.

He returned to the barrack-room, gave an order to the seven members of the patrol.

One hour later they left the dam.

At three in the afternoon Luc and Cray reached the left nostril. Cray rested, upright on the rock. Luc rigged a line across the place where they would pin the Oyster. It took ninety minutes to manhandle the Oyster from the pack-frame, set it and tie it to the pitons.

Above them was the two thousand feet of slab that jutted to form the mountain's nose, above that the great cavern of the left eye-socket where they would spend the night. A chimney ran vertically where the slab joined the face.

Cray pointed to it and Luc nodded.

They began to climb.

The sun was low when they brought the sled onto the first sleeve of snow. It had been difficult on the scree and the bald ground and, dragging at the inert weight of the sled, they had watched the snow come nearer through a haze of sweat and effort. When the runners touched the snow Farran held up a hand. They stopped. It was very cold and their breath broke in clouds across the sled. Below them they could see the tree-belt spread like a dark rug on the shadowing land and, where the chain curved, a corner of the lake.

The sun was low and the lake already in shadow when the sergeant and the patrol reached the end of the lake. But the sun was still bright on the upper face of Jalanath and on the snow peaks behind it.

The sergeant raised his binoculars, focused on the dam.

182

Then he brought the lenses slowly through the arc of the shore. Nothing moved except water-birds and the wind-shivering reeds. He completed the circle, taking the lenses across the base of Jalanath, along the opposite shore and across the dam, down the shore on which they stood until the red star on the cap of his second-in-command obscured his vision.

It was a place of peace. Yet every instinct was alert. He returned the lenses to the base of the mountain. He examined it. Then he raised the glasses very slowly, up the strange black bones of the mountain's face. An eagle soared. Snow appeared. He lowered the glasses, held them on the bridge of the nose. Something had moved, something that was unconnected with the flight of birds. He turned his head slightly so that the left eye of the face appeared. Two men were climbing below the socket.

He gave the glasses to his second-in-command, said something. The man examined the mountain, nodded, returned the glasses. The sergeant slid them into their canvas case. Then he walked a pace from the patrol, tried to arrange his thoughts.

The dam was a military installation. It supplied Su Tokai with a regulated flow of water. Therefore it had great importance. But the climbers were on the mountain. They did not threaten the dam. There could be no connection between the mountain and the dam. At this point he became confused, doubtful of his own conclusion. The glass bottle tilted across his mind. A man in a high hat and a red coat marched and was gone. The climbers were going up, not down. But if they had done something at the dam why should they escape up a mountain when they could walk up the Col that lay behind it? He shook his head, despising his own imperfect brain. He stared at the patrol but the faces were stupid, like those of the sheep they had burned in the village. Then he stared at the mountain.

The terrain was drawn on his mind like a map. Lebmann's Col could be reached from the summit. And the Col led to the Khurdo peaks, the glaciers and the frontier. This much was clear. He did not reason that it would be prudent to send a man to the dam and warn them of the presence of the climbers; or even to wait until the patrol-boat came on its evening circuit. He knew only that he could march up the Col and intercept the climbers, that he would do this on his own because he was afraid of the disdain of authority, that he hated the lower altitudes and yearned for the halls of cold and silence where he was truly at ease.

He gave the order.

The patrol turned inland from the lake.

At sunrise Luc and Cray left the eye of Jalanath and prepared to scale the last two thousand feet of the face; the sergeant and the patrol emerged from the cover of the firs above Shindi Kul; and Farran, Ardrey, Ricci and Kemmerich began the long upward haul through the snows of Lebmann's Col.

Ice and wind had slowed them and it was an hour past noon when Luc and Cray reached the top of Jalanath. There was no pyramidal summit and the ridge on which they stood was like the brink of an immense cliff. The wig which from the lake had made a white crown to the mountain's face was a snow plateau. They fixed racquettes. Then they crossed the plateau to where it formed a brow.

Standing on the brow, not speaking and panting in the thin air, they could see where the plateau was divided by a rift. The rift ran parallel to the ridge, a blue shadow in the glare. Beyond the rift the land rose into the north-eastern ranges and they could see the twin peaks of Khurdo as sharp as shark's teeth on the sky. Below them the land fell to a gully and the gully ran at a diagonal into Lebmann's Col.

Cray looked again at the rift. There you see it, Hadji had said that day in the Armoury. The outward evidence of a massive geological fault. This then was the point at which the face of Jalanath would break away and peel off like a mask?

He stared around him at the vastness of it all, shook his head; and Luc, watching him, said, 'Hard to imagine, isn't it?'

He did not answer.

They set off for the gully.

Two hours later Luc and Cray entered Lebmann's Col. They stopped, their faces enveloped in their own clouding breath. Below them was the great white cleft. Wind whined in the silence, weaving feathers of snow on the breast of the Col. Luc pointed. Very small on the whiteness four figures strained at the traces of the sled.

Farran dropped the trace, peered through the spindrift up the rise of the Col. He said with relief, 'It's Luc and Cray.' He waved and the two descending shapes waved in response. He bent to the trace again, retrieving it, saw something black and chain-like on the lower Col. His pulses raced. A spume of snow crossed his vision. He waited. The snow parted. A column of men trudged in single file up the Col, bent against the wind. At distance the men were as tiny as insects. He counted them. There were eight.

Ardrey joined him. 'The soldiers?'

'Who else?'

Farran focused his binoculars. A flat cloth cap, a red star, a dark face with black moustaches appeared within the rim. The man had some kind of insignia on the arm of his quilted jacket. The arm rose. It held binoculars.

The sergeant focused up the Col. Four men stood by the sled. One of them was staring down the Col through binoculars. He saw movement above the men and, raising his own binoculars, brought within their field two descending figures. Six men. He knew now that something very serious was happening. He lowered the binoculars.

Farran, too, lowered his binoculars. For a moment it had seemed as if their eyes had met and each had measured the other.

He went to the front of the sled, picked up the trace. He looked at his watch, at the sky, at the sun. Two hours of light remained.

'We have to hurry,' he said.

Luc and Cray rejoined them.

Farran pointed down the Col. and Luc nodded and bared his teeth and said, 'Yes. We saw them.'

They bent to the traces.

Now, with six men at the traces, the sled moved faster up the Col. The Col was curving with its rise. They could not see Jalanath and the lake; but the summit plateau of the mountain, Farran judged, was already below them. The snows were flushed and the sun was red.

The sun was red. Shaw watched it for a time. It made the four headstones glow with colour. He bent, touched the small headstone, opened the door in the wall of the grave-yard, walked through the temple garden and into the Communications Room. Zirkon Voyager was painting pictures on the screens.

He closed the door of his office, sat down at the desk by the transmitter. He looked up at the wall and the picture of the graveyard. Then he rose, pulled from the yarn of his jersey the stalk of the gentian, arranged the flower so that it drooped over the child's grave.

He sat again, began to drum nervously with his fingers. He knew what the fingers wanted to do, that the years of medicine and priesthood were now without meaning, that he was about to surrender to hatred. There was only one mountain, and its name echoed in his mind like an incantation. Jalanath. Jalanath. Jalanath. He closed his eyes and saw its face.

The face was in three-quarter profile. The lake was as dark as a grape. From here on the edge of the ravine they could look down through the gap in the Col and see the whole of the lake, its enclosing walls, the mountain, the little white bone that was the dam, the gorge.

Cray lifted out the transceiver from the unlashed end of the sled, set it down on a rock. Farran dropped his pack in front of the rock, sat on it. Then he removed his right, outer glove, spread the sheet of paper so that he could read the code, weighted it down with a piton.

He looked behind him. They were waiting.

He said to Kemmerich, 'Put your goggles on.'

Kemmerich did not move and he said, 'Don't you under-stand? The flash could blind you.'

Cray said with contempt, 'He understands. But he's having another attack.'

'Attack?'

'Of the Gentle Jesus.'

Farran stood. He said to Kemmerich, 'But we agreed.'

'Yes.'

186

'You saw what they did to the village. Don't they deserve it?'

'The ones that did it, yes. And they're down there in the Col.'

'And we'll take them,' Cray said. 'Tomorrow we'll take them. I promise you that. But it's only eight men. And that don't seem much for what we been through.' His face went ugly. He took Farran's arm, turned him toward the transceiver. 'So first we'll do Sue Tooky.'

Farran sat again on the pack. Across the grey metal of the transceiver he could see the mountain's face. There was meekness in it. Its beauty stabbed like a pain.

Kemmerich said, 'It's wrong. And you know it.'

Farran turned.

Ardrey and Ricci nodded.

'Time for the bang,' Luc said.

Wind came up the Col, flinging snow.

Farran said to Kemmerich, 'Put your goggles on.'

He reached for the key.

Shaw reached for the dial of the wall-safe, touched it, then withdrew his hand. He locked his fingers, cracked the knuckle-bones, smoothed his jersey, pulled his beard. He felt sick with the conflict. The need for vengeance was as strong as ever. Yet he could not bring himself to the final act. The destructive power of the Oysters was pinned to the face of Jalanath. Only he and Farran's team knew this. He could release this power, rid himself of the hatred like a man slaking a terrible thirst. But now the affair had moved from the shadows to a higher plane. The flood might drown more than the city of Su Tokai and a few thousand Reds.

He went to the window. Below him was the stone wall of the monastery and the path that led down to the camp. Sun struck the path, a slowly moving figure, an orb of silver hair. He rapped on the window-pane and Kate Shaw looked up, smiled, took another step.

He watched her, the hunched shoulders, the slow pacing of the sticks. His eyes went wet. 'Love you,' he said to the window-pane and the silver hair. The glasses blurred with condensation and he wiped it and the small figure reappeared. 'Love you. Love you. Love you.'

He saw her totter, reel against the bank, then fall. One

of the sticks slid down the path. There was a moment in which she sat there staring at the sun, in which he saw in her face the weariness of her burden. Then Arif ran down the path, lifted her to her feet, retrieved the stick, brushed her coat.

Shaw turned from the window. He was trembling. He had seen her fall a hundred times. But this time the pain, the pity and the guilt swelled against his heart like a bladder. He sat heavily in the chair, shut his eyes, clasped his arms about his body, began to sway.

When the emotion had passed he rose. Now there was only the old unquenchable anger. He knew what he was going to do. He went to the safe, manipulated the dial, opened it, took out the cassette.

'Try again,' Cray said.

Farran rubbed his ungloved hand. It was raw with cold. He completed another transmission. They watched the mountain. Nothing happened. He shook his head, stood, held up his red fingers.

'Let's have a go,' Ardrey said.

Ardrey sat on the pack, reached for the key.

Shaw put down the cassette on his desk. He opened a drawer, took out a folder. In it was a single sheet of graph-paper. He studied the co-ordinates. Then he looked at his watch.

He nodded with satisfaction. Then he put on his white surgical coat, slid the cassette into a pocket, walked from the office into the Communications Room.

They waited. The mountain brooded in the dying sun.

'Again,' Farran said.

They listened to the pulses of sound.

Ardrey sent the last number of the group.

Nothing happened.

'Again,' Farran said. He looked at them. Kemmerich's face was pale with tension. Ardrey's transmission had taken seventy seconds. Yet his own transmissions had needed eighty. Every hand varied. But ten seconds was a serious differential. He felt the anxiety grow. What margin would be tolerated by the receivers in the Oysters?

The pulses stopped.

They stared at Jalanath.

The face smiled in the pink light.

'I'm sure you made an error,' Luc said.

'In the first group.'

'I distinctly heard it.'

'Shift over,' Luc said.

Ardrey rose and Luc sat.

He began to send.

Shaw went to the screen. Zirkon Voyager, sailing through the ellipse of the West Himalayan axis, was transmitting. He stood there casually, as he stood most days, watching the moving panorama of snow, rock and sky. He could hear behind him the traffic and voices of the communications staff.

There were sunset tints on the screen. Somewhere in that great land mass was the mountain.

Luc turned from the mountain.

'The whore,' he said. 'The mangy whore of a mountain.'

Farran heard the hatred in his voice.

'Why don't she go?' Cray asked.

'Because we're doing something wrong,' Ricci said.

Farran looked at them. He saw their dismay. They were restless, rubbing hands, stamping feet, staring at the mountain. They were like children waiting for a firework that would not go off. Only Kemmerich was still.

'She'll go,' Farran said. 'I know she'll go.'

Shaw slid his hand into his pocket, fingered the cassette. Inside the cassette was the tape; and recorded on the tape in Morse code were the four groups of numerals that would trigger the Oysters. A transmitter was connected to the screen. It was a simple gun-metal box with two external features. These were a slot into which the cassette would fix and a locked flap that concealed a switch. A triangle could be drawn with Zirkon Voyager at the apex and Jalanath and Dhalabat at the points of the base. When the satellite was positioned within certain co-ordinates it would receive the code from Dhalabat, re-transmit it to the Oysters.

That time was now.

Shaw looked around him. Then he took the cassette from

his pocket, pushed it into the slot. Blue light from the screen touched his spotted hand. It was trembling.

Farran bent again to the key. Concentrate, he told himself. Good long-dash Morse. Even and perfect. He began to send. But the frustration was building. Another part of his mind was asking questions. Suppose the code was geared meticulously to Shaw's own hand? What was the duration of a dash? What was the space between characters? How much mutilation in transit would the Oysters accept? He reached the final group. Sweat ran inside his goggles. Maybe the frequency was wrong. Maybe the order of the groups was wrong. Maybe the dates were wrong and poor bloody Millicent hadn't died exactly seven days after the bloody padre. Maybe the bloody Lancer captain had answered the Last Bugle on an entirely different date. Maybe the headstones were nothing to do with it. And maybe the Oysters weren't H-bombs at all, were harmless lumps of iron.
He finished the transmission.
Nothing happened.
The mountain smiled.

Shaw looked around him again. Then he took a key from his pocket, turned it in the lock of the flap. The flap sprung open. A red switch gleamed.
He flicked it down.

'Let me help you,' Kemmerich said.
Farran turned in surprise.
The German's boot came in a swift upward arc, struck into the front of the transceiver. The transceiver leapt from the rock and into the ravine. They saw it shatter, coils and dials and metal pieces shooting into depth. Cray swung his fist and Kemmerich fell.
He stared up from the snow. 'Sorry,' he said through blood. 'No bang today.'

Shaw listened to the Morse pulsing in the gunmetal box, mentally translating the four coded groups into the events and facts they represented. These were the year of India's independence, the height in feet of Kangchenjunga, the year

190

of Mahatma Gandhi's death, and Colonel Hadji's army number.

The pulsing stopped.

'She's going!' Cray screamed.

He stared, fist poised, across Kemmerich's face.

Farran turned – into a core of intense white light. The detonations came, buffeting his body with waves of sound so that he began to reel and wander in the glare, lost in noise and light, this other sun expanding and the tremors coming up through the rock and into the limbs and the ground moving and the lungs sucked empty then filling with heat then sucked out again and now the glare orange and the sky a growing flower of fire and the noise mounting and the ravine a jaw of blackness in the glare and he like a sleepwalker in the black rain of pulverized rock and the face of Jalanath as submissive as a victim in the heart of fire still smiling and intact then breaking into new and fearsome contours and hideous in the moment of disintegration and the face falling and the snow-wig boiling and the steam and the fire and the black upflung rain fused into one single rising cloud and Ricci's face coming pale with terror out of the red-black avenues of light and saying, 'Oh my Jesus, Oh my Jesus, Oh my lovely Jesus.' Then the voice went as if flung on wind and Luc's face swung like a gourd down the sky and the voice was saying, "Look. Look. Look.'

Now there was a new and deeper noise. It bellowed beneath them. The lake was boiling like water in a cauldron. They could not see the lake, only the canopy of steam that covered it. Then the lake rose through the steam, not grape-dark but red from reflected fire, rising rising rising until it curled like a sea-wave, poised, then leapt at the dam. They saw the dam swirl like a white toothpick in the torrent. Then it was gone from sight and this wave that was the lake was moving through the gorge and its sound was like thunder in the ears.

Shaw looked at the screen. There was a solitary cloud on the lower mass. Unmagnified it was as graceful as a summer puffball, shot through with golden light. Then it passed from the screen. He flicked up the red switch, locked the flap, retrieved the cassette and put it in his pocket.

In his office he poured a tumbler of water. Standing at the window he sipped and watched the sunset. So that little cloud was the shape of vengeance? He felt empty. He put the tumbler on the desk, took the gentian from the top of the picture-frame, stood it in the water.

He had always loved alpine flowers.

Down in the lower Col the sergeant and the patrol could not see the lake and Jalanath. But they felt the tremors and heard the sounds, stood in the black rain and watched the immense cloud and the scarab of red light form on the sky.

Nightfall was near. They pitched tents. Then the sergeant went alone to a ridge. He could not know or understand what had happened, only that terrible primal forces had been released, that the men (these men who, despite their goggles, beards and bonnets, had seemed to be not Indian but European) were responsible.

He raised his binoculars, swept the upper Col. Nothing moved. Night was now their refuge. In the morning they would continue through the Col toward Khurdo and the frontier. They were aware of pursuit, the point from which attack must come; and because of this they enjoyed an advantage.

He brought the binoculars through a downward arc. To his right the eastern wall of the chain was divided. The divide, he knew, ran level from the chain, opened on to a rising traverse that rejoined Lebmann's Col at a point one thousand feet below its maximum altitude. At this point the advantage shifted. The Col narrowed, the air was thinner, the cold was greater, attack was unexpected.

Here he would prepare his ambush.

At first light Farran glassed the lower Col. There was no sign of the Chinese patrol.

'Maybe they gave it up,' Cray said.

Ardrey laughed. 'Or the bang scared them.'

Farran shook his head. The eight men had been cruel and professional. 'They'll come,' he said.

They waited two hours, deployed in cover with the Armalites. But the sun grew higher and there was no movement in the Col.

He glassed the Col again. He could see the V-shaped bite where the wall of the chain was broken, recalled that it formed an exit to the Col. But where did it lead? Anxiety grew. He slung the Armalite across his pack, pointed up the Col.

'Let's go,' he said.

At four in the afternoon Hadji sat down in the W/T Room at the camp, poured tea from a china pot, waited for the weather forecast and the news from Radio India. Petrie joined him.

The forecast ended.

Then the voice said: 'In the last hour Radio Urumchi, Sinkiang, has reported news of an unparalleled disaster in the south-west region of the province. The whole of the upper face of the eighteen-thousand foot Mount Jalanath detached itself during the sundown hour of yesterday evening and fell into the lake that lies below it. Millions of tons of water were displaced and, destroying the dam, surged through the walls of the Su-Fu gorge. Such was the force of the flood that it reached the nuclear city of Su Tokai within three hours. Observers say that the water came out of the darkness like a giant tidal-wave to engulf the city and its installations. No figures are yet available but it is feared that more than ten thousand people have perished. In the early hours of today geologists and army and government experts were taken by helicopter to the scene of the landslip. Peking has made no announcement of their preliminary findings or of the magnitude of the disaster. But unofficial sources in Hong Kong state that the destruction of Su Tokai is a calamity that will retard for a decade the Chinese nuclear programme. There is also an unconfirmed report from the same sources that intense radio-activity had been detected at the landslip, giving rise to conjecture that a rogue missile from Su Tokai, or even from its twin nuclear installation seven hundred miles distant at Lop Nor, may actually have struck the mountain—'

Hadji switched it off.

Petrie drew the pipe from his mouth, stuck it, still smouldering, into his breast-pocket. Smoke rose.

They stared.

Then Hadji went to the window, pointed with his beard at the crag and the monastery buildings.

'We need answers,' he said.

Shaw held up the X-ray picture to the light, shook his head.

'It's no good,' he said to Dr Azfar. 'You'll have to reset it.'

'He's a Marine Commando,' Azfar said in panic. 'He won't like it.'

Shaw gave him the picture.

'Will you tell him?' Azfar asked.

'Why should I? You did it, didn't you?'

Azfar's face went sullen. He left the annexe, the glass door swung. A green turban wavered behind the imperfect glass.

Hadji and Petrie entered.

Shaw stared. Fear touched him. For the first time he saw the savagery in Hadji's handsome face.

Snow was falling when they approached the top of Lebmann's Col.

Farran stopped the sled. In front and above them the Col narrowed and the walls rose like cliffs. The mist was low and they could not see the peaks, only a luminous white glow where the sun would be. Farran removed his goggles, peered through the snowflakes.

'You're an old woman, Farran,' Cray's voice said behind him. 'There's no one there.'

Farran raised his binoculars and, shielding the lenses with his hand, studied the Col.

'Not a living soul,' Cray said.

Farran turned.

'Make camp,' he said.

They did not move.

'We have two hours of light,' Cray said stubbornly. 'We can make the top by then.'

Farran looked at them. They were haggard with strain, wanting the top and the end of the long upward haul. He too wanted to believe in their escape. Yet there was danger. He knew this. The instinct was as real as the cold that gripped his bones.

He said, 'What do you think, Luc?'

Luc stared at the Col. He nodded. 'I think they are there.'

'Make camp,' Farran told them.

He studied the rock-walls and the great spur that ran up diagonally into the mist.

Then he touched Ricci's arm.

'Fancy a climb?' he said.

From the tip of the spur they could see through the wraiths of mist, down into the Col. There was a daub of colour on the whiteness, like orange-peel dropped in snow. He focused the glasses and the colour separated into four orange, two-man, pyramid tents. The tents were tightly grouped, each touching the other. Men were moving around the tents, stamping snow, tightening guys. The barrel of a light machine-gun protruded from the flap of the foremost tent.

The place of ambush, Farran saw, had been chosen with care. It lay off the bed of the Col, surrounded on two sides by rock. Yet the barrel could swing through at least one hundred degrees of arc, thus covering a great area of the Col.

He took the binoculars slowly up the Col, across its narrow bed, then down the wall that faced the Chinese camp. Snow drove rods across his vision. The wall was broken and eroded. There were steep slopes, cut with gullies and miniature ravines.

He examined them. Two of the gullies ended short of the Col. All of them ran down into exposed positions. But one had possibilities.

He re-examined it. It ran very steeply into the Col, entering it at a point almost opposite the tents. Its bed, he knew, would be filled with ice, then layered with new snow. It was perhaps two hundred yards in length.

He gave the binoculars to Ricci.

'You see the tents?' he said.

'Yes.'

'And the gun?'

'Yes.'

'Now take the glasses across the Col and up the slope.'

The glasses moved.

'Do you see the gully with the long sleeve of snow?'

'I have it.'

Farran watched him move the glasses up then down the gully.

'Well?' he asked.

Ricci wiped snow from the lenses.

'From up there,' he said, 'we could fire straight down into the tents.'

Farran shook his head.

'No?'

'No. We'd get half of them. The rest would run into cover.'

'What then?'

'Look again.'

Ricci looked.

'You'd get another silver cup,' Farran murmured.

They rose two hours before dawn. It was very dark and wind howled through the Col. They emptied the sled, stowed its contents in the tent. Each man put his skis and poles into the sled, slung an Armalite with a full magazine across his back. Then, taking the traces, they towed the sled through the awful cold toward the first ravine.

The ravine was sharp with rock. It took one hour to climb the slope of the Col, another twenty minutes to reach the top of the gully.

Snow began.

They could not see the Chinese camp, only the pallor of the snow in the upper gully and the wall of darkness. They removed the skis and poles from the sled. Then, the sled perched above the gully, they half-filled it with rock and pebbles from the scree.

Cray put the weight of his body against the prow of the sled, freeing the runners from the grip of ice.

'Jesus man,' he said, 'it'll hit them like an express train.'

Farran looked at the eastern sky. Now he could see the serrated edge of the range.

'Hurry,' he said.

Ricci removed his Armalite, gave it to Ardrey. Then taking a pole in either hand, he mounted the sled so that he lay face down behind the prow.

They fixed skis, dropped their poles into the sled, brought the Armalites to the ready. Then they positioned themselves behind the sled.

'Remember to fan out,' Farran told them. 'Leave a clear field of fire.'

He looked again at the sky, then down the long white

196

slope of the gully. The wall of darkness was dissolving. The tents made faint geometric shapes.

Farran bent across Ricci.

'Can you see them?'

'Yes.'

'Then go.'

They strained against the sled.

'Tally-ho,' Cray said.

The sled plunged.

Running, the gully fast as a downhill run and the cold like fire on the face, he saw the sled, propelled by its own weight, leap into the throat of darkness, saw it veer, bounce respond to the thrust thrust thrust of the ski-poles, leap again and through the snow-veils and into the white-dark maw of the Col and now the long and unrelenting bursts of the machine-gun throwing yellow on the tents and the tents yellow and palpitating in the dark and the sled skimming the white road of the Col and pointing at the tents and the machine-gun shedding fire and Ricci leaping from the sled and rolling like a ball into snow and shadow and they firing with the Armalites into the gun, into the tents, into the moving figures that lurched in and out of the yellow light and the sled driving black and undeviating into the yellow and now the gun stopped and the yellow gone and the triangles of the tents broken on the body of the sled.

They crossed the Col. There was no movement in and around the tents and they raked with gunfire the mass of nylon and humped bodies until the magazines were empty.

Ricci came through the snowflakes.

'That was marvellous,' Cray told him.

He offered Scotch and Ricci drank. Panting in the cold and the half-darkness, they passed the flask until it was emptied. Then they disentangled the sled, turned it on its side, freed it of rock and pebble.

Then they went down the Col.

After they had brewed up and eaten they struck camp, stowed the sled and fixed racquettes. The top of Lebmann's Col lay one thousand feet above them.

Sunlight was flooding the Col when they reached the Chinese camp. The snow had stopped. They began to

197

search, turning bodies, examining supplies.

'They didn't have much food,' Ardrey said.

Farran heard the pity in his voice. The elation had gone. Now there were only the dead in this white and silent place.

'They deserved it,' he said. 'Remember the village.'

Cray bent, picked up a cap with a red star. 'We oughta have a trophy.'

'Yes,' Luc said.

Ricci found a cap, brushed snow from it. Farran saw him fold it, unzip his pocket. Then he shrugged with self-disgust, threw the cap into the snow, went to the sled.

Farran followed him. Then, turning, he saw that Luc was bent across one of the soldiers. Something metal glinted in the sun.

He crossed the snow and his shadow touched the soldier. Luc looked up.

'No,' Farran said.

'No trophies?'

'Not that kind.'

'He has very good ears. Like yellow coral.'

The blade moved.

'Leave him,' Farran said.

The face went wolfish. Then Luc shrugged, closed the razor, left.

Farran looked down at the soldier. This was the man he had seen in the binoculars. His head bristled with cropped blue-black hair. He was young, sleek and strong as a wild-cat. Even in death he had power. Snow lay on the moustaches.

Cray said, 'He's a fierce-looking bastard.'

'Yes.'

'Some kind of sergeant.'

'Yes.'

They went to the sled.

Farran pointed.

The mist had lifted and they could se the twin peaks of Khurdo and, distant, the snow shoulder of Tuzluk.

'Ready?' he asked.

They nodded.

He picked up one of the traces.

'Let's go home,' he said.

CHAPTER TWELVE

On the third day they crossed the frontier and, trekking up the Tuzluk glacier, reached before sundown the first of the three refuge huts. Below the hut was the glacier bank where the Puma had debarked them.

There were bunk-beds, a transmitter, ample food and fuel in the hut. Cray opened the cupboard, and the two bottles of Johnnie Walker stood untouched on the shelf.

'Isn't that a sight?' he said.

'You'll get stoned tonight,' Ardrey said.

'We'll all get stoned.'

Later, the hut warm and they sitting at the wooden table in the yellow lamplight and the stove hissing and the Scotch diminishing and Ethan Cray wearing the cap with the red star, Farran said, 'We have to send the HQ signal.'

'No hurry.'

'Let them sweat it out.'

At Headquarters, Baer asked, 'Any word?'

'No.'

'Do you think—?'

'I think nothing,' Hadji said roughly. 'I wait.'

'Suppose they get caught,' Baer whispered. 'Caught and questioned. I get nightmares about it.'

'Don't we all,' Petrie said. He began to fill his pipe, stabbing viciously with his thumb into the bowl.

In the morning the range and even the valleys were white with mist and Farran knew the helicopter could not come.

He waited until mid-morning. Then, the team standing around the transmitter, he sent to HQ Dhalabat: ARRIVED HUT ONE. ALL WELL. WEATHER UNSAFE CHOPPER.

Arif received the message in Shaw's office. He wrote it down, acknowledged it. He sat there for a moment, staring at the wall and the square of lighter paint where the photograph of the gravestones had hung.

Then he lifted the telephone.

Hadji was the first to enter the office, then Baer and Petrie.

Arif gave them the pink signals slip and they passed it from hand to hand.

'Thank God,' Baer said. He returned the slip, then locked his fingers so that they should not see the tremor. 'Thank God.' He knew he was emotional. Perhaps it was the altitude? He said, 'Do you know—?'

'We know,' Petrie said. 'You prayed all night.'

'They'd never had stood it. Not Chinese torture.'

'No man could.'

Arif sat again at the transmitter and Hadji pulled his beard. He deliberated. Then he said, 'Send this.' The voice was very cold. CONGRATS AND WELCOME. PROCEED HUT TWO IF WEATHER PERMITS.

Arif sent it.

Petrie said to Hadji, 'Feel better?'

'Much.'

Hadji went to a cabinet, opened it. He asked Arif, 'Did he keep a drink here?'

'No.'

'Let's go down to the mess.'

In the mess Baer watched Hadji pot a red and fail on a colour. Hadji stood back and Baer set down his glass of whisky on the edge of the billiards table, bent to take his shot.

Hadji held up a hand, picked up the glass from the edge, put it down on a table. He said severely, 'We don't do that here, Baer. Suppose you knocked it on the cloth?'

Baer flushed.

Arif said gently, 'It's a very special cloth.'

'It is indeed,' Hadji said with pride. He stroked the nap. 'This is the Viceroy's table.'

'The who?'

'The Viceroy of India.'

'I didn't know that,' Petrie said with interest.

Arif explained, 'It's the original billiards-table from Viceroy Lodge, Simla.'

'You don't say?'

Hadji nodded. 'And you wouldn't believe the trouble we had getting it up here.'

Baer looked at the great mahogany legs. He tried a joke. 'What did you use?' he asked. 'Elephants?'

'Of course.'

Baer stared. They're taking the piss out of the stupid Yank, he told himself. But the brown faces were serious. He looked around the room. The walls were decorated with pictures and relics of the old Imperial past. He felt uncertain. There were things here he would never understand.

'Your shot,' Hadji said.

Baer shook his head. 'Don't feel like snooker,' he said.

He gave his cue to Arif, picked up his drink, took it to the window. He stared out into the sunlight. The Indian flag, flickering in wind, seemed for a moment to reform into the Union Jack. He heard the balls click and Hadji saying, '—to think that Viceroys and Generals and even Kings have played on this table. I often think of that when I play a shot.' Baer felt the incredulity rise again. Had he heard nostalgia in that vibrant voice? He sipped his drink. The relief had gone. Mountains were exploding, waters flooding in his mind. They could still find out. What if they arrested the President when he got to China? The whisky turned to acid in his stomach.

Hadji said behind him, 'One will never be sure.'

'No,' Baer said. 'Never.'

'Six men. Going their separate ways. Possessed of this terrible knowledge.'

Baer turned.

Hadji stroked his nose, leaving a smear of blue cue-chalk on its tip.

'The situation,' Petrie said from the table, 'was always there.' He potted a black. 'We have only to face it.'

Now free of the sled they made good time to Hut Two.

'It's the life of Riley,' Cray said with pleasure. His face was ruddy. 'Ski, sun, plenty chow and' – he opened a cupboard to reveal two bottles of whisky – 'lots of highland gargle.'

He took off the cap with the red star, flung it on the table.

Farran said, smiling, 'You'd better not wear that to-morrow, Ethan. Someone might shoot you.'

He watched them chose their bunks, unfold blankets, empty packs. Luc primed and pumped the pressure-stove. The tension had gone. They were relaxed, proud in their different ways of a mission completed. Even Kemmerich had his soldier's pride to sustain him.

Later, around the table and intimate under the lamp and the wind pulling at the hut, they talked of the future.

'Me,' Cray said, 'me to quit the army. I have their word on that.' He laughed so that the scar-tissue crinkled on his face, bunched his fists. 'Try my luck with the pros.'

'You'll do well,' Luc said.

Farran nodded. 'You're still young enough. Why not?' He saw the answer in Cray's glass of whisky. He looked away and said to Luc, 'What about you, Luc?'

Luc poured whisky in his tea, stirred it. 'I have a year to do,' he said. 'But after that—' He shrugged. 'There isn't much for the Belgian Army. Not any longer.'

'So?'

Luc smiled. 'I'm a mercenary at heart. Wherever there's a war – that's where I'll be.'

'And you, Alan?'

Ardrey flexed his fingers. The bandages crackled.

'Alan?'

'The army, of course.'

Farran saw the confidence in his eyes.

Ardrey said shyly, 'I'm looking forward to it.'

Cray laughed. 'You'll be a goddam general.' He ruffled Ricci's hair. 'What's for you, Ricci? You going to grow spaghetti-trees?'

'Acres and acres.'

'There's money in it.'

'But he don't need money.'

Ricci laughed.

'You crazy bastard,' Cray said with affection. 'But you going to break your neck. You know that, don't you?'

Wind tore at the door.

Farran said, smiling. 'We don't have to ask him what he'll do.' He drank some Scotch. 'There'll be the Ferraris—'

'—and then the ski-jumps.'

'—and then the bloody Wall of Death.'

'—and then the Cresta.'

'—and the six somersaults without a net.'

'Definitely the Cresta.'

'No more Crestas,' Ricci said, laughing.

Cray put on the Chinese cap. 'D'you think we'll get a medal?'

'Sure to.'

'Old Hadji'll pin it on before we go.'

Wind yelled.

They listened.

Then Kemmerich said, 'And you, Dick? What will you do?'

Farran looked at him. He said quietly, 'No more climbs.'

Their eyes met.

Farran said: 'There are a few things still to do. The old ski-tours, places I've been happy in.' He drank his Scotch, watching Kemmerich's face. 'Ghosts to look for.'

Kemmerich nodded.

Farran saw his eyes brim with tears.

'We'll go together,' Kemmerich said.

They were quiet for a moment.

Then Cray laughed. He pulled off the Chinese cap, stuck it on Kemmerich's head. 'You horrible Kraut,' he said. Kemmerich smiled. The red star glinted. Cray rose, went to the cupboard.

'Let's bust another bottle,' he said.

In the morning the mist was still low.

Farran sent to HQ: VISIBILITY BAD. PROCEEDING HUT THREE.

They waited.

The reply came: CHAMPAGNE READY.

By noon the mist had cleared.

They ate, high in the pass, on the shore of an ice-stream. Then they began the long ski down to the refuge.

Ski-ing through the perfect day, the snow good and the packs light and the Karakoram revealed above them, they made a chain on the whiteness, Farran leading and each man in harmony with the man in front, the sun laying blue shadow on the white and the blades sibilant and true on the undulating land. There was joy in this downhill rush and, soon, they could not contain it. Kemmerich began to sing. Farran heard the baritone voice lift into 'Lili Marlene':

Underneath the lamplight
By the barrack-square—

He heard Cray and the others take up the song. He too began to sing. The melody crossed the snowfields. Its poignant phrases seemed to echo in the peaks. The voices swelled. In them were all the sunlit snows of youth; other places, other times where the beauty was so intense that song was needed to express it. They began to swerve, accenting the bars so that the chain of ski-ing men swung on the snow to the rhythm of the song.

—My Lili of the lamplight
My own Lili Marlene

The song ended. They stopped on the shelf above the valley, not speaking, smiling through the plumes of breath with the pleasure of the run.

Then Kemmerich pointed.

Below them, small with distance, were the hut, a helicopter, a little group of men.

'Ready?' Farran asked.

They smiled. He saw their pride.

'Then off you go.'

He knew they would make this final run with speed and style. He waved them on and Kemmerich laughed, kick turned, leapt from the shelf onto the first reaches of the slope. Luc followed, then Ardrey and Ricci, then Cray. Farran felt Cray's ski strike hard into his ankle. His own skis slewed, ran into the rock that grew like a black reef across the shelf. He fell, rolled; and, rolling, heard Cray whooping like an Indian on the slope below. The sound grew faint. He sat up, aligned his skis. He brushed snow from his face and neck. His bonnet and one of his poles had gone. He searched, retrieved the pole, knocked snow from the bonnet. Then, edging the skis, he prepared to lever with his hand.

Below him he could see the five black figures swooping on the lower slope. They reached the plateau, made a wide circle around the helicopter, stopped. He smiled, thrust with his hand into the snow.

In that moment he heard the gunfire.

It seemed to come from the plateau. Flashes, pale in the sun, were spurting from the shadow of the helicopter. He saw the five figures wilt under the fire, fall to the ground. 'No,' he whispered in denial of the sight. 'No. No.' Shock held him rigid on the snow.

Some men in combat suits came from the Puma, went to the bodies, sprayed them with fire. Then three more men came from the hut. They lifted the bodies into the helicopter. The engine surged. The rotors turned. Snow was flung. The Puma lifted.

He crawled into the cover of the rock, snatched off the coloured bonnet, pulled over his head the white hood of his parka. The Puma turned, flew slowly over the shelf. Men were staring from the perspex; searching, he knew, for a sixth skier. It turned again, flew east to where the land was broken and ravined. He could see the shadow scurrying on the snow. Then the shadow stopped. Now the Puma hovered over the blue zigzag that was the mouth of a crevasse.

The door of the cabin opened. Something black and limb-waving fell through the air and into the crevasse. Farran began to count, whispering as the shapes fell: 'Two, three, four, five.'

The Puma went.

Farran watched until it was gone into the haze of distance. Then he stood. He vomited into the snow, wiped his face with trembling fingers.

Then he skied down the slope. Hig legs were weak from shock. He fell twice.

When he reached the hut he threw off his skis, went inside. He closed the door, stood with his back to it.

He stood there in his aloneness until the cold moved up from the concrete floor.

During the night, the hut dark and the bunk-beds empty around him, he surrendered to grief. The wind also grieved, soughing in the valley, entering the hut and filling the darkness with its sobs.

At first light he left the hut. There were fifteen miles between the hut and Dhalabat. He would go to the Shaws. There was nowhere else to go.

205

It was dusk when he reached the slopes above the camp. Opposite, across the bowl in which the camp lay, were the lights of the monastery and the hospital. Below, defined by light, was the perimeter fence and the main gate.

Ski-ing high on the slopes of the bowl the shadow went black and the snow waved like white cerements in the falling night. He circuited the bowl until he was above the crag and the hospital. Then he made a long, descending traverse down to where the snow-line was. Here he removed, tied and shouldered his skis, began the walk down the scree and sodden grass to the path that looped the hospital.

He followed the path until he reached the gateway. He could see the pillar and the board that was nailed to it. But now the board read:

DHALABAT MILITARY HOSPITAL
Director: Dr A. N. Azfar

He felt the first foreboding. He opened the gate, went in, leaned his skis in the angle where the pillar met the wall. Then, avoiding the hospital entrance, he walked around the flanking path to the door that opened onto the Shaw's quarters.

It was unbolted. He entered, passed through a small flagged hallway and into the living-room.

It was empty. He stood in the doorway, staring. There was no furniture, no carpets on the floor. The fireplace was dead. The Chinese collection had gone but Kate Shaw's pictures were still hanging on the wall at the farther end. These and the grey ash in the fireplace and the few scraps of worthless rubbish that littered the floor were the only signs that people had lived here.

He walked into the centre. His boots made echoes in the great stone-and-timber room. Shadow leapt. He stopped, stood there in the silence. It was so cold that his breath formed grey wraiths in the air. He could smell the decaying odour of the stone.

He went to the farther wall, stared at the pictures. In the half-darkness they had no colour. Even the prettiness had gone. Anger rose, then pity. They had taken everything. But these they had left; with contempt because they had no value.

He turned, crossed the room. His boots moved through the litter. There were crumpled letters, strands of coloured wool, some printed crochet-patterns, a calendar, a batch of old medical journals. His boot struck something. The object sprang from the stone with a metallic ring. He bent, picked it up. It was a steel knitting-needle. He fingered it, touched its point. He began to shiver. Fear for the Shaws possessed him. He turned the needle in his hands, hesitated. He could not discard it. He slid the knitting-needle into the pocket of his parka, preserving it like a memento. Then he crossed the room into the hallway, went out onto the path.

The path led through the water-gardens, past the lily-pool to where the temple roofs stood dark on the sky. Below the temple was the wall, and in the angle of the wall the graveyard.

The four headstones were pale ovals in the shadow. He did not know why he had come to this mildewed place, only that in his fear it had drawn him. He went nearer to the stones. *Answered the Last Bugle*, one of them said.

It was then that he saw the two new graves.

They lay behind the headstones, parallel to the wall. They were crude six-foot mounds, beaten down with the flat of a spade. There was no name, no marker, not a flower, not a cross.

He had no tears. They had all been shed in the night of the hut. He stood there until he heard Arif's voice speak behind him.

'Farran.'

He did not turn.

He heard Arif step nearer.

He said, still without turning, 'Did you do this?'

'No.'

'The soldiers at the helicopter. Were you one of them?'

'No, Farran.'

He went to one of the graves, bent to the soil that filled the stone surround, picked some primulas. He dropped them on the two mounds.

'A bit of sentiment,' he said in despair. 'A few flowers. What difference will they make?'

The temple bell rang. Across the valley they were still enacting the pretence.

Arif said, 'Things happened. Political things. We all became – terrified.'

Farran was silent.

Inside his pocket his fingers locked around the steel needle. In my way I loved her, he told himself. The beginning of a kind of love. She was older. She was useless as a woman. I met her once. It was a kind of love. He saw her silver hair in that moment, the ugly ankles, Cray's cheroot and Ardrey's bandaged hands, bodies falling through the air, the ogre that had formed from the mountain's breaking face.

He said, 'I can't take much more. There's been so much.'

'Do you want revenge?'

The novice bell rang again. He felt his utter emptiness.

'Farran?'

'I want to go,' he said. 'Just go. That's all.'

Arif took his arm and he turned obediently.

'I'll help you,' Arif said.

An hour later Arif came for him.

They went out into the night. Snow was falling.

'They're still searching for you,' Arif said. 'All day they've been out in the passes. They know you used Hut Three last night.'

A window bloomed in the darkness. Dr Azfar's sleek black head appeared.

'From now on,' Arif said, 'he'll have to practise on Indians.'

'How so?'

'They've closed the School. This time tomorrow there won't be a foreigner left.'

They began to walk.

'Keep with me,' Arif said, 'and you'll be all right.'

There was a convoy of four Indian trucks in the inner courtyard of the temple. Snow covered the canvas. A sentry stood at the gateway. Doors opened in the buildings, throwing yellow washes on the snow. Soldiers crossed and recrossed the yard.

'Audacity,' Arif said. 'It always pays.'

They climbed into the truck that was fourth in line.

Arif sat in the driving-seat. He pointed to the rear. There were four large cans, some paper-wrapped parcels.

'Petrol,' he said. 'Food. And a pair of trousers.'

'Trousers?'

'You're wearing the regulation combat-suit. They'd spot

you a mile off.' He touched Farran's sleeve. 'You can keep the parka. But you have to change the trousers.'

Farran nodded.

'Here's some money.'

Farran took it.

Now the engines were revving.

'They're going to Lakh,' Arif said.

'The airstrip?'

'Yes. Tomorrow there'll be three big transports. They'll fly the foreign troops out.'

Farran turned.

'No,' Arif said. 'It's too near, too obvious. They'd be watching. We have to do the unexpected.'

'Which is?'

'The Cease-Fire Line. Cross over into the Pakistani zone and you'll be safe.'

'But I have no papers.'

'You will have.'

Arif started the engine.

'You see, Farran,' he said, 'they expect you to make for the Consul at Srinagar. That's where they'll concentrate.'

The trucks moved forward. Arif stopped in the gateway, said something in Urdu to the sentry. The man saluted, stepped back.

Arif accelerated. The headlamps cut channels of light out of the mountain road.

'You see?' he said, smiling. 'Was easy.'

They followed the trucks. The red tail-lights glowed in the night. Already the wipers had made thick shelves of snow on the windshield.

The trucks turned right at the junction toward Lakh.

'But we turn left,' Arif said.

He drove for a time until the lights of the camp came near. Then he stopped.

'I leave you here,' he said.

He got out.

'Take this key,' he said.

'A key?'

'To a houseboat.'

Farran took the key.

'Yours?' he asked.

'Yes. An investment. But she isn't let at the moment.'

209

Arif gave him a scrap of paper. 'I've written it down. She's named Pride of Kashmir. And she's moored on Naini Lake.'

'Naini Lake.'

'Yes. At six thousand feet. The drive will take two hours. And it's signposted.'

Arif pulled up the hood of his parka. Snow made crystals on his cheeks. 'Now listen. I'll try to pinch your passport from Records. But in any case someone will come for you with papers. It may be hours, a day, even a week. But someone will come for you. I promise you. He'll take you through the Sassar Pass to the Line.'

Arif held out a hand. They gripped.

'You promised me a medal,' Farran said.

Shame touched Arif's face. 'I know,' he said. 'I'm very sorry.'

He turned, walked into the darkness.

It was dark in Hadji's office. But the snow had stopped and a pale starlight from the window glimmered on the steel cabinet.

Arif unlocked the central drawer, drew it out. He searched, located Farran's passport. He closed and locked the drawer.

Light flooded the office.

Hadji entered, then Petrie, then two soldiers.

They did not speak for a moment. Petrie removed his hat, beat the wetness from it. Then Hadji held out his hand. Arif gave him the passport.

Hadji murmured, 'Where is the truck, Arif?'

Arif did not reply.

'Answer.'

Arif was silent.

Hadji riffled the pages of the passport.

'We found his skis,' he said. 'We checked with Quarter-master. The issue number's tallied.'

'They were Farran's all right,' Petrie said.

Hadji pointed to a chair. 'Sit down, Arif.'

Arif sat.

'I'm waiting, Arif.'

Snow slid down the roof.

Hadji shrugged. 'Shut the door,' he said to the soldiers.

It was nine o'clock when Farran reached Naini Lake.

He left the truck in the cover of a group of giant plane trees. Then he followed the path.

This was the end of the tourist season. His boots rustled in the drifts of fallen leaves. But the air was warm after the heights. Across the lake a small hotel cast yellow pennies on the water. There were a few floating gardens where melons and tomatoes would grow. Shikaras glided on the breast of the lake. The shape of a mosque was outlined on the night-sky. Most of the tourists had gone and the houseboats, moored stern to prow, made dark clusters in the shadows.

Arif's investment was tied in a narrow creek, near to a willow. *Pride of Kashmir*, the nameboard said, *Sanitary Fitted*.

Farran went aboard, unlocked the door on the starboard side. It led direct into the dining-room. There was a smell of sour rice, charcoal-smoke and cooking-oil. But it had great dignity. A bay window with panes of engraved glass gave a view of a small deck and the length of the lake. Mahogany furniture filled the room. There was a fireplace and a pile of logs, kindling and old newspapers.

He lighted the oil-lamp. Then, holding it high, he went into the main bedroom. There was a big mahogany bed, carved with oriental plane leaves, covered with a bright Tibetan rug. But it was cold and damp. He took the rug, the blankets and mattress from the bed, carried them into the dining-room and arranged them in front of the fireplace.

Then he built the fire, lighted it. He watched the flames lick the logs, held his hands into the warmth. Then he unwrapped the food-parcel, ate.

When he had eaten he removed his parka and the trousers of the white combat-suit. He put on the black ski-pants that Arif had provided. Then he turned down the oil-lamp so that only a faint amber glowed in the room.

He lay down on the mattress, pulled up the covers. He could feel the slight movement of the houseboat. Water lapped gently against the hull. The flame of the logs threw unstill shapes on the walls and ceiling. If he turned his head he could see the bay window and the moonlight entering so that each pane reflected a separate diamond on the floor.

He closed his eyes. This was the moment of aloneness. He could hear the sound of his own respiration, but not the breathing of the five sleeping men, the stirring of a limb, the swallowing of spittle. These sounds were missing. He had been one-sixth of a single, breathing, living cell. But now he was alone. He turned uneasily in the roads that led to sleep. Petrie's voice said, 'I offer you – adventure.' Then: 'There is a price to pay.' A face came, a white oval in a hood of fur, a wisp of silver hair. She smelled of lavender. 'Take care, Farran.' A green turban shone like an idol's emerald eye. He stroked her silver hair. 'There is a price to pay.' Bodies lay in a cold crevasse, preserved for an eternity. 'I paid,' he said to his god. 'How I paid.' The face of Jalanath fell through a core of fire.

He slept.

He was awakened by a sound.

He came abruptly from sleep, sat upright. The fire was low but the window was still a bright rectangle in the darkness. He listened. The houseboat knocked against the wood piles of the mooring. He relaxed, looked at his watch. It was four in the morning. Someone would come, Arif had promised him, perhaps within hours. The lamp was out. He got up, replenished it from the oil-can, lighted it. The room went amber. He put a log on the fire, poked in a few bits of kindling. He watched the flame lick. Then he lay back.

The sound came again.

It was unmistakably a footfall. It came from the deck. He sat up, listened. He left the mattress, put on his boots and parka, went out onto the deck.

There was no one there. The lake was luminous in the moon. A few lights gleamed. It was very cold and the willow rustled in the wind.

He walked around the narrow deck, stopped outside the bay window. He sniffed. An odour touched his nostrils. It was putrid. It reached also at another sense. This evil stench lay in the memory. He had smelled it – where? His neck-hair crept. Someone will come for you. The words took on another meaning. *Someone will come for you.*

He wheeled.

Dorje stood behind him.

He was a square of fur against the moon. Farran stared.

212

Then Dorje slowly turned and the mongol face was cruel in the light and the long black whiskers trembled like wire. Wind touched the greasy fur, bringing again its evil smell. He held no weapon. The hands reached out, gripped the fur of the parka, jerked. Farran felt his face thud into fur. Then the arms enfolded him. They stood there locked. The arms constricted. He felt the man's terrible strength. His ribs bent. His lungs emptied. The spikes of fur were in his mouth. Then Dorje lifted him, held him high for a second, flung him through the bay window.

He felt no pain. There was only the glass-shattering noise and he rolling and the shapes of the cabin tilting in the amber light. He got to his feet. His eyes were blurred. Then they cleared and he saw a monstrous shape leap through the ragged square where the window had been.

Dorje came toward him. He lifted the oil-lamp, smashed it into the coat. The fur flared like a torch. The pock-marked face went yellow-red. Then Dorje ripped the coat from his body, tossed it with contempt onto the mattress. An arm swung. Farran felt his wits scatter with the impact. Then the arms enfolded him again. The mattress surged into flame and he saw Dorje's lips part and the carious teeth yellow in the glare.

'This time the end, heh?' Dorje said.

The arms tightened. The breath left his body. His ribs bent inward. Dorje leaned. Now his spine was curving inward with the pressure. He knew it must snap. He began to claw at Dorje's lower body. His hand touched something sharp in the pocket of his parka. He thrust his hand into the pocket and his fingers grasped the steel knitting-needle. He jabbed the point into Dorje's flesh. Dorje gasped The grip went loose. His arm was free. The mongol face leaned into glare. He pushed the needle hard into the left eye.

Dorje did not scream. The needle was in his brain and only an inch of the fragile steel protruded from the eye-socket. He turned full-circle, as stiff and jerky as a puppet.

Then he fell.

Farran stepped across him. Smoke and flame engulfed the room. He climbed through the broken bay and onto the deck. The air was cold and sweet. Wind fed the fire.

He jumped onto the piles. Heat waved against his neck. Boatmen were running down the path.

When he reached the plane trees he got into the truck, sat there with his face in his hands. Tremors rode through his body. Pain gnawed at his ribs. Now he was abandoned. There would be no messenger from Arif. Outside the refuge of the truck and the dark of the trees was a vast and hostile land. He did not want to venture there, or move or meet its dangers.

The fear passed. But his brain was tired. Think, he told himself. Think. What is your situation? Arif, he knew, would not have willingly betrayed him. But Dorje had come in the night. So they had obtained knowledge of his plans. They would wait for Dorje to report his death. And when Dorje failed to report they would make inquiry, learn of the burning of the houseboat. Dorje was missing, so Dorje was dead. But they would not know if he too had died in the fire. I have time, he told himself, a little time to profit from their uncertainty.

He started the engine. Arif's gentle voice spoke within him. *We have to do the unexpected.* That was good advice. He reversed the truck from the cover of the trees and onto the lake road. He would retrace his route, drive boldly back toward the camp and the airstrip at Lakh.

Driving on the mountain road and the angle of the truck tilting he saw in the driving-mirror the curve of Naini Lake. Arif's investment was still blazing in the darkness.

It was mid-morning when he reached the road-junction above Lakh. Below was the bowl, as grey and bleak as a dead crater. He could see the runway, some huts and a concrete building, a compound in which were lines of vehicles. Two of the three transports were already on the apron. A fuel-tanker moved between them.

He got out of the truck, went to the edge of the road. The flag by the control-tower streamed in wind. There was a circuit-road, a perimeter fence, an entrance-gate with a guard-box and a red and white weighted pole. It was very exposed. No truck or man could enter without challenge. Despair touched him. He went back to the truck.

In that moment he heard the engines.

He walked to where the road looped. Below, on the Dhalabat road, a convoy was climbing. It came slowly through the banked snow. He counted. There were a staff-car with a pennant, six trucks, two open and five covered lorries. This, perhaps, was the final exodus from the camp.

He went back to the truck, got in. He reversed into the branch road so that the nose of the truck abutted on the airstrip route. Then he pulled the hood of the parka over his head, put on his dark sun-glasses.

He waited.

Now the engines were querulous on the steep road.

He started the engine, put the truck in gear. The staff-car passed, then a truck, then another. They were closely spaced. The last of the trucks passed, then an open lorry that was packed with singing men. He nosed forward. A long gap had opened between the second and third of the covered lorries. He let in the clutch, accelerated into the space. Somewhere a man shouted.

The convoy circled the bowl, began the descent. Men stared down at him from the tailboard of the lorry. The convoy stopped.

Exhaust-fumes broke in the wind. Another song began. A door slammed. Boots crunched on the road. Farran felt the sweat form. Convoy regulations had been broken. If an NCO came . . .

A whistle blew. The boots retreated. The door slammed again. The tailboard moved away from him. He took the truck forward. His mouth had dried. Another stop would indicate they were checking every vehicle. But the convoy did not stop. He passed through the gate. The weighted pole made a red and white vertical and the guard was already in his box.

The convoy entered the compound. Farran studied the lines of parked vehicles. There was a space between a snowplough and a tractor. He waited until the tailboard slowed. Then he turned out of the line and into the space.

He got out. Men were springing from the trucks and lorries, dragging kit. Two NCOs came from the concrete building. He could hear a distant Tannoy voice, the whine of an aircraft-engine. Now the men made a moving group in the compound.

He joined it.

The building was filled with a mass of shifting men. Noise beat on the walls.

'We've been here two bloody hours,' a voice said.

'This bloody wind—'

215

Farran looked around him. There were peeling walls, a door with a broken hinge and a view of a choked lavatory, a coffee machine and a litter of paper cups. Condensation ran down the big glass departure doors, made pools on the floor. There was a high wooden desk by the doors. Two armed Indian NCOs stood by the desk. Through the blurred glass he could see one of the transports, men loading kit. A windsock pointed in the wind.

'If this wind don't drop,' someone said, 'we don't get off.'

Farran walked into the mass of men. He felt relief. He was not conspicuous. Most of the troops, like himself, had beards and burned mountain-faces. He went to the coffee-machine, filled a cup. Drinking he looked over the rim, searching the crowded hall.

A man in a green parka with an Olympic Games emblem on its breast came from behind a pillar, pushed his way through the groups. He carried a clipboard and a document-case. This was Crosbie, the Senior British Officer.

Farran went to him.

'Colonel Crosbie.'

Crosbie turned.

'Hello, Farran,' he said. He stared. 'You look rough.'

'Yes.'

Crosbie looked around him, over Farran's shoulder. 'Where's the squad?'

'They're not here.' He heard his voice tremble. 'They went on ahead.'

Crosbie checked the folios on the clipboard. A man with a freckled skin joined them.

Crosbie said to Farran, 'You know Maddox?'

'Yes.'

Crosbie gave Maddox the clipboard. 'You've made a balls-up, Tom. Farran's not down here.'

Maddox checked. 'Oh, Gawd.'

Crosbie asked, 'Do you have a Boarding Pass?'

'No, sir.'

'No Boarding Pass?'

'No.'

'Oh, Gawd,' Maddox said again.

Farran removed his sun-glasses, wiped them.

'You do look rough,' Crosbie said.

Farran watched the doors. An Indian in civilians had joined the NCOs.

'Are you in trouble?' Crosbie asked.

'Yes.'

Crosbie smiled. 'Been robbing the Bank of Bombay?'

Farran shook his head. His ribs throbbed with pain.

'Well?'

'Not that kind of trouble.'

'What then?'

'Political.'

The smile went.

They waited.

Farran said, 'I can't tell you now. Perhaps I can never tell you.'

He saw the coldness in their faces. A wave of nausea rose.

He said in desperation, 'I have to get away. If I don't get away—'

Voices were coming from the noise, a snatch of German. He felt himself sway.

He said thickly, 'If I don't get away they'll kill me.'

Maddox's face came close. 'You're as pissed as a coot.'

'No. No, no.'

'Wait a tick,' Crosbie said. He touched Farran's arm. 'Are you serious?'

Farran nodded.

Their faces were unyieldng.

'Please help me.'

The lavatory door fell from its hinge. Men were laughing.

An Indian voice shouted in anger, 'The English have smashed the lavatory—'

Crosbie said slowly, 'We have a man here—' He tapped the clipboard in Maddox's hand. 'What was his name, Tom?'

'Reid.'

Crosbie nodded. 'Broke a thigh yesterday. So can't get off yet. Dr Azfar's got him.'

'Poor devil,' Maddox said.

'You can have his pass, Farran.'

'Thank you, sir.'

Crosbie said to Maddox, 'Give it to him.'

Maddox hesitated. He was a paper-man. He hated an irregularity.

'Tom.'

Maddox produced a green Boarding Pass.

Farran took it.

Crosbie said kindly, 'But I can't get you through that gate. You do understand that?'

When the wind dropped they opened the glass doors. The Tannoy spoke. Cold gusted into the hall. Farran took his place in the column of shuffling men. He put on his sunglasses. He could see the Indian in mufti, the two NCOs. He looked away. Crosbie and Maddox were watching. Some Scandinavians were banging on the coffee-machine. His limbs were trembling. His mouth was dry. But the hope was rising. A dozen paces, a walk across the apron, safety. He felt exultant. Crosbie nodded, smiled at him. He looked back at the desk.

Shock rode through him.

A tweed hat with a coloured feather leaned between the NCOs. The hat lifted and Petrie's face turned into the light. He was staring at the column.

The column moved. Farran watched the desk. Each man proffered his Boarding Pass. One of the NCOs examined it, read out the name. The second NCO checked it with a list. Petrie studied each man, nodded. The man passed through to the apron and the aircraft.

The column advanced.

The little pile of Boarding Passes grew.

The voice recited names.

'Slater.'

'Westbrook.'

'Moorhouse.'

Now he was resigned, like a man going to his execution. He reached the desk.

The NCO took his card.

Petrie stared.

'Reid,' the NCO said.

The second NCO ticked the name.

Farran felt his heart leap. He moved forward.

'A moment,' Petrie said.

He stopped.

'Take off your glasses,' Petrie said.

He removed them.

They stared. He saw the gleam of recognition in Petrie's eyes.

218

The NCO looked up from the list.

The man in mufti opened his jacket.

Then Petrie turned away, shook his head, pulled out his pipe.

Farran walked through to the apron.

The aircraft lifted into cloud. It was very cold in the cabin and moisture ran on the curves of the metal shell. Beyond the window there was only whiteness. He sat there with his eyes shut and his fingers locked in his lap.

When the aircraft levelled he opened his eyes. The cloud was below. It shone in sun. The aircraft banked. He looked down the wing to a rift in the cloud.

The Karakoram lay beneath him. The ice-peaks burned with the fire of diamonds. They reached at him from violet shadow. Then the cloud closed and they were gone.

He knew he would not see them again.

EXTRACT FROM THE LONDON
EVENING STANDARD

CHINA STRIKES NUCLEAR RICHES

Standard Foreign News Desk

China, in its first reference in six weeks to the
Mount Jalanath landslip disaster which killed
more than thirteen thousand people, today published news of an incredible geological discovery.

The New China News Agency, in a report moni-
tored in Hong Kong, stated officially that the
fallen face of the mountain had exposed an
enormous vein of uranium. The uranium is rich
in the isotope U235, the rarest explosive in-
gredient used in the production of nuclear
weapons.

The Chinese Prime Minister, Chou En-lai, said
in a birthday message: 'Out of loss and suffering
has come immeasurable wealth. The People's
Republic of China has now ensured for the fore-
seeable future its thermonuclear programme.'

Also announced was a celebration march by the
People's Liberation Army in Peking's main
Avenue of Eternal Peace.

A Selection of General Fiction from Sphere

A Selection of Crime Thrillers from Sphere

Two Great Novels by Burt Hirschfeld from Sphere

Fire Island   45p
This is a number one bestseller from the greatest storyteller
since Harold Robbins. New York's beautiful beach resort
is a sun-soaked playground for the bored and rich, where
the wealthy, the housewives, the hippies all come to find
freedom. This is the story of six friends who share a
summer house every year. It is a story of friendship, of
love and of passion, money, murder, joy and despair.

Cindy On Fire   50p
This great novel is the story of a girl who is alone in a
decadent world where she brushes with the jet-setters and
the drop-outs. She rejects her middle-class background and
struggles to find herself. She has to become a prostitute to
support her lover who's a drug addict. She hungers after
more and more lovers and eventually becomes involved
with revolutionaries in Chicago. It is a story of youth, sex,
despair and a kind of freedom.

All Sphere Books are available at your bookshop or
newsagent, or can be ordered from the following address:

Sphere Books, Cash Sales Department,
P.O. Box 11, Falmouth, Cornwall.

Please send cheque or postal order (no currency), and allow
7p per copy to cover the cost of postage and packing
in U.K. or overseas.